IN THE WOODS:

A FICTION FOUNDRY ANTHOLOGY

In the Woods: A Fiction Foundry Anthology edited by Robert Lewis

This book is a work of fiction. All events, incidents, characters, names, businesses, places, and other entities depicted in these stories are either fictitious or are used fictitiously.

"Widdershins" by Hollie Snider was originally published in 2012 by Evil Jester Press in *Evil Jester Digest Volume One,* edited by Peter Giglio.

All other stories appear here for the first time.

Cover art: Leighton Buxman
Design and layout: Robert Lewis

Published by Polymath Press, a trade name of Polymath Enterprises, LLC. Please direct all inquiries to Polymath Press, P. O. Box 461870, Aurora, CO 80046-1870, online at www.polymathpress.com, or via email to editor@polymathpress.com.

First edition
November, 2023

ISBN(paperback): 978-1-961827-02-8
ISBN (eBook): 978-1-961827-03-5
Library of Congress Control Number: 2023949032

IN THE WOODS:

A FICTION FOUNDRY ANTHOLOGY

Edited by
Robert Lewis

POLYMATH
— PRESS —
Aurora, CO

Other works by Fiction Foundry

Fiction Foundry Presents: One
edited by Amity Green and Henry Snider
Published 2015 by Strigidae Publishing

Other works by Robert Lewis

Case Files of the Rocky Mountain Paranormal Research Society
Volume 1
by Robert Lewis and Bryan Bonner
Published 2023 by Polymath Press

Contents

INTRODUCTION

This is not your average anthology. Sure, it has some similarities to others. The stories do have a common theme, and I've compiled and edited them just as any other anthology editor would. However, its purpose is a bit different from others, its stories are perhaps more varied than in others, and it followed a strange path to publication. Nevertheless, everyone involved is quite proud of the final product and we all hope you enjoy the stories you're about to read. But before we get to those, a few words of introduction and explanation seem to be in order.

This anthology is a product of Fiction Foundry. Though it looks from the outside a lot like any other writers' critique group, Fiction Foundry is a bit different from most. It was founded in 2012 with a simple mission statement: "Fiction Foundry is a group of experienced writers, editors, and layout artists coming together to share their work for final peer feedback with the goal of attaining professional publication for every member."

Though short, that statement represents a diversion from Fiction Foundry's predecessor. Our group was founded by the

Snider family, former members and officers of the Colorado Springs Fiction Writers Group (CSFWG). But while the older group was dedicated simply to making writers better—whatever improvements that might entail—Fiction Foundry's goal is much more specifically geared toward publication preparation. As such, members in Fiction Foundry are typically more advanced in their craft than in many other writers' groups (though we are open to newer writers and some members have not yet achieved professional publication credits) and critiques from the group are, to put it bluntly, brutally honest. Our goal is not to coddle anyone's feelings but rather to get written works ready for submission to professional markets. Don't get us wrong, though. Our meetings are still filled with good-natured writerly shenanigans. By the same token, while most groups are desperate enough for members that anyone can join, we maintain an audition process as a condition of membership. All are welcome, but our members must demonstrate a willingness and ability to receive critiques and improve their work.

In fact, if you'll permit me to use this introduction partly as an advertisement, Fiction Foundry is always looking for new members. I encourage any writers reading this to visit us online at www.fictionfoundry.org and consider sitting in on a meeting to see if we're the right group for you.

Fiction Foundry has published an anthology in the past. It's called *Fiction Foundry Presents: One*, edited by Amity Green and Fiction Foundry co-founder and past president Henry Snider. Its purpose was to serve as a sort of business card for the organization. A place where our members could showcase their work. Unfortunately, it's long out of print at this point and second-hand copies aren't all that easy to come by.

In 2021, the very same Henry Snider announced a new Fiction Foundry anthology—the one you're reading now—with much the same purpose. But its path to publication was fraught, which is why you're reading it more than two years later. Submissions were open to any current or former member of Fiction

INTRODUCTION

Foundry, and there were no rules regarding genre or style. The stories just had to prominently feature "the woods" in some way or other. Not every member or alumnus chose to contribute, of course. We have numerous members spread across two distinct meeting groups, not to mention quite a roster of alumnus members, so it would be impossible to get everyone's work between the same covers. But the submissions that did come in, I think, represent a decent cross section of our membership.

As the submissions rolled in and following a competitive selection process, Snider announced yours truly as a co-editor for the anthology and the editing process began. However, due to a confluence of events beyond his control during that time, Snider had to step down as President of Fiction Foundry and as editor of the anthology.

And I stepped in. As luck would have it, I was at the same time in the process of founding Polymath Press. So the anthology, though delayed, was moved to its new home at my new publishing house, and I took over editorial duties. I want to thank all the contributing authors for their patience as we got this project put together, and I hope they're as proud of the final product as I am.

Now that you understand where it came from, you're in a better position to understand why it's a bit different from most anthologies you've read. For one thing, it's not limited to a single genre. Though it skews a bit to the dark side due to a current overrepresentation of horror writers in Fiction Foundry, you'll find a good mix of horror, fantasy, dark fantasy, and more. Because of that, you'll probably find some stories in here that aren't what you typically read. Personally, I think that's one of the great advantages of Fiction Foundry. Because our members work in numerous genres and come from all walks of life, the critiques during our meetings represent opinions from all over the literary world. And the stories in this anthology, similarly, represent an eclectic mix of literary voices. As editor, I was thrilled to read stories that represented something of a divergence from my usual literary diet.

Some of these authors have been professionally writing, editing, and publishing for decades. For some others, the story in this anthology represents their first published work. But for all of them, it's our collective hope that you enjoy the stories, that you discover some new authors, and that you get a taste of what the Fiction Foundry members are capable of.

Arranging the stories into an order that makes any kind of sense was a challenge. My first thought was to put them in alphabetical order. However, that would have resulted in clusters of stories from the same genre, not to mention a run of three stories in a row from the Snider family. Instead, I've arranged them in such a way as to provide a varied and textured reading experience. I hope I've succeeded.

Finding cover art for such an eclectic genre-hopping book was a similar challenge, and I'm forever grateful to the amazing Leighton Buxman for, I think, perfectly capturing the blend of styles and stories you're about to read. Sometimes there really is a "perfect" artist for a book, and I think this was such a case.

So just what are you in for in the pages to follow? I don't want to spoil anything, but just to whet your appetite a bit: we've got forest spirits, haints, mental illness, parasitic spiders, werewolves, out of control plants, evil forces, reincarnation, humans with animal ears, witches, and Lovecraftian horrors. And all of them can be found…*In the Woods*.

Robert Lewis
October, 2023

THE BOTTLE TREE

John H. Howard

Ronica gasped. The knife in her hand clattered to the floor.

"You okay, Ronnie?" Aaron asked. He looked up from the other end of the counter, where he was chopping peppers. "Cut yourself or something?" He set his own knife on the cutting board and stepped over to inspect his wife's hands. She didn't resist as he examined them for blood. Finding none, he turned each one over and gently massaged the palm with the pad of his thumb in small circular motions. Normally, this got some sort of reaction from her—a loving smile, a soft shiver, a promise of something more to come later. This time, nothing. In fact, she hadn't even looked away from the chicken she had been preparing, which lay splayed open on the counter before her.

"Ronnie?" Aaron asked. A worried frown creased his brow. "What's wrong?" He squeezed her shoulder.

This seemed to snap her back to the present. Her eyes took a long moment to focus on his. They were wide, her pupils dilated. "I have to go," she whispered.

Aaron laughed, thinking it was a joke. "Okay, I'll bite.

Where are we going?"

"No." She pulled her hands from his. "Not you. Just me. The chicken, it—I have to go." She hurried over to the coat closet. She started to reach for her favorite black flats, then changed her mind and grabbed her sneakers instead, the ones with the thick soles.

"You going for a run?" Aaron asked in confusion. He glanced back at their half-prepared dinner.

Ronnie pulled out her favorite purple fuzzy jacket and slipped it on.

"No," she said, reaching for her purse. "I have to go home."

"You are home."

"Home home."

"Wait, right now?" Aaron asked. He came to stand before her. It was their one-year wedding anniversary and they had been planning this evening for weeks—a nice dinner, candlelight, soft music, maybe some dancing in the living room.

"Yes, right now." Ronica reached for her keys on the hook by the apartment door, but Aaron was faster. His hand closed around them before hers did.

"Want to tell me what's going on?"

Ronica looked up at him. Her pecan-colored eyes were filled with worry. "It's Momma," she said. "She's in trouble, maybe hurt or...worse."

Aaron cocked his head like a dog trying to understand the strange utterances its human was making. "How do you know that? Our phones are off for the evening."

Ronica broke her gaze, cast her eyes to the floor. "I...I can't explain. I'm not sure you'd believe me. And even if you did believe me, I'm not sure you'd still..." She let the sentence hang unfinished between them.

"What, are you psychic or something?" Aaron joked. It was his nature to try to cut tension with humor. It was one of the things Ronica said she loved about him. He cracked a smile when she looked up, but she didn't smile back.

"No, I…" Once again, she let the words die before speaking them.

He looked behind her, to their half-prepped dinner, the pans on the stove awaiting a flame, his piles of chopped peppers and onions, her chicken, nearly ready to go into the oven.

Aaron grinned. "Don't tell me the chicken told you."

Ronica's expression didn't change.

Aaron's grin faded. "I was joking."

He followed his wife as she led him over to the chicken. Its belly lay open, a mound of wet, shiny giblets on the counter next to it. She pointed. "Look at the liver."

The tiny organ, which should be grayish-pink and smooth, was instead ashen, scarred, and shriveled. It looked almost fossilized.

"So what?" Aaron said. "The bird was clearly sick."

"And this?" Ronica pulled aside some tissue to reveal a fully-formed brown-shelled egg.

"Okay, that *is* a weird thing. I've never heard of a store-bought chicken having an egg inside it, but I don't suppose it's outside the realm of possibility."

Ronica reached into the chicken's abdominal cavity and pulled out the egg. She held it up next to her face. It was the exact same shade as her own ochre skin. "This is not a coincidence," she said. "This is a message."

Aaron found himself frowning again, not understanding anything that was happening right now. He opened his mouth and closed it again, not knowing what to say, an unusual and uncomfortable situation for him.

"This is me," Ronica said, shaking the egg. She pointed at the chicken. "That's my Momma. Something's wrong."

Aaron felt a nervous laugh threatening to burst forth. He forced it down. "Why don't we call and check on her before we drive six hours one way?"

Ronica sighed. "Aaron, you know Momma doesn't have a phone." She threw the egg in the trash bin under the counter.

"The only way to find out is to go there."

Aaron felt the evening slipping away, all their plans clattering to the floor like Ronnie's knife, which he suddenly remembered. To stall for time, he bent over and picked it up from where it lay on the chipped black-and-white tile they kept talking about replacing but never did. Aaron set the knife next to the chicken, trying to figure out how to get their evening back, even if they had to order in. "Then call one of the neighbors and have them check on her."

Ronica sighed. "Aaron, that's...not possible. You know she lives halfway between Ass End of Nowhere and Bumfuckville. And even if she didn't, she doesn't have many friends. At least, none willing to go to her place after dark." She held out her hand. "Please let me have the keys. I'll be back in two or three days."

Aaron's spirits fell. All their planning, for nothing. He'd been looking forward to tonight practically since their honeymoon.

Ronnie must have seen the disappointment in his face. Her expression softened. "Honey, I'll come back as soon as I know everything's okay. I promise."

Aaron steeled himself. "No. If you absolutely have to go, then I'm going with you. I'm your husband. And that's final."

Aaron expected her to give in. It had always worked before. But this time, she resisted.

"And I'm your wife and I say you're staying here."

Aaron's resolve crumbled. He hadn't been expecting that. "What? Why?"

"Because," Ronnie said, shifting her weight. "I...don't know if I can keep you safe."

Aaron started to laugh, but his wife's serious expression stymied it.

"Ronnie, I made you a promise when I married you. Whatever this is, you don't have to go through it alone. Your family is my family. I want to be there for you. Don't push me away when things get difficult."

Ronnie put her hands on either side of his face, kissed him gently, then looked him in the eye. "Aaron, my love. I didn't marry you for your speeches and even though that was beautifully heartfelt, I don't have time to do this with you. So…get your shoes on and let's go."

A wide smile split Aaron's face as he pulled his own sneakers out of the closet and slipped them on.

"I'm driving, though," she said, snatching the keys from him. Then she sighed. "And I guess I'll have to fill you in on the way. There's a lot you don't know."

"About?"

"Me." Ronnie said. She opened the apartment door and stepped out, leaving Aaron to follow.

His smile faded.

"So you mean to tell me that I've been married to a Hoodoo princess all this time? That's kinda hot. Did you ever…use your powers on me?"

Ronnie sighed. "First of all, no, I've never cast a spell on you. That was all me. And second, there's no such thing as a Hoodoo princess. Have you been listening at all to what I've been telling you? Or are you just trying to figure out ways to get me into bed?" She shot her husband a sideways glance before returning her attention to the road.

"Both, actually. The latter we can work out later, but in answer to your first question, your ancestors were from Africa, which I kinda sorta knew already…"

"Smartass."

"…and your family is of something called the Gullah tradition, which I didn't. And, in fact, have never heard of, honestly."

"Of course you haven't," Ronnie said, inching the car's speed up a little more. "It's not something that you would have studied in prep school."

That stung a little, but Aaron resisted the urge to snap back at her. He reminded himself that she was stressed and that their differences sometimes created some incidental friction that wasn't the fault of either one of them. "You're right," he said, "but I'm willing to learn anything I can about you in order to better understand who you are and why we're suddenly driving all night to get to your mom's house."

Ronnie sighed again. She'd been doing that a lot during the last several hours. So far, she had driven the entire way, barely stopping, except once to pick up some fast food for dinner and another time to pee. Aaron knew she was anxious and driving was one way she felt like she had some amount of control over the situation, so even though he offered to take over, he didn't push the matter when she turned him down.

"I know," she said. "And I appreciate it. I appreciate *you*. I have to keep reminding myself that it's not your fault that there are things that you don't know about. That you and your ancestors had completely different experiences than me and mine."

"Of course," Aaron said, and was rewarded for his empathy when Ronnie reached over and squeezed his hand. "But what I'm really interested in is this magic you mentioned. If you're not a Hoodoo princess, then what are you?"

"I was kind of a prodigy," she said. Ronnie was matter-of-fact. She said things as they were, rarely exaggerating, so Aaron knew she wasn't bragging. "It just came naturally to me. Momma said the spirits whispered in my ears." She shrugged. "I don't know about that, exactly, but it just...made sense to me. Like a puzzle where you can see how all the pieces fit together."

"What is it, though?" Aaron pressed. "How does it work?"

Ronnie laughed. "That would take years to explain, but in short, it's an understanding of nature and the world we live in, both the seen and unseen, and all the connections that exist between, well, everything."

"And the chicken was part of that?"

Ronnie nodded. "The universe reaches out to us all the time, sending us messages. If we're open and accepting and know how to read them, we can have a more thorough relationship with it. The chicken was an unmistakable message."

"No offense, but I hope you're wrong about that."

"So do I," Ronnie said quietly.

The car sped up and Ronnie stopped talking.

A few hours later, they pulled off the highway. Asphalt roads turned to crushed stone, became dirt. Ronnie clearly knew this area well. Aaron had only been out this way once before when they'd come down for their wedding. It was the only time he had met Ronnie's mom, but she had seemed to take to him right away. She had given her blessing to their union, something that Aaron would never forget, because it involved scented oils, a rope, and a smear of chicken blood on each of their foreheads. Ronnie had brushed it off as humoring her old mother and her out-of-date ways, but at the same time had taken it seriously. The memory took on a different meaning now in light of Aaron's newfound knowledge of his wife.

Ronnie turned slowly onto the dirt path which led to her old home. It could barely be called a road. Aaron was glad for the all-wheel drive and high undercarriage on their SUV as it bounced along the pitted path. Old-growth forest loomed on either side, seeming to grow larger in the stark blue-white glow of the halogen lamps. Cypress trees stood tall on either side of the path, ancient sentries watching over the place. The occasional low-hanging vine brushed the roof of the car.

If ever there was an elder wood, this is it, Aaron thought. He yawned mightily. It was pushing three in the morning. He was bone-achingly exhausted. Ronnie, on the other hand, seemed wide awake. She sat straight in her seat, her eyes big and alert, focused on the road in front of them. He hoped they'd find that

Ronnie's premonition had been wrong and they'd surprise her very healthy mother, who would somehow be overjoyed to see them at this insane hour, and then quickly rush them off to bed and let them sleep until noon.

The light of the headlamps fell on a rough wooden structure hunched among the trees, barely large enough to be called a cabin. The roofline sagged and the entire thing leaned slightly to one side, but somehow it held itself together. In any other setting it would come across as quaint. *Fix it up a little and some people would pay a lot of money to rent a place like this*, Aaron thought.

The SUV jerked to a hard stop in front of the porch. Aaron grunted as momentum pressed him against the seatbelt. Ronnie slammed the gearshift into park and killed the engine. She jumped out, the headlights still on, illuminating the house and surrounding trees in stark relief.

Aaron forced his tired body out of the car. Something ran away through the underbrush.

"Oh, no!" Ronnie cried.

Aaron turned to where she was kneeling on the ground in front of what looked like the metal skeleton of a Christmas tree. A "trunk" about the girth of a length of rebar stuck up from the earth, smaller branches of wire and metal jutting out from it at various heights. "What's the matter?" Aaron joined his wife.

In front of Ronnie were broken bottles of all different hues; shards of green, red, brown, blue, and clear glass sparkled in the dirt and grass. Aaron remembered the tree from his first visit here. Each branch had been decorated with a bottle, a metal rod through the mouth of each one so that they hung upside-down on it. He had admired it as a folk art piece. Ronnie had called it a bottle tree but hadn't said anything else about it.

"Somebody did this," Ronnie said. Her voice trembled, whether out of fear or anger, Aaron wasn't sure.

Aaron scanned the broken bits of glass. It certainly seemed deliberate. There was no way the bottles could have just fallen from the tree, even in a strong storm. One or two maybe, given the right conditions, but not all of them. "Who would do this?" he asked. "And why? It was so cool." He rested a hand on Ronnie's shoulder. "At least it's easy enough to clean up. And we can go out tomorrow and get a couple of six-packs or something and repla—"

The look Ronnie shot him over her shoulder was venomous.

Aaron jerked back his hand at that look.

"Replace it?" Ronnie stood and faced him, her eyes dark, even in the glare of the headlights. "Is that what you were going to say?" At his uneasy nod, she poked his chest with a sharp finger. "You might be somebody where you come from, but you don't know anything about anything down here. And you'd do well to remember it." She turned on her heel and with long steps made her way to the house.

Aaron had never seen this Ronnie before. The Ronnie he knew was kind, patient, loving, caring, calm. Who was this woman who had just lashed out at him with such fury? He was slow to follow her onto the creaking porch.

"Dammit!" Ronnie cried from the front door.

Aaron's instinct was to rush to her side, ask what was wrong, and try to figure out how to make it better, but now he hesitated. He was becoming more unsettled by the moment. It was becoming difficult to deny that something was very wrong.

"Momma! MOMMA!" Ronnie banged on the front door. It swung open onto a yawning black space that even the car's headlights couldn't pierce. "Oh, God," She muttered. "This isn't good." She disappeared into the gloom.

Aaron shook off his unease and rushed onto the porch. A line of white powder crossed from one side of the porch to the other, except in front of the doorway, where it had been brushed away. He paid it no mind, stepping into the darkness of the house.

From his initial visit, he knew that he was standing in the living room. It had a green, earthy smell that was indistinguishable from the woods surrounding the house except for an underlying mustiness, the lingering aroma of last evening's dinner, and a very faint metallic scent. He felt around on the wall to his left for a light switch but found only bare wall.

Suddenly, a light like a small white sun flared to life in the middle of the room. The flashlight function on Ronnie's phone filled the space with a cold, stark, electronic luminescence that bleached the room and its furnishings of color.

The light shone in his eyes, blinding him momentarily. He tried to block it with his hand and failed. "She doesn't have electricity, remember?" Ronnie said.

Now he did.

The light washed over the rest of the room.

"Help me find her," Ronnie said.

Aaron activated his own flashlight function.

The house contained only a few rooms: living room, kitchen, two bedrooms, a walk-in pantry, and a single bathroom—Momma had indoor plumbing and running water, if not electricity—so it didn't take long to find her body. Aaron was searching Ronnie's old bedroom when his wife called out.

"Aaron, help me!"

He rushed to Ronnie, who was kneeling by what he at first took to be a pile of clothes on the floor by the open cellar door.

Except it wasn't a pile of clothes.

"I can't tell if she's breathing," Ronnie said. Her voice was strained. "Help me turn her over."

Momma wasn't a large woman, but she wasn't light, either. It took both of them to turn her onto her back. Her clothes were wet and sticky. Ronnie raised her light so they could see better.

Aaron gasped at what it revealed.

It looked like Momma had been mauled by a bear. Her clothing was shredded, nothing more than strips in places. Her body mutilated, deep gashes marring her face, torso, and arms. One eye was gone, a hollow socket staring up at them. A white tooth peeked through a ragged tear in one cheek. She was soaked in blood.

Aaron shuddered. He looked at his hands, which shone reddish-black in the electric light from Ronnie's phone.

He frantically wiped his hands on his shirt and jeans. The metallic smell that he had detected upon entering the cabin was much stronger now and he realized he had been smelling Momma's blood. There was so much of it.

"Aaron!" Ronnie chastised. "Help me! See if you can find a pulse."

Aaron forced himself to ignore the stickiness on his hands and the blood pooling beneath Momma's chin and pressed his first two fingers to her neck. He had once been trained in CPR for a job as a lifeguard and he called upon those long-unused skills now.

After a long time of searching for a pulse in Momma's neck and not finding one, he felt first one wrist and then the other.

"I...I can't find a pulse," he said. "I'm sorry. We need to call 911."

Ronnie was surprisingly calm. "You do it," she said, and stood. "But first, help me move her into the bedroom."

"Should we? I mean, that's disturbing the scene. Even if it was an animal that did this. Once the police show up—"

"*If* they show up, they'll look around and take our statements, but won't do shit that matters. Now help me move her. Don't make me do this by myself."

Aaron reluctantly hooked his hands under the dead woman's arms while Ronnie took her legs. They struggled to lift her but managed it. As they carried her to her bedroom, Aaron said, "It's the police's job to look into stuff like this. That's what they do. They *have* to."

Ronnie huffed. "If she were white, maybe. *Rich* and white? Sure they would. But the crazy old black Hoodoo woman who lives out in the woods by herself? They'll be glad she's gone, even if most of their mothers did come to her for a charm or potion for love, marriage, money, an easy birth, or to soothe a colicky baby. Or to avoid having a baby altogether."

They laid Momma on her bed. Aaron's hands were even stickier now and he was pretty sure that the scent of blood was now permanently stuck in his nose.

"So call 911," Ronnie said, arranging her mother's limbs so that her legs were together and her arms were crossed over her chest. "You're probably right that we need to, but right now I have something to do."

Aaron was taken aback at both her vehemence and nonchalance. "What in the world do you have to do right now?

She stopped halfway through the door and turned back to him. "Find out who did this."

"*Who?*" Aaron was stunned. "Clearly an animal did this. Didn't you see the claw marks?"

"This wasn't an animal," Ronica said. "This was intentional. Planned. Now do what you need to do and give me the space to do what I need to do." With that, she stepped through the door.

Aaron ran to catch up with her, but as he came out into the hallway, he caught sight of Ronnie stepping around the puddle of her mother's blood and disappearing into the cellar.

"What the hell?" he asked aloud. His question died in the still night air.

Aaron made the call on his cell phone. He had to step outside to get a signal, and even then, it wasn't a great one. The call was choppy and broken and he had to keep repeating himself to the dispatcher to make himself understood. He stayed on the porch so he'd be close to the door in case the bear—or whatever had attacked Momma—came back. Or in case whatever was rustling around in the underbrush decided to take advantage of the open door. As he was trying to communicate with the dispatcher, something else occurred to him. He wasn't sure if predatory animals could smell blood from miles away like sharks could in the water, but as soon as the call ended, he stepped back inside the house.

Whatever had attacked Momma had knocked the door askew, so he had to lift up on the knob in order to get it to fit into the frame. As it fell into place in the frame, Aaron shivered a little at the thought that he could have narrowly missed being attacked by a cougar or a wolf or whatever else lived in these woods.

Ronnie was still in Momma's bedroom, bent over her poor mother's body. At first, Aaron thought she was crying and started to back out to give her some privacy, but quickly realized she was talking. Her voice was too soft to hear clearly but it didn't sound like she was speaking English. Transfixed, Aaron stayed put, half in and half out of the room.

Ronnie dabbed her thumb in a bowl in her hand, which Aaron hadn't noticed before, then smeared something dark across her mother's forehead. Then she made a vertical line down across her mouth with the same substance. She said something else, then put her ear to her mother's lips. In the gloom of the bedroom, it almost looked as if the dead woman's lips moved.

He blinked, then rubbed his eyes. When he opened them again, Momma's lips were still.

According to his watch, it was a little after five in the morning. He had been awake just shy of twenty-four hours. He was definitely seeing things.

He made his way into the living room, purposely avoiding looking at the dark puddle by the cellar door. He sat down on the couch to wait.

Then Ronnie was shaking him.

"Aaron, honey. Wake up."

He forced open dry, heavy eyelids and wiped away the wetness on his chin. "Are the police here?" he mumbled, trying to force himself back into consciousness.

"No."

"What time is it?"

"Going on eight."

Aaron sat up straight. He was awake now. "What the hell? I called them hours ago!"

Ronnie sat down next to him and put her hand on his. "I told you, Hon. They're not going to do anything. Not for us. We're on our own."

"So, what now?"

"I'll call the coroner. Momma knew him. He's a good man. He'll come for her."

"And then?" Aaron was hoping she'd say they could sleep the rest of the weekend.

Her face darkened. Instead, she said, "We find the person who did this."

"What...what do you mean? This couldn't have been done by a person."

"You're right. It may not have been done by a person, but a person caused it."

"What do you—"

"The bottle tree. The disrupted salt at the front door. Someone had to do that in order for them to get in."

"Them?"

"The haints."

"The...?"

"Haints. Like...forest spirits."

Aaron laughed. "You're saying fairies did this? Or was it elves? Or gnomes, with their pointy red hats?"

"No. Not like that. Spirits. Ghosts."

He started to laugh again but choked it back at her serious expression. "You're..not joking."

"I told you what I am. Who I am. You believed that."

"Yes, of course. I—"

"But not this?"

"Spirits aren't real."

Ronnie's eyes flickered. "We don't have time for this, Aaron. I don't have the luxury to convince you, to explain everything right now. But now you're a part of this and we have work to do."

Aaron suddenly felt lost, adrift, floating on a sea of doubt. He found himself in a strange world outside the boundaries of the one he knew and had grown up in. A world he hadn't known existed. He thought briefly of those old maps that marked everything beyond the borders of the known world with *Here there be Monsters.*

Here there be Monsters, indeed. He looked to Ronica, his wife, a woman he had known for more than half a decade, yet seemingly didn't know at all. Who was this woman who stood before him and spoke of magic and spirits? Who was this woman who had looked at him with such ferocity just a few hours before? He had never seen this version of her before. And what about the woman he had known? The gentle, loving, patient woman he had fallen in love with? The woman he married and with whom he hoped to start a family some day? Where had she gone? Was she real, or just a fiction created for him?

"I...don't understand. Any of this."

Ronnie sat down next to him, put her hand on his leg. He flinched at her touch and she put it back in her own lap. Something like sorrow appeared in her eyes but was quickly replaced by resolve.

"I know you don't," she said. "But I need you to trust me. Like you always have. I'll keep you safe."

"Safe?"

"We have to make sure Momma's buried. The right way. So she can't be..." Ronnie shook her head. "Never mind. At any rate, in the meantime, until she is, we have to keep her safe. And keep ourselves safe. Because the person who did this could come back. Probably will, in fact."

"You keep saying someone.... Who would—or could—do this?" Aaron gestured in the direction of Momma's body.

Ronnie started to speak but was cut off by a pounding at the door. Ronnie closed her mouth into a hard line and looked up.

After a few good tugs, the front door fell open. Ronnie jumped back to avoid getting hit by it. Then she stayed planted, staring through the open doorway, frozen in place.

Aaron stood and went to join her. "Ronnie, who is it? Is it the coroner?"

It wasn't the coroner. Instead, a young black woman about Ronnie's age stood on the porch, her hair fashioned in dreadlocks. Her eyes flicked from Ronnie to him. Her mouth spread into a grin.

"Valeria," Ronnie said.

"Ronica," the woman on the porch said, saccharine-sweet, her eyes finding Ronnie again. When she spoke, her voice was low. There was something sensual about it. Aaron imagined wrapping himself up in it like satin. "I'd heard you'd come back. I wanted to come over and say hi. How's your momma?"

"We just got in a few hours ago and we didn't tell another living soul that we were coming. How'd you find out?" Ronnie bit off the question. Her tone was cool.

Valeria looked skyward. "Oh, you know. A shift in the wind, whispers in the trees, a little bog boy told me." Her gaze drifted lazily back to Aaron, but nothing about this woman indicated that she was anything less than intelligent. "I see you got yourself a nice white boy. At least very well off, if not rich, I'm guessing. Just like you always said you would. I heard you'd done well for yourself in the city, but this...." She looked Aaron up and down and sucked her teeth. "Good for you, Ronnie."

Her words stung Aaron. *Just like she'd always said?*

Ronnie reached over and grabbed Aaron's hand in her own. "This is Aaron. We've been married for the last year," she said. "Happily. And, yes, we're doing okay for ourselves."

Valeria looked past the couple at the state of things. Her eyes found the broken door. "I heard your husband mention a coroner. Is it a bad time?"

"It is, actually. Momma was...she passed away unexpectedly.

I'm here to settle her estate."

Valeria put on a somber face. "I'm so very sorry to hear. I always liked your momma. She was like the mother I never had."

The sound of car engines drew everyone's attention to the dirt drive. A shiny black hearse appeared through the trees, followed by a Sheriff's car, the lights dark.

"You have visitors," Valeria said, turning back to face the couple. "I won't keep you. I hope you'll come by and see me once you get everything settled. I'm living at my auntie's old place. You know where it's at."

Valeria stepped off the porch. She took her time descending the steps, taking each one deliberately, as if she were the lady of the house making her grand appearance for a ball. As she passed them, she greeted both the coroner and the sheriff's deputy. The deputy's eyes followed her slim form as she passed by. Valeria stepped off the drive and disappeared among the trees.

Aaron let his hand slip from Ronnie's as the coroner and deputy approached.

"Miss Ronica." The coroner was a tall, thin, dark-skinned man, slightly past middle-age, Aaron guessed. The man removed his navy-blue fedora, which matched his suit jacket and slacks perfectly, to reveal a clean-shaven head. He held the hat to his chest with one hand as he shook her hand with the other. "I'm glad to see you again. I wish the circumstances were different, though."

"Thank you, Lenny. So do I." Ronnie introduced Aaron and Lenny and Lenny shook Aaron's hand. His grip was firm and confident.

The deputy stepped up on the porch behind Lenny. A white man, he looked as though he'd been carved from a boulder. His mouth was a thin line. "Miss Ronica," He tipped his head in her direction before turning his icy blue eyes to Aaron.

"Jimmy." There was less warmth in her voice than there had been for Lenny. "Thank you for coming."

Jimmy grunted something about just doing his duty. Neither Ronnie nor Jimmy offered a hand.

Ronnie led the men inside. The Sheriff's deputy noted the half-broken door but didn't ask about it. Ronnie showed them to her mother's body. Aaron stayed on the periphery while Ronnie filled them in on the events as they had transpired, leaving out the parts about haints and coercing her dead mother to speak. Instead, she speculated aloud that some sort of animal, a bear perhaps, had broken into her mother's house.

When Ronnie finished, Jimmy asked Aaron a few cursory questions, the deputy's cold gaze chilling him more deeply than a frigid day. The entire time, though, Aaron got the distinct feeling that the man was just going through the motions. This made him angry, but he kept it to himself.

Once Jimmy was finished interviewing them, the couple was asked to wait in the living room until he and Lenny had finished their investigation.

After some time had passed in silence, Aaron said, "A nice, rich, white boy, just like you always wanted, huh?"

Ronnie sighed. "I knew that wouldn't get past you." She turned to face him as they sat on the sagging sofa. "It's just one of those things you say when you're a kid. Like how boys say they're going to be astronauts and marry supermodels when they grow up. I'd actually forgotten about that. I met you and... that was it. Not having to worry about money is nice, but it doesn't matter. I know how to get by because I've done it all my life. If the money were gone tomorrow, we'd be just fine. Just as long as we're together. Thing is, we never get what we think we want as kids. Sometimes…sometimes we get better." She took his hand in hers. "Aaron, I'm actually glad you came down here with me. I don't think I'd be able to get through this on my own."

Aaron squeezed her hand, his anger deflating. He felt stupid for letting Valeria's words get to him. "It's fine," he said. "I get it."

Ronnie squeezed his hand back. As if in response to his

thoughts, she said, "Don't let Valeria get to you. She likes to do stuff like that. She always has. Don't let her come between us."

"I won't," Aaron said. "Promise." He smiled and kissed her. They sat in silence for a time, listening to Lenny's and Jimmy's voices in the other room. Finally, Aaron said, "Valeria, huh? Her name sounds like—"

"A poisonous plant?" Ronnie said. "Right? I always thought so, too."

They both burst out laughing.

Some time later, after Lenny and Jimmy had taken Momma's body to the coroner's car and Ronnie and Aaron had received a stern lecture from the Sheriff's deputy about moving the body, Aaron was sure they'd finally get some time to rest. He sank onto the sofa with a loud groan.

Instead, Ronnie grabbed her purse, smacked him playfully on the knee, and said, "C'mon. We've got shopping to do."

Aaron groaned again as he sat back up. "How are you still standing?" he asked his wife.

"Because I have to."

"No, you don't. You *have* to rest. You can't keep going like this for much longer. Besides, your mom just died. How are you not falling apart?"

Her face darkened at that. "There'll be time to grieve later. Right now we have to go."

Several hours later, an exhausted Aaron brought in grocery bags while a seemingly inexhaustible Ronnie carried in a gallon of paint and a couple of brooms.

As he unloaded bags of rice, multiple canisters of salt, six-packs of root beer, and a wide variety of other items that didn't seem to have any relationship to each other, Aaron asked "Why are we staying here again? It's not like we can't afford a hotel."

"Because this isn't over. She'll be back tonight."

Aaron slammed a canister of salt down on the linoleum counter and turned to his wife. "Enough talking around the subject, already. What isn't over? Who will be back tonight?"

Ronnie set the paint can down on the porch before leaning one of the brooms against the side of the house, right next to the door. She had explained to him that some types of haints were obsessive-compulsive and would be compelled to count the number of bristles in the brooms, hopefully keeping them occupied until sunrise, at which time they'd have to seek shelter or be burned up in the sun's rays. "Haven't you figured it out yet?" At his shrug, she answered the second question first. "Val. That wasn't a friendly social visit this morning. She came to check on her handiwork. To make sure that the trap had been sprung."

"What in the hell are you talking about?" Aaron threw his hands up, exasperated.

Ronnie made her way to the kitchen at the back of the house, sidestepping the sticky red-brown pool by the cellar steps that they still hadn't gotten around to cleaning up. She set the second broom outside the back door before shutting and locking the door. Then she leaned against it and crossed her arms. "Valeria and I grew up together. In fact, we were born on the same day. So, of course we were destined to be best friends. That's just how it works. We did everything together. We even dressed alike when we could.

"When my momma and her auntie started teaching us Hoodoo, it became clear pretty quickly that I was a quicker learner than she was. It all just...made sense to me. As if every new thing I learned was a piece in a gigantic puzzle and I could see exactly where it fit. Val picked it up but much slower. She struggled with it. And made mistakes. Nearly got herself disemboweled by a plat-eye in the shape of a wolf when she wandered too close to the swamp one night."

"A what, now?"

"A shapeshifting mist haint."

"I feel like I wouldn't want to run into one of those."

"It would kill you before you could blink."

Aaron felt the blood drain from his face and considered suggesting they stay in a hotel, but Ronnie continued her story as she helped put things away.

"I think it was more salt in her eye that I didn't care about it as much as she did. For me, it was a fun hobby, but I didn't take it too seriously. Val, on the other hand, lived for Hoodoo. I think she was addicted to the thought of having so much power at her fingertips.

"The final straw for her, though, was that it became clear to both of us that her Auntie Flora preferred me to her. She'd praise me for things like filling my bag with certain wild herbs and flowers while scolding Val for not filling hers fast enough. Or bringing back the wrong ones. She'd take me out into the woods to teach me things while leaving Val home to have lunch or supper ready for us when we got back. To be fair, I did ask Flora to bring her along, but she flat-out refused."

"She sounds like a real piece of work," Aaron interjected. "Kind of like some of the nuns I had as teachers in school. You knew who their favorites were pretty quickly."

Ronnie nodded and continued her story. "At any rate, you can guess where this is going. We went from best friends to worst enemies. She started ignoring me in school. She'd sic small but troublesome spirits on me to pinch me and pull my hair. One time she took me dreamwalking, and then left me behind. I had to find my own way back to my body. I nearly became a haint myself that time. Anyway, I finally got sick of her behavior, so one day I retaliated by moving the forest around so she'd get lost in it. And she did. For three days."

"You did what?" Aaron asked.

Ronnie continued as if she didn't hear him. "Auntie Flora put it back to rights when she realized what I had done," She said. "And I got the tongue lashings of my life, one from Auntie and one from Momma. So after I graduated school, I left for the city and never looked back."

"I understand maybe a tenth of what you're telling me," Aaron said. "But it doesn't matter. What does any of that have to do with what you said about springing a trap?"

Ronnie pushed herself off the door. "Come with me," she said, and made her way to the front of the house, once again avoiding the now-congealed pool of blood.

That's going to be a bitch to clean up, Aaron thought, stepping around it himself.

Outside, Ronnie led him to the bare bottle tree. She pointed at the broken glass at its base. "Bottle trees are used to trap haints. They get stuck in the bottles until morning, when the sunlight kills them. Someone broke all the bottles on purpose and..." she led him to the house and pointed to the floorboards, where a line of white grains stretched from one side to the other, except in front of the door. "...and swept away the salt in front of the door, letting them into Momma's house."

"Salt?"

"Spirits can't cross it. You'll also notice that the porch ceiling is white."

Aaron looked up. "Yeah, so?"

"It used to be blue."

Aaron remembered this was true and recalled remarking on the lovely light blue shade when he had been here before.

"Someone painted it," Ronnie continued. "And did a quick job of it, by the looks of things." She pointed to some drip marks along the edges of the boards. "Haints can't cross water, either, so porch ceilings are painted a particular shade of blue—haint blue—to confuse them and keep them out."

"But why would someone do that?"

"To lure me here."

"And you know this was Val somehow?"

Ronnie nodded.

"I'm sure I'm going to regret asking this, but how?"

"Momma told me. Last night."

"But…she doesn't have a phone and you said you didn't get a call from her." Aaron had never felt so confused.

The corners of Ronnie's mouth turned up into the ghost of a smile. For the first time in the last day and a half, she appeared tired. "I didn't say she called. You were there, Aaron. In the room with us. You saw."

"You saw me?"

"Do you have to see your hand to know it's there?"

"Of course not."

"So, same thing."

He chewed on this for a minute. He had a hundred questions but didn't know which one to start with. Trying to sort through his thoughts felt like wading through a murky swamp.

"Are you saying your, uh, dead mother spoke to you?" He was sorry to state it so bluntly but didn't know how else to put it.

Ronnie nodded.

"I don't—" he started. He rubbed his face with his hands. His exhaustion felt like a force of nature at this point. He stepped through the open front door and fell onto the sofa. "I don't understand anything that's happening right now."

Ronnie followed him in. She sat next to him and put her hand on his leg. "I know you don't, honey. I know this is all new and strange to you."

"That's one way to put it," he said. "I mean, I'm seriously starting to wonder if one of us is crazy. I don't think I am, because I'm pretty sure that the dead can't talk. So I don't know what to think."

"If they still have some breath in them, they can," Ronnie said.

"I'm going to be real blunt with you right now and tell you that I don't know what the hell you're talking about."

"If the dead have any air left in their lungs and you know

how to do it and they're not *too* dead, they can sometimes be co-erced to talk. Momma still had some breath in her. Just enough for one word. And she hadn't been gone that long, so..." Ronnie shrugged. "I needed to know and she told me. Confirmed my worst fear, in fact."

Aaron rubbed his eyes, wondering if he was going to have to have his wife committed when they got home.

Ronnie slapped his knee. "C'mon, Sport. We have work to do."

Aaron groaned.

"You can sleep later," Ronnie said. "But right now we have to prepare. Grab a root beer and a paintbrush and let's get to work."

A few hours later, they had done as much as they could. The porch was repainted, the door was rehung, the blood pool was cleaned up, the bed sheets changed, and the salt barrier re-placed. Also, the bottle tree had been resupplied with fresh-ly-emptied root beer bottles and Aaron had to pee. Out of an abundance of precaution, they had even painted the window-sills haint blue, so spirits couldn't cross them, something Mom-ma hadn't done.

"We have a few hours to sleep," Ronnie said. "But we have to be up by dusk."

"Dusk?" Aaron didn't bother to stifle his yawn.

"That's when she'll come for us."

"Oh, okay." Aaron couldn't pinpoint exactly when all of this had become completely normal.

After double-checking that all the doors and windows were locked, they stumbled back to Ronnie's old bedroom, which her Momma had kept up for her. They found fresh sheets on the bed when they pulled back the hand-made quilt. They had bare-ly kicked off their shoes and lay down before they were both asleep.

Aaron thrashed. He couldn't breathe.

He tried to wake but struggled to come up from the black depths of sleep. His consciousness felt like it had an anchor attached to it, dragging him down. And it felt like something was pressing on his chest, as if someone were sitting on it. He tried to move, but his muscles wouldn't respond.

When he was growing up, Aaron suffered from night terrors. He would awaken from sleep screaming and thrashing with a vague sense of having had a horrible nightmare but being unable to remember it. Sometimes his mind woke up before his body and he lay there for anywhere from a few seconds to agonizing minutes, completely unable to move. He had eventually grown out of them, but the sense of the experience remained. It was horrible.

This was worse.

Aaron was aware of shouting, his name repeated over and over. A struggle that felt like it was right on top of him. Then, eardrum-bursting screeching.

The weight lifted and was gone.

Aaron forced open his eyes just in time to see what looked like a skinless woman squeeze through the miniscule space between the almost-closed window and sill into the darkness beyond. The awful screeching faded into the night with her. The room smelled sweetly of rotting meat.

"Aaron!" Ronnie shook his shoulder. "Aaron, please wake up!"

It took Aaron several long moments to regain control of his muscles. Just like when he'd been a kid, he felt locked out of his own body, aware but unable to move. He groaned and forced himself to sit up. His entire body felt as if it were made of lead.

"What...was that?" he gasped. His chest didn't seem to

want to expand.

"A boo hag," Ronnie said. She went to the window and peered out after the creature, then down. "God *damn* it, Val, you bitch!"

"A what now?" Aaron rubbed the sleep from his eyes, forced himself upright, then joined his wife at the window to see what had made her curse, something she almost never did. The windowsill had been repainted white. In the weeds below, a dull knife glinted orange in the light of the late evening sun. Aaron surmised that the knife had been used to slip the lock and that same someone had repainted the sill so the creature could get in.

"It's kind of like a vampire, only it feeds on your life energy. But that's not important."

"Isn't it?"

"We overslept!" Ronnie pointed to the dark woods outside the window.

Aaron uttered a curse of his own. "What do we do?"

Ronnie slammed the window shut and locked it. "Try not to die."

The living room had two windows, one that looked out upon the rutted dirt driveway in front. The other faced the woods and the setting sun.

The sun wasn't completely down yet. There was still a hint of pink and purple above the trees, but in the woods, it was night. An impenetrable inky blackness filled the spaces between the trees. A chill was starting to settle in. A thin fog crept out from the trees, tendrils like misty fingers reaching tentatively into the cleared space around the house. Blinking fireflies lit the darkness, and the chirping of the crickets filled the empty spaces between trees. Otherwise, the forest was still. No wind rustled the leaves. No animals scampered through the underbrush. No birds flew overhead in the purpling sky.

For more than an hour they moved from window to window, patrolling the interior of the house opposite one another, trying to monitor the entire perimeter at once. They watched for any movement among the trees. All they saw was the light fade into inky blackness.

Yet, there was an undefinable sense of wrongness to the darkness among the trees, as if something were watching and waiting for them to reveal themselves.

At one point, they found themselves in the back of the house at the same time.

"See anything yet?" Ronnie asked.

"Believe me, you'd know if I did." Aaron grabbed a bottle of root beer from the fridge and popped the cap off before taking a long swig.

At that moment, the quiet stillness was shattered by their car alarm.

The headlights flashed on and off, piercing the darkness in the house with blinding blue-white light, casting stark flat shadows across the furniture and walls.

Startled, Aaron dropped the root beer onto the floor, where it foamed onto the well-worn wooden boards.

The pair quickly made their way back to the front of the house and eased up to either side of the front window, trying not to reveal themselves. Outside, a Val-shaped silhouette appeared in every flash of the beams, smashing bottles to the ground.

Each time she did so, something new appeared: a dog-eared cat creature the size of a wolf; a flaming skull which, despite its empty sockets, seemed to pierce the wall to gaze right at them; a young girl who had buttons for eyes, clutching a crude burlap doll with a painted face; something that seemed made of mud and sticks with stones for eyes. To one side, the tendrils of mist coalesced into an enormous wolf with glowing red eyes. The skinless woman that Ronnie had chased out of the house earlier was there, too, crouched low to the ground like a feral animal. Her exposed muscles glistened red whenever the lights flashed on.

"Oh, my God," Aaron muttered. He had never been truly terrified before.

"Even God doesn't dare to come out in these woods at night," Ronnie said quietly.

"Ronnie!" Val yelled, smashing another bottle. Something made of moss with writhing tentacle-like vines for appendages appeared before her. "I know you're in there! Come out and finish this! Come get what's comin' to ya! Been waitin' ten years to settle things between us. I ain't waitin' no longer!"

"I'm calling 911." Aaron sat down out of sight, his back against the wall, and pulled his cell phone out of his pocket.

"It won't do you any good," Ronnie said, still staring outside.

She was right. He had no signal. Even the emergency call option wasn't available. That hadn't been the case last night. He cursed.

"What do we do?" he asked.

"I go out there and settle things," Ronnie said. "What else?"

A sledgehammer of fear slammed Aaron in the guts. "Don't." His plea came out as a whisper. "Please. Don't go out there."

"She won't stop." Ronnie sagged wearily. "You've seen the lengths she went through to get me back here. *She killed my Momma*, Aaron. She made damn sure we had something to settle. So I'm going out there and I'm not coming back in until it's finished, one way or another."

Aaron stood and grabbed her arm, a little harder than he intended. But he was scared, desperate. "As your husband, please. I'm begging you. Don't go out there." He knew his wife well enough to know that she was going to do what she was going to do, but he at least had to try.

Ronnie looked at him for a long time, her eyes black holes. When she finally spoke, her voice was low and dangerous. "You may be my husband, Aaron, but you don't have the right to keep me from this."

A wind whipped up inside the living room, blowing old papers and magazines around. Aaron released his wife, suddenly more afraid of her than the woman outside who wanted to kill them. The wind grew in strength. Pictures in frames blew off the mantel above the fireplace. A highbacked chair toppled over. The heavy wooden coffee table skittered sideways.

"Okay, Ronnie, you've made your—oof!"

Ronnie extended her hand and the wind punched into Aaron like a fist, knocking him back several feet and slamming him against the wall. The force of the blow knocked the air out of him and he crumpled to the floor like a dropped rag.

Ronnie stared at him a moment longer, then turned without another word and strode to the doorway.

She opened the door and stood there, illuminated in silhouette once a second by the flashing headlights.

From outside, Valeria whooped. "Here she comes! Gonna give me the ass-whoopin' I deserve! Come teach me a lesson, Ronnie! I got it comin'! I been a baaad girl!"

Ronnie bent over the threshold of the door and made a complex sign with her hand. Then she stepped out and was gone.

Aaron scrambled to his feet and ran after her—*there might be just enough time to stop her, drag her back into the house*—and slammed up against something solid. For the second time in as many minutes, he got the breath knocked out of him. Aaron stumbled backwards, his head ringing from the impact. He shook it off, then crept forward carefully, hands out in front of him, and encountered an invisible barrier blocking the doorway. He felt around all sides and could find no opening.

At his feet, in the dark space between the lights flashing a symbol glowed light blue on the threshold. He tried to touch it, but it shone brighter and his hand bumped up against the invisible barrier again.

"What the hell did she do?" he asked no one. He banged his fists against an obstacle he couldn't see, yelling his wife's name, but she didn't respond.

She stood in front of Valeria now, a rising wind whipping their clothing around their bodies. The haints encircled the pair, but Ronnie didn't seem to notice. Her attention was focused on Valeria.

Where Aaron stood behind the invisible wall, the wind didn't touch him.

"She locked you in, huh?"

The unexpected voice from behind him made Aaron jump nearly out of his skin. He cried out and spun around, nearly falling down in the process.

Momma stood in the hallway, as she had been in life.

Except not quite, as she disappeared every time the headlights flashed on.

"What the fuhhh—"

Momma chuckled and stepped forward.

Aaron pressed against the open doorway, unable to go anywhere, and tried not to wet himself.

"First time ya face a haint is always the scariest," Momma said. "Guess I'm one now, too, huh? She looked down at herself, plucking at her skirt. "Always kinda wondered what it'd be like."

"How are you...how is this...?"

"Oh, honey, I'm tied to this house. I'm part of this land. I been here longer than some of these trees. Some o' those haints outside are no stranger to me. I've fended them off before. Just...not all at the same time. And that's what got me."

She took a couple more steps forward. "Can you set this chair to rights, Son? It's my favorite spot. I think I'd like to sit it in one last time."

Aaron's fear over the apparition started to subside. He set the chair back up as she had asked. But he still stepped back quickly at her approach.

She sighed as she settled into it. "You're a good boy, Aaron. I liked you from the moment I set eyes on you. You're polite, respectful, and you have a kind heart. And you love my daughter deeply. I felt that in you first time we met. Ronnie done right by you."

Aaron beamed at the praise, forgetting for a moment that he was conversing with a ghost.

Something crashed outside and one of the headlights went out. Aaron rushed to the window. Outside, Ronnie lay sprawled on the ground in front of the SUV. Val stood over her. The haints circled around them, closing in.

"Oh, my God! Ronnie!" he cried. He turned back to Momma. "I need to get out there!"

"Ronnie can hold her own," Momma said. "For a few minutes, anyway. Thing is, though, she can't win this fight. Val's got too much misplaced anger and jealousy and spite in her. And it's just grown all these years, festered like a sore she couldn't leave alone. She kept picking at it and picking at it and it got infected and now that infection is in her blood.

"And not that she was ever weak, but that infection inside her makes her stronger. Of the two of them, she was always the short-sighted one. She wanted the power for its own sake. So the magic resisted her."

The spirit sighed again and rose from her chair. Aaron made room for her at the window—his fear of her was fading quickly. Together they gazed out at the battle beyond. "Val never realized that the person she should have been angry at was herself," Momma continued. "She'll never understand that killing Ronnie won't fix her problems."

Outside, Ronnie gained her feet. She gestured and Val flew backwards a dozen feet. One heel snagged a root and Val tumbled several times before coming to a stop. She rose a moment later, blood running from her mouth. She wiped it away, looked at it, and laughed.

"Ronnie, though…she didn't care about the power," Momma said. "So the magic craved her, threw itself at her like a desperate lover. But still, she's not strong enough. She needs you, though she don't know it."

"What am I supposed to do?" Aaron asked.

The spirit turned to him, raised her finger, and pointed at him. Instinctively, he wanted to shrink away but forced himself to stand his ground. "Your name has power. Your namesake was the brother of Moses, one of the greatest prophets who ever lived and whose teachings our faith is based on." Momma reached out and touched his forehead. Or would have, had it not passed through his flesh. It felt like a cold electric shock where her ghostly finger met his skin.

"You'll know what to do when you need to know it," she said. "Now go out there and save my daughter. Save your wife."

Between one blink of the headlight and the next, she was gone.

Aaron still didn't know what to do but he knew he had to act.

First things first, he thought. Ronnie had warded the door but not the windows. He picked up the heavy coffee table and threw it. The front window shattered, sending glass everywhere.

Ronnie responded immediately, directing the wind to catch the glass shards and send them tearing through the haints, shredding those closest to the house. Their screams faded with their forms.

"Well, isn't that sweet," Val purred as Aaron climbed through the window. "The prince has finally decided to come rescue his princess."

"We're not afraid of you, Val," Aaron lied. "Please go home and leave us alone." He moved to stand next to Ronnie.

"What are you doing?" Ronnie asked him. "Get back inside where you're safe!"

"No. My place is next to you. No matter what happens."

"How very fucking sweet," Val said. "But trust me, Ronnie. He wouldn't have been safe in there, either. Just saves me time and energy, is all. This way I can kill you both and still get a full night's sleep."

Aaron forced down his fear despite the knowledge that there was a very good chance he could die tonight.

"No, Val." Ronnie said. Her voice was iron. "You leave him out of this. He has nothing to do with us."

"Sure he does," Val said. "You love him. So if I kill him before I kill you, I get to watch you die twice. And that'd just be *so* satisfying."

"Bring it, bitch," Ronnie said through gritted teeth.

Val grinned. "You asked for it." She gestured and the remaining haints moved in.

The giant mist dog was the first to fall. Ronnie pulled a burlap bag from a pocket and threw it at the creature's feet. "Have some sulfur and gunpowder, fucker!" she shouted. The bag burst, filling the air with the putrid scent of rotten eggs. The dog form howled and faded away like fog in the morning sun.

The button-eyed girl hugged her doll close, then charged at Aaron. As she ran, her face transformed into something out of a horror movie. Her mouth opened wider than humanly possible. Her teeth were filed to points. Her button eyes honed in on him.

As she closed in, she swiped at Aaron with abnormally long fingers that possessed too many joints. The fingernails were curved, sharp claws.

Aaron dodged to one side and nearly fell. The girl's momentum carried her past him. She stopped and turned back to face him with those nightmarish button eyes. At least her head did. The rest of her body stayed facing forward, eliciting in Aaron a horror unmatched by anything he had seen thus far.

"The doll, Aaron!"

"What?"

"Grab the doll!"

Then the child's body swiveled while her head stayed laser focused on him.

Aaron barely had time to react when she charged again.

He dodged her attack again—barely—but managed to

reach out and grab the doll from her grasp as she ran past.

The moment he did, the girl's body collapsed like a rag doll, sprawled on the ground, limbs sprawled in all directions, blank button eyes staring up at the trees.

As soon as the girl was down, the doll in his hands bucked and kicked. Its painted face came alive and the thing snarled and tried to bite his hands.

Instinctively, Aaron pulled at the doll's head. The burlap tore. Cotton stuffing spilled to the earth. The doll went limp and still like the child had a moment before.

Panting, he threw the remains of the doll as far from him as he could, then scattered the stuffing across the ground.

And looked up just in time to see a flaming skull flying right at him, jaw open wide, screaming. A red-orange spectral trail streamed behind it.

Aaron dropped to the ground and the skull missed him by inches.

The skull spun in midair and made another charge.

Ronnie stepped between Aaron and the skull, spit in her hand, and then blew on it. The saliva became a geyser of water that erupted from her hand, enveloping the haint.

The skull's flame went out and the thing, screaming like a tortured soul, fell to the ground, where it smashed apart.

Aaron got unsteadily to his feet.

Only one haint remained, the figure made of mud and twigs.

It turned and ran, disappearing into the underbrush.

"Just us now, Val," Ronnie said, blood dripping from her brow. The earth drank it up where it dripped.

"Well, that wouldn't be a fair fight, now, would it?" Val crossed her arms.

Behind her, the underbrush came alive.

Literally.

Dozens of tiny creatures cobbled together from sticks, mud, and leaves rushed out from the forest, led by the first one, which was now brandishing a tiny stick sword. Some of the things ran upright on two stick-legs like little people, others stampeded on four legs like dogs or horses.

Then they were climbing up on the couple, stabbing and pinching, even biting with tiny sharpened teeth made of stone.

Aaron swatted at them, knocking some of them to the ground, but they climbed right back up his legs, onto his torso, arms, neck, and face and resumed stabbing and biting. He felt like he was being stung all over his body all at once. Every time he knocked one to the ground, two more took its place.

Beside him, Ronnie was crying out in pain and swatting the creatures away but ultimately having no more luck fending them off than he was.

Aaron pulled one of the things from his face just as it stabbed at his eye with its sharp little sword. Angry more than scared now, he threw it to the ground as hard as he could and stomped on it, feeling the satisfying crunch of sticks under his foot. When he finally stopped, the creature was in pieces.

He pulled another off and crushed it. Then another, and another.

"Ronnie!" He tried to get his wife's attention to show her what he had discovered, but the stick creatures were dragging her to the ground by their sheer masses. Her screams rang through the forest.

Aaron tried to move toward her, but he, too, was suddenly being pulled down by the haints swarming over his body.

He managed to stumble to just within reaching distance of his wife before he finally collapsed. He stretched a bloody hand toward her.

She reached back. One fear-filled eye peered out from the mass of murdering stick creatures. Her hand was slick with warm blood. Aaron gripped it tightly.

He tried to tell her he loved her, but a three-legged stick haint stabbed him in the tongue as soon as he opened his mouth. Biting its little arm off gave him intense satisfaction.

This is it, he thought. *I never thought "'til death do us part" would come so soon. But at least we're together at the end.*

Aaron watched the blood on their hands intermingle. He thought briefly of children that would never be born. He had never thought seriously about having kids before, but now he wanted to weep for the lives that would never come to be as well as the future that would be denied him and Ronnie.

A drop formed from their combined blood, grew, stretched into a single drop, and then fell to the dusty earth. From the soil a tiny blade of grass sprang forth, starting as a yellow-green shoot before deepening in color and stretching toward the sky.

From within the mass of writhing stick bodies, Ronnie's eye grew wide.

"Aaron," she gasped out. "I need you."

What a weird thing to say at a time like this, Aaron thought. "I need you, t—"

"Not like that!" Ronnie cut him off. "I need to borrow from you."

"I don't understand," he said. "You're not making sense."

"I need to borrow your energy," she said. "Your life force. I don't know what'll happen, but it's our only shot."

"Anything you need," he choked out, still not understanding what she was asking of him. He felt lightheaded and fuzzy. It was getting hard to talk.

Ronnie clamped down on his hand, hard. He felt bones grinding together under her grip. Then, he felt a *pull* at something deep inside him and then that same something being drawn from him. He felt himself being emptied of something vital, something that was inherently *him*. The loss of it sapped his energy and he became exhausted, weary beyond anything he had ever known. He had never wanted to sleep so badly in his life. And yet he knew he couldn't.

He sensed a gathering of power, like thunderheads forming directly above.

"What are you doing?" Val's voice floated on the night air

as if in a dream. "Stop it! Stop it right now! I forbid it!" Aaron sensed power in her words, but Ronnie ignored her command.

Then, Ronnie pressed their hands to the ground and he felt raw power disperse like an electrical charge into the earth. Except it wasn't an electrical charge. It was something else entirely. Something ancient and powerful.

A heartbeat later, the ground began to shake and groan and Aaron had the sense of something massive and impossibly old looming over them.

Then, he felt something rip itself from the earth and with a thunderous crash set itself back down again.

The stabbing and biting and stinging suddenly stopped and the stick creatures tripped over themselves in a frenzy to escape.

Aaron breathed a sigh of relief to see the swarm of tiny haints running back toward the forest.

They didn't make it.

A tall cypress, stretching higher than the trees around it, tore a root from the ground and slammed it down in the midst of the creatures, crushing them to splinters. Then a second root broke forth from the ground and smashed another group that the first one had missed. Those that weren't obliterated were sent flying, disappearing into the underbrush or falling apart upon impact onto the hard ground.

"No!" Val screamed. Her cry was accompanied by a streak of lightning and a crack of thunder in the sky above them. "My children! What have you done?"

"Survived." Ronnie's voice was raw. She pushed herself to her feet. Aaron could tell she was barely able to stand but that she was trying not to let it show for Val's sake.

Then, another flash of lightning and the giant cypress was burning. Had he been asked about it later, Aaron would have said that the screaming he heard was himself or Ronnie, possibly Val, and definitely not the tree that ignited like dry tinder.

Because that would have been ridiculous.

Still, now, in the moment, the tree certainly seemed to be

screaming. It sounded like the wind howling through the eaves of an old ramshackle house. Its branches waved wildly although there was no wind.

The trees around the cypress seemed to lean away so they, too, wouldn't burn.

"No!" Val screamed. "You will not leave this place!" Each word was punctuated by a flash of lightning and a crack of thunder and now the woods were burning all around them.

"One of us won't," Ronnie growled. She kneeled and slammed her hands to the ground, digging her fingers into the soil. Cracks like veins spread outward from her hands. The ground shook and split. The veins grew and spread.

The fear on Val's face as one of the veins zigzagged towards her was most satisfying. *Good*, Aaron thought. *Let her be afraid for a change.*

Val took a step back, then two, as the crack approached.

But then, it stopped short.

Ronnie was visibly confused. "What the hell?" she muttered. She dug her fingers in even more. The crack in the earth spread another few inches, but no further.

Val threw her head back and laughed. She sidestepped the crack and moved to where Ronnie knelt. "You used to be so much stronger than me," she said. "I used to envy your power, the things you could do. How you made it seem so effortless. But now you're weak and out of practice." Val leaned down and spoke right in Ronnie's face. "Gentrified." Her eyes searched Ronnie's. For what, Aaron didn't know. Ronnie met her eyes with an iron gaze.

Val frowned, clearly unsatisfied. She straightened and raised her hands toward the sky. "You're done, Ronnie." Then, she spun and danced away from the woman who had once been like a sister. Lightning arced overhead. The clouds swirled around, like an upside-down whirlpool. The lightning intensified, jagged streaks of crimson, blue, green, and violet shattering the sky. The wind at ground level picked up, catching up and tossing last autumn's dead leaves around. The hair on Aaron's head and neck stood on end. It felt as if the air were building up a charge.

And when all that pent-up energy was discharged, Aaron knew they'd be obliterated.

Then, just as Momma had promised, Aaron knew what he needed to do.

He accepted Ronnie—the whole of her. And chose to trust her. All of the rest of it, all that she had kept hidden from him, didn't matter. During their wedding, he had vowed to devote his entire life to keeping her safe, no matter what. So that's what he had to do. Even if it meant *giving* his life.

With that decision, all of his doubts fell away.

"No, Val," he said. "We've just won."

He grabbed Ronnie's hand and clamped it tight. At the same time, he placed his other hand on the ground, digging his fingers in as Ronnie had. Then he sent his energy forth.

It left him in a rush, half flowing into Ronnie for her to guide and the rest into the ground itself, to complete the circuit.

One of the cracks in the earth angled toward Val, eliciting a gasp from her. She instinctively took a couple of steps back and the crumbling earth veered to one side of her.

Val, after watching the zigzagging earth pass harmlessly by her into the forest, turned back to them. And laughed.

"Oh, that's funny!" She said. "That's really funny! I told you you were weak, out of practice. Even with your husband's help, you can't get it right. You can't kill me, no matter how hard you try. Because I'm stronger than you now. So much stronger! And you were so, so close, too." She held her finger and thumb close together. "You were this close to being rid of me forev—"

A vine shot out of the darkness of the forest and wrapped around her chest and waist. Half a breath later, another wrapped around her throat, shutting her up.

Four more vines entwined themselves about her wrists and legs. Together, they lifted Val off the ground, where she hung suspended for a long moment.

"Goodbye, Val," Ronnie said. "Forever."

The vines retracted into the woods and Val was gone. Some distance in there was screaming and a great thrashing of trees that seemed to go on for a very long time.

Ronnie looked after her onetime childhood friend, regret in her eyes. Then her face closed off.

She gripped the earth even tighter and squinched her eyes shut tight.

Aaron felt the energy being pulled from him, but not as much as before. He watched as the wounds in the ground knitted themselves back together. In a few moments, they were all but gone. Only faint scars remained where the cracks had been.

Overhead, the lightning slowed and stopped. The clouds quit circling and the air gradually lost its charge.

Ronnie opened her eyes and turned her attention to her husband. "Aaron, my love?"

"Yes, hon?"

"You're kind of crushing my hand."

"Oh! Sorry." Aaron forced his hand open. He hadn't realized how hard he was squeezing. "I feel like that was a close one," he said.

"If you hadn't acted when you did, we'd be dead right now," Ronnie said. "So, yeah, you might call it that."

Behind them, the sound of high wind through eaves caused them to turn at the same time.

The cypress was still burning.

"Oh my God!" Ronnie jumped to her feet, then spent the next several seconds scouting the ground for something. Before Aaron could ask what she was looking for, she bent down and scooped a handful of water from a puddle. Then she tossed it into the air as high as she could while saying something that sounded like a prayer, but in a language Aaron had never heard.

A moment later, Aaron felt drops on his face and arms. The drops became bigger and then they were in a downpour.

After a few minutes, the rain extinguished not only the fire on the now-singed cypress, but also the ones in the other trees that had been started by the lightning strikes.

The sound of a breeze through leaf-laden branches on a summer evening floated to them on the air.

"You're welcome, old friend," Ronnie said to the singed cypress as rain ran down her face and soaked her through. "I'm just sorry we brought that upon you. May your branches grow strong and your leaves be ever full."

"Old friend?" Aaron asked. The rain felt good, refreshing after the evening's adventures. Ronnie opened her mouth to say something, but Aaron held up a hand. "Know what? Never mind. That's not even the weirdest thing you've said this weekend."

A shuffling sound drew their attention to the far side of the drive. The boo hag hovered at the edge of the woods.

"She must have hidden in the underbrush when the fighting started," Ronnie said. "I lost track of her in the chaos."

The boo hag cast them a baleful look, then coughed out something that sounded like "Find me, Ronnie. Follow the old trail." Then she turned and disappeared into the trees on all fours.

"What are we going to do about her?" Aaron asked.

Ronnie's expression had darkened. "We'll deal with her tomorrow. She won't be back tonight."

"How can you be sure?"

Ronnie pointed at the sky, which was starting to lighten. "The sun'll be up soon and if she's not back in her skin by then, she'll die."

"If she's not back in her—okay, *that* might be the weirdest thing you've said this weekend."

"Let's get some sleep. It's been a long couple of days."

Aaron yawned. "Feels like it's been a week."

They slept most of the next day, waking up a couple of hours before sunset. They ate, drank some root beer, and showered. Only then did Aaron ask his wife what her plans were to take care of the boo hag.

"The sun's almost down," Val said." She'll be leaving soon to feed. I know where to find her skin."

"Is she...?"

"Not coming back here," Ronnie said. "You don't have to worry."

An hour later, Aaron was following his wife through the woods. She followed some trail that he couldn't pick out. They used old incandescent flashlights that Ronnie had found to guide their way. They cast a comforting golden glow ahead of them. Aaron was nervous, but he felt if he could survive the events of the previous few days, then he could survive just about anything.

After some time, they came to a cottage deep in the woods. It was in extremely poor repair. The porch sagged, the roofline dipped in the middle, and the weathered and grayed clapboard siding was falling off in places.

"Val, what'd you do to this place?" Ronnie said under her breath.

Aaron followed Ronnie onto the porch. The ceiling was haint blue. It seemed to be the only thing about the house that was well-maintained.

Ronnie hesitated at the door. "Auntie Flora's place," she said, her hand on the knob. "At one time, my second home. The Val you saw wasn't the same person I knew back then."

Aaron put a gentle hand on Ronnie's shoulder. "I wish I'd gotten to meet that Val," he said.

Ronnie turned grateful eyes to him and smiled thinly. Then she turned the knob and stepped inside.

The inside of the house was as bad as the outside. The furniture was ripped and sagging. Yellowed wallpaper hung in strips. The ceiling had collapsed in one spot where a leak had developed and never been fixed. Flies buzzed around something in one corner that may once have been a raccoon. The entire place reeked of rot and mildew.

"Watch where you step," Ronnie said unnecessarily. She pointed to a section of floorboards that was splintered and looked like they could give way at any time.

Aaron followed his wife deeper into the house. The decay was worse here. It was as if the jealousy and anger that had consumed Val had infected the house until it had died of it.

Ronnie led them into the cellar. The walls were wood and river stone and the floor was packed dirt, except for where a few rough boards had been laid for a floor. A filthy heap of a mattress lay in a corner that was sectioned off by clothes hanging from the pipes above. Val had obviously been living down here.

The opposite end of the cellar, however, was pristine. Wooden shelves along one stone wall were laden with meticulously labeled jars containing things that made Aaron's stomach turn over. Similar shelves holding thick leatherbound books stood against the facing wall. One of these books lay open on a darkly stained table resting against the short wall between the other two.

Ronnie stepped over and looked at it. "Jesus Christ," she whispered.

Aaron stepped closer to look over her shoulder at the page, but it was all gibberish to him.

Ronnie slammed the book closed and threw it onto the floor. "She found a way to make a boo hag." Ronnie's voice was raw. She didn't take her eyes from the book. They were very wide. "I didn't think it was possible. It shouldn't *be* possible." After a few breaths, her eyes found Aaron's. "We really need to find that skin."

They spent the next hour searching the basement. Val assured him it would be there but wouldn't explain how she knew.

Finally, Aaron discovered a loose stone in one wall. When he pushed on it nothing happened. But when he tried to pry it out with his fingernails, half the wall swung open. He hesitated before ducking inside. In the far corner was a heap of what looked like old brown leather. He reached out with a shaking hand and held it up.

A wrinkled brown face stared at him, except the eyes, nostrils, and mouth were empty holes. He screamed and dropped the thing, backing out of the hidden room as quickly as he could, knocking the back of his head on the low entry in the process.

"I take it you found it," Ronnie said, putting a hand on his shoulder.

He could only nod and rub his head and point into the secret space.

"Be right back." Ronnie ducked inside.

Aaron watched from where he stood, feeling guilty for not being brave enough to accompany his wife, but also knowing that she was far better equipped to handle this situation than he was.

"I can't believe she did this to you, Auntie Flora," Ronnie said. She pulled a blue canister from the bag at her hip, turned the skin inside out, and sprinkled salt generously on the inside of the thing. Then she put the skin back as she had found it. "I hope you feed well tonight. It'll be your last time."

Ronnie stepped back into the cellar and pushed the entrance closed behind her. "Let's go." The sadness of finality hung heavy in her voice.

"I'm sorry for all this," Aaron said.

Ronnie met his eyes. "Thank you. But the one who should be sorry is dead now."

Aaron had nothing to say to that.

Ronnie was quiet during the walk back to Momma's house. Aaron left her to her thoughts and memories.

Momma's funeral a few days later was uneventful. Aaron could tell that Ronnie was touched by the number of people from all walks of life who showed up to pay their respects to the crazy old black Hoodoo woman, as more than one person called her, not without affection. She was brought to tears more than once. Ronnie would express to Aaron later that she had found peace and comfort in the fact that her mother had touched so many lives.

Ronnie donated Momma's property to a local conservancy group with the stipulation that it never be developed and that it be left to be reclaimed by nature.

The long drive back home was mostly quiet and uneventful. This time Ronnie let Aaron drive while she alternated between sleeping and watching the scenery pass.

Trying to lighten the mood, at one point Aaron said, "You owe me an anniversary dinner, you know."

Ronnie looked at him for the first time in miles. She managed a wan smile. "I suppose I do. This wasn't much of an anniversary, was it?"

"Well, it certainly was...memorable. Just maybe for future ones let's not almost get killed by forest spirits, okay?"

"Well, that sounds boring."

"Boring is my middle name."

"From now on, it's your first and last names, too, Mr. Boring McBorington."

They shared a much-needed laugh and started to relax.

As they pulled into their spot at their apartment complex, life started to feel normal again. Aaron looked forward to putting the events of the last week behind him.

"By the way, you get to clean up the chicken you left out," he said, as they gathered their few bags from the trunk of the car.

"Pretty sure that's your job, considering I saved your life at least a dozen times last weekend," Ronnie said.

"So this is how things are going to be from now on, huh? You holding that over my head and completely ignoring the fact that I came to your rescue in the end?" Aaron closed the back and they started for the apartment.

"Yep. Because that's how marriage works."

"Doesn't seem fair."

"Nobody said life or marriage was fair, my love."

"Still seems like I'm getting the short end here."

"I'm sure we can find some way to ease the sting of reality," Ronnie purred.

"I suggest starting with that lost anniversary dinner," Aaron said, smacking his wife on the backside as he followed her through the door.

Three hundred or so miles away, something opened its eyes for the first time. It saw green leaves and brown trunks. It heard birds singing, squirrels chattering, insects chirring all around. It smelled fresh loam mixed with damp leaves. Somewhere in the distance it heard an animal die violently. It was home here, it sensed. Familiar. Comfortable. Safe.

It sat up and looked down at itself.

It saw twiggy brown-barked arms and fingers and legs and feet. Small yellow-green leaves sprouted at intervals along its limbs and viny tendrils encircled its arms and fingers. With new hands, it felt its trunk-like body, carved wooden face, and the woven grassy runners like dreadlocks that served as hair.

Memories trickled back from before.

A battle.

Defeat.

Being torn apart by living trees. Pieces of meat scattered across the forest floor. Crimson blood painted across verdant leaves.

Using the last of her power to cast her life force out into the woods in one last desperate attempt to stay alive in some form or other. Then, as awareness faded, finding a pile of discarded twigs and vegetation, settling in, binding them to her essence.

Then it remembered the consuming anger. The burning jealousy. The cold need for revenge.

Features that strongly resembled Valeria's smiled as the creature began planning.

AMANI'S ANSWER

Sangita Kalarickal

Translucent spots floated before Adeni's eyes in a slow dance of impending doom. The torrid heat seemed to suck every bit of moisture from the land, even the sweat. Some days were worse, though. Decades ago, Zym had known real weather, rains feeding crops and blessing the land with plentiful bounty. But Adeni had not seen such things in all her seventeen years. She knew of this from Mandissa, the old grand priestess who, as a child, had watched rains come down several times a year. Adeni stared into the stark empty sky again. No clouds lingered today, only the deep blue which made her see spots after she had gazed into it for a while.

She wanted to meet the oracle and yet was dreading the encounter. Something about a seer always seemed daunting. Though she was adept at magic and spells, the supernatural always gave her chills. At the same time, they were out of options. Everything they had tried led to nothing. Only more years of famine and despair. Crops drooped from mysterious diseases. Rivers and lakes dried up. Ironically, if not for the terrible snowstorms, they may never have survived. Animals had started disappearing, almost all hunted up. Berries and roots were never enough to sustain people. Mothers lost their babies, and babes, their parents. Even tears dried up. Adeni shook her head, wanting those memories to fly away from her.

Adeni's gait slowed as she approached the copse which extended several hundred yards as far as she could gauge. The daylight on the meadow from which she approached melted into darkness among the trees. Her heart beat fast and her pulse quickened. Entering the Amani woods led her to another place entirely. This was a world where famine and drought never struck. Lush green extended into the sky, and Adeni squinted, looking up. She could only see a few patches of blue. Light filtered through the foliage. A songbird twittered far away. Strangely enough, the song echoed. Adeni scanned the landscape, wondering how to proceed. No clear trail could be seen anymore. She gingerly lifted vines to peer under and walk on, deeper into the forest. As she proceeded, her heart slowed to a steady, calm rhythm. It took her several minutes of pulling at vines and branches and venturing further before she encountered the legendary tree.

Keia, the tree of eternity, the tree of knowledge, the tree famed to grant wishes. All fables she had heard since she was a little girl. Her heart began racing again. According to lore, the oracle lived somewhere near Keia. Adeni stopped. This was no ordinary tree; this one had no single trunk. Instead, the base gave rise to several trunks, all fanning outward. Dark, broad leaves began close to the ground, large and hugging the branches. Adeni stroked one of Keia's trunks gingerly and dusted its crumbled bark off her fingers.

She warily touched a broad leaf nearer her and stroked the central vein. Now to find the oracle. Perhaps she had a house at the base of the tree. Adeni swung onto one of the trunks to peer into the green denseness.

"Hello?" Her voice came in a croak she was sure never

even carried past the next bough.

She ventured deeper into the Keia over the outer trunks, her heart sinking deeper as well. This was a stupid idea. Coming here all by herself, following a legend she had heard growing up. There was not a mere single known version of the legend.

An oracle—she can tell you the future, if you ask. And if you leave her a gift.

A nymph, aye! She has golden eyes and will lead you astray. Never, never look into her eyes!

She's a mighty witch, she is! She has counter spells for any that you can use.

But there was one thing all agreed on. All fables insisted that the entity never grew older, never died. Just lived on for all eternity, gathering wisdom.

Adeni shivered despite the pleasant weather. She knew she was being silly; she had her own arsenal of spells. Adeni was training to be a healer under her grandmother, High Priestess Mandissa. A couple more tests and she would have been ready to earn her own staff. *Perhaps Grandmother will relent after this quest and let me have the staff without those grueling tests.*

How long she dug deeper into the woods, she didn't know. All she knew was the light filtering through the canopy of leaves above was growing faint. Her limbs were weak from navigating and climbing branches of the single humongous tree. At her helplessness and hopelessness, tears started stinging her eyes. She felt in her bones that this was a futile journey. And that she was lost. There was no way out of the forest and no real way ahead.

She chose a broad spot on the branch and squatted. How hopeless! She saw no sign of a dwelling. No sign of a person nearby.

An owl hooted deep within the woods. The sudden sound made her lose her footing and slip, flattening her body against the bough. For a moment Adeni lay on the branch, her long braids, satchel and her silver locket which had slipped out from under her tunic, all dangling mid-air.

"Oh god-darnit!" Adeni said as she pulled up the satchel and rested her bottom on the branch. Each hair in her several braids bristled with static electricity. She looked down at her right hand, the sleeve of which was rolled up beyond the elbow. Goose bumps. *What…?*

She spun around. There was no one. Yet there was someone.

It was not anywhere behind her, or in front. It was an omnipresent feeling of a person that engulfed her. Her hand flew to her neck and clutched the locket dangling from a thin silver chain. The locket, a silver band fashioned in the sign of infinity, yet with a twist, an elaborate mobius. *The inside becomes an outside, what is out is in, you are one with the universe forever.* The locket belonged to her great-great-grand aunt Maeveleh, the grand Healer of Zym. Adeni believed—no, knew—it protected her. Growing up, she heard tales of her aunt coming to these very woods on the way to finding her lost staff. Had Maeve, as she was often known, encountered this oracle?

How do you possess the locket?

It was a voice within her head. No, heart. No, her own voice. In her ears. A booming yet gentle voice. Wide-eyed, her gaze darted from tree branch to tree branch. What enchantment was this?

Where did you get it?

The voice was louder this time. Only, it wasn't a voice. Not exactly. "Who are you? Show…show yourself!" cried Adeni in utter fear. "Who are you?"

There was a clear sigh in answer.

Ah. It's been so long. I've almost forgotten my own name. That locket…it's been so long since I've seen it.

Adeni's grip on the locket tightened. This recognition of the locket scared her. Especially since it was clear that this person could see her, but she couldn't see anything save silhouettes of leaves. "How…? Show yourself!"

I am with you, around you, within the forest, I am Keia, I am the Amani woods.

"You are the forest? Are you…the oracle?"

Oracle? There is no oracle here! It's just me, trapped here. How did you get the locket?

"It is mine. Belonged to my great aunt Maeve, who was the greatest healer Zym has ever known, so don't you dare try to take it from me!" Again, Adeni's voice rose. Fear engulfed her, yet she was curious too, the two emotions causing a conflict within. Her grip around the silver locket tightened until her knuckles shone pale. She could swear she heard a sigh. A faint relaxing of the forest, the Keia leaves moving just a tad bit towards her. "Who are you? Who trapped you here?" Again, the sigh. This time it was louder.

It happened when the sorcerer tried to kill Maeve. I jumped in to save her, and the curse hit me instead. I should've died but…not everyone is lucky.

There was a distinct pause as if the entity was trying to remember. Adeni waited. Loneliness emanated from the tree. Like mist slowly riding the breeze, after a night of snowstorm. And a deep sense of sadness.

Keia sucked up all that I knew, my consciousness and memories. I have been waiting all this while. Waiting, watching. All these years. Such a long, lonely wait. My bad luck, watching everyone that I loved die. And I was left behind here….

Adeni tried to grasp this person's narrative. She had heard the story of Maeve and her encounter with the sorcerer who killed the only person she ever loved. Far'ai. So, was this Far'ai? As Far'ai's life left his body, the Keia tree entangled its own life with his consciousness. Adeni had heard that such a magic was possible but never knew anyone who was able to trap his consciousness into a tree. Strokes of luck. This was magic far beyond her understanding.

Far'ai continued, speaking of his times with Maeve, of him accompanying her here. Of the times before Maeve and of the times after. Shadows lengthened. Adeni's heart sank deeper and deeper the more she heard, heavy with immense sadness that seemed to radiate from the tree.

A teenager, she had only just begun her training as a healer, starting with herbs and small spells. She was good—no, she was one of the best. So young, yet she could already heal people's bodies when struck with natural diseases or broken bones. But being a healer meant a lot more. Her learning was just beginning, her path still long and unclear. The quest to find an answer to the disease of the land was her first step.

Asking the oracle seemed a brilliant idea. Now, as she listened to Far'ai's narration, dejection filled her. There was no oracle, no seer. There would be no answer to the land's plight from this forest. She sat still, rubbing her locket between her fingers. Dark shadows filled the forest. The owl hooted again, this time from farther away.

Adeni swallowed. She had heard the entire story and understood the implication. It all meant something ominous. Frowning, she stroked the branch she was sitting on. She stretched out her fingers and made a face as bark again crumbled into her fingers. Something was not quite right. Far'ai had stopped. She realized that her thoughts had drifted on and she wasn't really listening.

You didn't answer. Why are you here?

The tears that were threatening to roll took on a life of their own. "I...I thought..." and then her shoulders shook trying to stop the sobs. Sitting atop the dark Keia trunk, Adeni told the tree what brought her there. She spoke of the land, its affliction, the droughts and the famines. She described the first day she chose her assignment.

Mandissa smiled and shook her head. "This wouldn't work, little one. No oracle can tell you what happened, let alone give you an answer to the problem. Let's find another assignment for you."

"But what is the point? I want to make a difference, High Priestess!" Adeni almost stamped her foot in defiance, using her grandmother's title to address her.

"You have all your life. What's the hurry?" Mandissa's eyebrows arched at the way her grand-daughter used "High Priestess."

Adeni clenched her teeth, knowing that her sneer had not escaped the older woman, who had kindly chosen to ignore it. "I won't live long enough if this famine continues anyway. This is urgent, can't you see?"

Now, Mandissa glowered at her protégé. "Of course, it is the most urgent issue of the land. But the Council will solve the problem. We need you to concentrate on your training."

"The Council! Hmmph," said Adeni, waving her arms about before storming out.

Continuous badgering for a couple of days, and Mandissa eventually relented. Adeni got three days to return with a solution, after which she'd have to attempt whatever mild task the High Priestess and her council came up with.

Adeni's tears of failure now flowed unchecked down her cheeks. "We are doomed, I think. The Council is looking for a solution, but I doubt they can come up with something fast enough. A bunch of stuck-up morons!"

Again, the now familiar silence ensued for a few moments. Then the slow deep voice of Far'ai came through to her, clear as if he was sitting by her on the bough.

You did right. Keia is intimately tied to the land. For the past several decades I have been Keia's soul. Now I am tired and grow weary easily. Everyone has his time. Mine is now. It's time for me leave for the Kingdom of the Clouds, where the rest of my loved ones await me. I cannot sustain

Keia anymore.

Adeni's eyes grew round at this disclosure of doom. She looked down at her hands which now held the red, disintegrating bark of the Keia. The dying tree broadcast Far'ai's exhaustion. Keia was trying hard to hang onto Far'ai but Adeni sensed that the old gent had no desire to struggle for life. His energy depleted, he was slowly beginning to give in to the call of the Clouds.

"Is there no way out? No way to save Keia? To save the land?" she asked, but this time the words barely emerged from her lips, her thoughts going around in circles going over every possible story she had heard, every chapter of the healing book she had memorized, every page from the book of spells that she recalled.

Hmm. Difficult. Yes. There is only one way. But it is very difficult. In fact, it is almost impossible.

The cool atrium was a welcome change to the heat outside and Adeni was happy to step into the high priestess's room. The cool marble floor shone and the fountain in the center of the room babbled happily. Billows of white curtains framed the windows, enhancing the bright, happy and cool effect of the room.

"Welcome back, welcome back." Mandisa's voice rang clear through the atrium as she strode in, beaming at her granddaughter. Adeni went on her knees before the elderly lady.

"Grandmother," Adeni said, bowing her head.

"What did you find, my dear? Is there an oracle? Is there a solution to our problem?"

Adeni gulped as she stood. "Before I tell you about my quest, grandmother, I need to hear from you directly. Who exactly is Far'ai?"

A frown developed between Mandissa's eyes. "Was, my little dove…*was*." Her eyes clouded over. She sighed, clearly not noticing Adeni shaking her head. "The story of Far'ai is lost in the ages. He was the companion of Maeveleh, our great healer. Maeve had managed to defeat the Dark Wizard ages ago but it is well known that she never took any companion after Far'ai. Lucky for us the lineage of healers and priests continued with her brother, else all that our ancestors earned in collective knowledge would have died with Maeve." Mandissa reached out and touched the locket around Adeni's neck.

Again, Adeni shook her head. "Far'ai is around, grandmother. Though not for long. He is with Keia, and Keia is dying."

Mandissa's frown deepened and she sat down facing Adeni as the younger woman began narrating her experiences from the past three days. Shadows lengthened as they conversed softly. Evening breezes lifted the sheer white curtains in swaying waves and the conversation and arguments between the two ladies grew muffled, entangled in the swell of the fabric.

Hot winds from the lowlands blew past Adeni's face. She licked her lips and considered taking a sip from her leather canteen but decided against it. She could go a bit longer without collapsing from dehydration. But then again, she would resolve the crisis of the land. Fertile land would return. Changing her mind, she tipped her head back and took a long gulp from her canteen. Behind her, her family shambled on, as if dragging their feet could delay the event they were going to solemnize. Mandissa, eyes swollen from hours of crying the previous night and from holding back unshed tears, walked as close to Adeni as she could.

Adeni's siblings carried the equipment needed for the ceremony. One carried a flute denoting air. Another bore a large canteen of water. Her sister held an earthenware pot. Mandissa's grip on the firesticks tightened. Fire, the final element under the sky, would complete the ritual.

The retinue came to a stop on the outskirts of the forest. Adeni, dressed in white muslin, her long hair braided tight with strips of colored cloth and leather boots, looked resplendent and ready. Standing at the edge of the Amani woods, she turned to Mandissa.

"For the land and for her children, a life to be set free, a life to be saved," she chanted.

Tears pooled in Mandissa's eyes. She blinked and released them. As they flowed down her wrinkled cheeks, she repeated the chant, "For the land and for her children, a life to be set free, a life to be saved…." Then with a deep breath added the rejoinder in a whisper: "A life to be given freely."

Adeni shook her head. *No tears, grandmother.* She then proceeded to hug each of her family, looking deep into their faces. Immense sadness clutched at her heart, holding her back.

To leave all of them behind. To let each one of them go.

Her feet suddenly felt heavy and her throat parched. She then abruptly turned and focused her gaze on the woods, where Keia stood, where Far'ai waited for her.

A life to be set free, a life to be saved.

The group set up the ritual. Mandissa gave her a quick hug and turned. Adeni knew she wouldn't have been able to face her granddaughter's sacrifice. The grand priestess then raised her staff to the sky and began her chanting. The tune was haunting, a moaning set to a slow rhythm.

Adeni stepped into a dance to the tune and faced the forest. She was ready.

Ready to take Far'ai's place.

A life to be given freely.

WOODLAND SIGNS

Josh Snider

Warmth.

Light.

A damned bright one.

Darek groaned loudly, rolling onto his back.

"Ninety million miles away, through an entire forest, and you still find the one fucking gap in my curtains?" Tired fingers fumbled to rub at his stinging eyes.

Silence answered his annoyance. A shadowed room met his wandering gaze, save for the single sunbeam streaking across from the picture window. Dark oak log walls stood tall, begging the thought of how many stories they had been witness to over the decades.

The old bed creaked as Darek sat up and stretched. A heavy sigh filled the air as he shrank back down before standing. Scratchy fibers of a second-hand rug met tender feet as he strode to the window, pulling the curtains open.

Streams of light poured through pine branches into the room. Vibrant greens and browns filled the view, scrub bush ringing the edge of the clearing. Dirt, near black with nutrients and ready for planting, filled the space up to the house.

No stranger's face waiting for him to open his home to their greedy eyes. No monsters lurking to lunge at him. Just the serenity of nature, the same as he'd left it the night before when the curtains closed him into the safety of the cabin bedroom.

Overslept. Again. He glanced at the clock as it blinked at him having lost power sometime in the night. Darek grunted, looking up through the trees at the sun, past its mid-day peak. His gaze lingered a moment as cogs spun in his mind. *Could work inside.*

Darek spun as half-finished projects flooded his thoughts. The partially built dresser sagging sadly in the corner, the light switch hanging from its haphazardly attached wiring, boxes half-heartedly emptied and discarded. Another sigh as he chose to ignore the bedroom projects and trudge into the bathroom.

Darek hit the switch, waiting for the dim bulb to flicker to life. Pale light revealed more of a closet than a bathroom. The clawfoot tub had been crammed in by some previous owner, now wedged firmly in the corner and barely leaving any room to sit on the toilet without his knees pressing uncomfortably into the side. The shower head hung loosely from the wall as its only support came from the exposed pipes that ran into the floor and below the house. He wondered how many leaks awaited discovery below his feet and shuddered at the thought of crawling around in the dark.

Darek didn't fear the shadows themselves; they brought a soothing peace to the world. Rather, he feared what waited in the shadows of his mind, which sought existence in the darkest corners of his reality. A shudder ran up his spine, heart quickening at the idea. A quick shake of his head brought him back into the moment. He tugged at the sink drawer, pulling an orange bottle out and downing a couple of the pills inside. A familiar calm washed over his mind with the movement. He glanced up.

The reflection of a worn, sunburned face stared back at

him from the mirror. Short salt and pepper hair topped his head, slicked back with the previous day's sweat and grime. He grimaced, squinting at the visage. The face contorted and squinted back, seeming to twist in on itself more than Darek thought he had.

"Who are you glaring at?" He stepped back from the mirror and pulled off his sweat stained tank top to reveal a pale, scrawny form covered in bruises and cuts, both fresh and scabbed over, covering his flesh.

Amidst the aching chaos was a strange addition. Old, yet new. Darek ran a finger along the line where flesh raised into a scar.

Where did you come from?

He looked down from the mirror, confirming the scar was real and not some trick of the light. It was small, maybe an inch long, and thin. Flesh pulled taught around it as if the wound had long healed but no injuries came to mind in the area, much less a scar.

"Working too hard." He shrugged it off. "Speaking of…." Darek turned on the shower, stepping in and letting the steam engulf him, thankful he had started the repairs by upgrading the cabin's water heater.

As the scalding water ran over his shoulders, melting away the previous day's stress, he thought again of what was left to do.

Plant the garden, and preferably not oversleep the cool morning air to do so.

Finish the dresser along with the rest of the furniture he'd ordered.

Put the kitchen sink back together.

His thoughts swirled with the tasks as puffs of steam rose from the bottom of the tub. Slowly he drifted into creativity. The fun in buying a new home. Deciding the flow of each room and how he would find the exact right angle to put the couch for maximum relaxation and minimal glare of the TV he had yet to purchase.

Soap foamed as his ideas grew, drawing frustration as the suds slid into his eyes and derailed any useful thought.

"God damn it." Darek rinsed a hand, swiping it across his eyes.

The water started to cool. Even the new heater was unable to keep up with his aching body's demands. Darek rinsed quickly, hoping to avoid the soon to be chilly water, and the worsening aches it would bring.

Drying off, he glanced at the foggy mirror. In the distorted reflection he seemed different. Broader shoulders, standing taller, and much darker eyes that sent a chill up his spine. A quick wipe of the towel revealed his clean, but still battered, form.

Darek exhaled sharply, heart pounding in his ears. He swiped the towel across the mirror again, then a third time to confirm the reflection wouldn't suddenly change back into the darker version of himself. He wrapped the towel around his waist and headed to the kitchen.

He took note of the unfinished projects here too. Cabinet doors falling from their hinges. The one below the sink sat open to reveal torn apart plumbing with no end in sight. The only parts of the kitchen that felt whole were the table and its single chair. Even the dingy yellow fridge felt ancient and on its last legs.

No sink meant cooking was not an option. Darek stared into the fridge. White take-out containers glared back, foam and cardboard blending together into a wall of depression eating. He grabbed the frontmost box and shook it to confirm the day-old and fridge-dried Chinese inside. He sat and popped a piece of chicken into his mouth, chewing far too long as he ruminated.

He glared at the cabinets and their peeling paint. He'd bought this house months ago, planning to fix it up into his own little retreat. A safe haven from the stress of the outside world, a place to calm the growing terrors of his mind. Instead he'd brought the stress with him and let it taint the work done so far, avoiding necessary projects in favor of hiding from the to-do list in his nightmares.

A heavy groan escaped between chomps on the jerky-like chicken.

So much to do, so little will to do it.

Darek's eyes looked between the sink and the cabinets. Both were equally as annoying, being among the first projects he'd chosen to take on and abandon.

Sink first. I need to be able to wash dishes and not eat this… garbage. He sneered at the open container before throwing it in the bin.

Darek quickly dressed, his clothes stiff with dried mud and sweat.

Need to do the wash too. He grimaced at the stench of stale body odor that washed over him and shivered, feeling the need to shower again already. Old boots slid on easily as the worn leather stretched to accommodate his foot once more. Bits of dirt flaked off onto the rug, adding to its scratchy texture, and crunching underfoot as Darek trudged back to the door.

He gave a final glance over the ramshackle home and its overbearing repairs. A quick nod and he yanked the keys to the sedan out front from their hook. The door fought against his initial tug, finally releasing with a piercing squeal as the hinges ground against the movement.

The screech was soon joined in song by birds and bugs, all singing out at the top of their voices. Darek cringed at the sudden assault on his ears. For as much was wrong with the cabin, it still held the silence in.

Darek strode towards his black sedan, ignoring the dusty coating it had acquired in the many trips to town and back. Familiar fear gripped his chest at the idea of going into town. So many people, even in a small mountain town. Too many. He needed to ground; that's what the therapist said. Panic can't take hold if you ground.

Darek looked at the forest around him, shadows growing

darker by the second. Bird song turned into a discordant cacophony of screeches and screams. Black figures darted from tree to tree, hiding in the bushes and scrambling up trunks. Darek clenched his fists.

Just a hallucination.

He took a deep breath in and closed his eyes. The symphony of terror assaulting his ears released its hold. Screeches turned back into gentle whistles and calls.

Another look around brought some calm to his mind as the song of nature quieted some at his presence. Darek savored scent of pine as the clean air helped to purge the negativity from his thoughts. The sunlight was a little less blinding as he smiled, happy to be starting once again on his dream.

One more calming breath and he stepped into the car. It turned over easily, rolling into motion as the trees and foliage seemed to part and reveal the dirt road ahead. A soft grin settled on Darek's face as he drove, rounding the corner from his driveway to the road.

Gravel crunched and shifted loudly under the weight of the vehicle as he rounded the first corner. The sun fell steadily into the dark trees, swallowed whole by the shadowed figures.

"Geeze it gets dark early up here." Darek focused on the sinking globe in his rearview as it fell behind the mountain.

He followed the winding mountain road through the canyon. The thick wall of pines broke into a clearing of tall mountain grass and wildflowers. Darek slowed to a stop. In the middle of the clearing stood a doe and her fawn, grazing lazily. He smiled at the calm scene. Streams of sunlight added a movie quality to it. Both deer lifted their heads, eyes trained directly on him.

The dark orbs shined in the evening light, glistening with caution before the pair turned and ran into the woods.

Darek sighed before continuing and finishing the drive into town in silence. Long shadows stretched beyond him as if the trees were reaching directly into town.

He pulled into the convenience store, receiving a cheery smile from the old woman behind the counter who watched him park. He stepped into the rapidly cooling air, breathing in the scent of the pines, still untainted by larger towns. Darek gave a small smile back to the woman and stepped into the shop.

She called out to him in the warm, raspy voice of a friendly old smoker. "We're s'posed to be closin' soon, but if you don't make a mess I won't rush ya." She gave a light wave, her floral dress flowing from the movement.

"Thanks." Darek said, nodding at her.

The old woman smiled again and turned to sweep behind the register.

Darek wandered into the paint aisle, looking over the meager offerings. A rich brown caught his eye, drawing him to pick up the can. The spot on top glinted faintly in the fluorescent light, as if still wet. Tinges of red showed through the brown.

Wasn't mixed very well. Darek shrugged before turning towards the brushes.

A reflection of movement caught his eye in one of the metallic handle pieces. The misshapen dark head of someone standing directly behind him. Darek stepped to the side, thinking another patron must have come in after him, though he hadn't heard the bell.

"Sorry." He muttered as he shuffled to the side.

The figure shifted with him, staying just behind his right shoulder. The way it moved sent a shiver up Darek's spine. The limbs seemed to flow, as if just dragged along and not moving on their own. He froze, icy tendrils spreading from his neck where frozen breath blew across his flesh. Shadows danced at the edges of his vision as panic took hold. Darek spun to face the figure.

Nothing. Just another set of shelves with more basic home improvement supplies.

He chuckled, blowing out a harsh breath to calm his heart.

"Just another hallucination." Darek reminded himself.

"Doc said they might still happen for a bit, even in a small town away from stress."

A sudden voice startled him. "You okay dear?"

Darek spun to face the old woman. The paint can fell from his fingers, spilling across the floor.

"Oh, dear! I didn't mean to give you a fright." She smiled warmly, hands raised in a gesture of peace.

"Shit." Darek fell to his knees to grab the can. "I'm sorry, just jumpy."

The paint flowed into an ever-growing puddle, the dark brown streaked with rusty red lines that stretched and crossed like veins. Darek's eyes followed the flow to the old woman's feet.

Dirt covered and scarred flesh met his gaze instead of shoes. Muddy footprints lead back to the counter where she'd been standing when he came in. Behind the counter stuck out a pair of white shoes, speckled with blood.

He looked further up to see her floral dress had hidden specks of red amongst its pattern, though the bottom hem was soaked through.

"I'm, uh, just gonna go." Darek stood, eyes kept low to hide his fear.

He closed his eyes for a second to right his balance, though when he opened them again the store lights had gone out. Only a dim bulb tried to fight the encroaching shadows over the door.

"Oh deary." The old woman's voice took on a deep, rumbling undertone. "Don't go so soon. Why don't you dance with us in the dark a while?" She snatched his hand, nails digging into his flesh.

Darek yelped, trying desperately to pull away from her grasp. Her face had sunken in, skin pulled taught over bone. Her warm smile replaced by a smirk of the darkest intentions.

"Get off, you old bat!" He shoved the woman hard to the ground.

She let out a scream of surprise and pain. The store lights

returned to normal. He looked to the old woman laying in a puddle of plain brown paint. Darek's gaze darted from the stunned woman to the empty space behind the counter and back. Her leg was broken and twisted, her foot now up near her shoulder.

"Why?" She whimpered.

"I'm so sorry." He muttered. "I—" Darek fled the store, ignoring her cries for help.

Warmth.

Light.

A damned bright one.

Darek rubbed at his aching head. A low groan escaped his throat as memories of the previous night came flooding back. The old woman, her ghastly visage, the broken leg he caused in a panic.

"Fuck."

Darek sat up, realizing he just left her there. His inability to tell psychosis from reality finally hurt someone. In a haze, Darek jumped from the bed, snatching his phone from the bedside table, and called his psychiatrist.

"Doctor Hinks' office." The assistant, Julie, answered in her usual strained, sweet tone.

"It's Darek, I need—"

"I'm sorry, Doctor Hinks has a patient currently Darek." Her tone shifted to one of pity and annoyance. She had tired of his emergency calls long ago.

"Listen, I need to talk to him now. I think… I think I hurt someone." Darek's voice trembled.

An extended silence answered his plea.

"Hello?"

A click, then Doctor Hinks' voice. "Darek? What happened?"

"Oh, thank god." Darek breathed in slowly. "The meds aren't helping, and coming out here feels like a mistake. There's so many shadows, and noises, and still people in town, and—"

"Darek." The doctor cut in. "Julie said you hurt someone?"

A pit settled in Darek's stomach. He stood, pacing around the dark room.

"Y-yes. An old woman. I was buying paint to clean up the house."

"Okay, good. Tasks keep your mind focused and keeps it from wandering dangerously. What else?"

Darek paused a moment. "Well, the lights went out, and the counter lady turned into some kind of demon. She wanted me to dance in the dark with her, and I shoved her. She fell and her leg snapped and was at this really bad angle and I just left her there."

A short pause broken by hastened scribbling answered him.

"What do I do?" Tears welled in Darek's eyes as the full weight of his actions hit him.

Doctor Hinks gave a heavy sigh through pursed lips. "You need to call someone and make sure she's okay Darek. Then go to the police station, tell your story there, and let the courts do their work. In the meantime, I'll have a new prescription sent over for you."

The knot in Darek's stomach tightened. "But then they'll know. They'll know who I am and what's wrong with me. I'll have to leave again. Don't make me go back to the clinic, please." Images of the inpatient psychiatric facility flashed through his mind.

The dull gray walls, the bland food, and the constant questions asked at all hours of the day. Long dark shadows that grew as lights out approached through the never-ending hallways.

"I can't go back." Darek whispered.

The doctor sighed. "It's okay Darek, just a minor slip up. Maybe she's fine and it just looked wrong in your panic. Just go and make sure she's okay, yeah?"

Darek nodded.

"Darek?"

He breathed deeply. "Okay, yeah. I'm sure she's fine. I'll call now." Tears fell from his eyes. "Thanks."

"Just call me ba—" Doctor Hinks' voice was cut short by Darek ending the call.

He sat on the bed, body shaking violently. His nerves were fried, and now he was relapsing. Psychosis was the final nail in the coffin of his old life. No friends, no family, no steady job outside of some freelance digital art. He'd crumbled from a life of leisure to one of constant fear of the next episode.

"You were supposed to help me!" He shouted, through the window at the forest. "Getting away into nature was supposed to be a cure!"

The trees waved leisurely in the breeze, uncaring.

Darek stared at the edge of the woods, afternoon sun streaming through every break in the branches.

"Okay." Darek wiped his eyes and sniffed. "Okay."

He pulled up the number for the local sheriff and called. The line rang a few times before a gruff voice answered.

"Is this an emergency?"

Darek swallowed. "No, well yes. Maybe?" Every nerve felt alive with panic.

"What's the address of your potential emergency?" The man sounded annoyed at his lack of specifics.

"It's the old general store and hardware shop on the edge of town."

"I've told you kids to stop going out there. Who is this? Is this Jim's son? He's gonna beat you bloody, I swear—"

Darek cut him off mid rant. "No! I was shopping there last night for some basics and… The old woman seemed like she wasn't doing so well. I wanted to make sure she was okay."

A deep grumble came through the line. "Listen, I don't know who you are, but prank calls are not taken lightly here. There is no general store here. There hasn't been since the Shar family left."

"What? No, I was just there. I was buying—"

"Goodbye sir." A heavy click echoed in the receiver.

"What the fuck?" Darek stared at his phone a moment.

No store? The image of the old woman lying in a puddle of paint flashed through his mind. *No, I'm not that crazy.*

Darek rushed to put on his clothes before storming out of the house. Bright sunlight filled his vision, the sound of chirping birds assaulting his ears again.

"I'll just go there and call again from the shop." He slammed the car door behind him. "That'll prove where I was."

Darek sped down the gravel driveway, turning quickly onto the dirt road without looking.

Warmth.

A light.

A damned bright one.

Darek groaned, rolling over and rubbing his eyes.

Wait.

He froze, fingers pressed into his eyes.

He jolted up, panic dulling the ache in his body. His worried gaze darted around the room, the covers tossed free of the bed. Dust and sweat covered his body again, mixing into a disgusting mud on his sheets. More grime under his nails. But no memory beyond driving away.

Darek stood, urging memories of the day before to come forward. He had woken the same way, showered, and left for… something. Trembling fingers rubbed at his temples as his mind stopped dead at the end of the driveway.

Breathe.

A deep inhale brought some sense of clarity, though memory stayed far from his grasp.

"Okay." Darek opened his eyes again. "It was just a nightmare."

He grabbed the curtains and yanked them open. He was met once more by the forest. Deep brown trees, green covered pine branches, dark scrub bush. The same view he'd fallen in love with, but the sun was once again beyond its midday height.

Darek checked his phone. No outgoing calls to Doctor Hinks or the sheriff.

"Yeah, just a nightmare." The missing time forgotten in his relief, Darek looked once more at the empty dirt waiting to be planted, then at the clock still blinking midnight.

Useless piece of junk.

He shook his head, going once again to the bathroom, ignoring the still unfinished projects demanding his attention along the way.

The same weathered face in the mirror greeted his entrance, adorned with a bit more stubble than the day before. Once again pulling off his shirt Darek stopped partway as his eye caught another scar on his chest. This one connected with the middle of the first, not quite overlapping it.

His heart drummed loudly in his ears as an uneasy feeling settled into the pit of his stomach. He ran a finger along the new scar again. It felt the same as the first, long healed and the skin only slightly raised and discolored.

Darek's breathing became shallow as he studied them, his mind wrestling with the scars that had not been there previously, as well as his lack of memory of the day before.

"Okay." He took a deep breath, holding it and rubbing at his face. "Okay, they're just scars, and it was a long day yesterday. That's all."

Darek talked himself out of panic mode. Slow, deliberate breaths brought a small sense of calm back to his shaking body. He turned and kicked on the hot water, stepping under it to wash the stress from his body and think.

He fought to bring the tasks at hand back to focus, ignoring what he couldn't explain.

Furniture. Decorating. Repairs.

Make a doctor's appointment.

The thought made his heart skip a beat, worry for his potentially slipping mind drowning out the needs of his home.

Breathe, Darek. You've made it this long without a panic attack, don't break now. In.

The steamy air filled his lungs.

Out.

He sighed loudly, willing the unnecessary stress out with it.

In.

Another breath brought the stench of rot, overpowering the clean smell of soap, and with it came the overwhelming sense of dread. Darek's eyes flashed open, locking on the figure in the mirror again. Except this time, it wasn't a reflection of the bathroom. More like a window. The figure seemed to be standing in the woods, jet black tree trunks and branches interlocking in a shadowed web behind him.

Scalding water did nothing to ease the chill clawing its way up his spine. Fetid air stuck to the inside of his lungs, refusing to leave no matter how hard he tried to exhale, muscles contracting painfully on his overfull lungs.

Those shadowed eyes glared into his from behind the foggy mirror. Bloody scratches being etched into its chest, a dripping shard of glass clenched tight in the figure's fist.

Its gaze kept him locked in place as the water seemed to get even hotter, beyond what he could stand, burning his skin while icy tendrils of fear pushed through his body. He could feel the flesh blistering on his back, skin sloughing off in large strips as his core froze, heart slowing with the chill. Nausea ripped through him as fear dug its claws deeper into his mind. Finally, the agony pushed the rotten air from his lungs in a heart-wrenching wail, darkness covering everything in sight save that horrible version of himself. Even in the fog of the misty mirror Darek could see the wicked grin plastered on his own face.

He fell from the shower, retching between the sobs that wracked his body. As he lay on the cool tile, vision returning to normal, he tentatively probed at the edges of his back. The skin felt smooth and soft.

He slowly stood, bracing on the counter, and wiped at the mirror. Nothing but his own fear-stricken face. He twisted and turned, inspecting every inch of his back. No peeling flesh, no blisters, just the same bruised and sore back he knew.

Halting breaths came slowly in the damp air. A shaking hand fumbled through the sink drawer, pulling the prescription bottle free and popping two pills into his mouth. Darek swallowed them dry, sucking in a deep breath after.

Ground yourself. It's just your mind grasping for understanding of your stress.

Doctor Hinks echoed in his ears.

He turned off the shower and stepped in front of the mirror again, splashing cold water from the sink on his flushed face. His heart rate fell into a calmer rhythm, no longer pounding deafeningly in his ears.

"Okay." Another splash of icy water. "Okay."

Dragging his hands down his face Darek stood up straight again, feeling the panic ebb from his mind.

"So much for having a project helping me." He grumbled, pulling open the door to step out in a wall of steam. He trudged to the kitchen, feet slapping wetly on the hardwood floor.

The kitchen that greeted him felt different, wrong. He stopped, focusing on the feeling, trying to work through it, to ride it out calmly.

There's nothing wrong here. It's just your mind processing.

Darek repeated this over and over, closing his eyes as he fought to get control over the rising panic. Opening his eyes, he scanned the room to prove it was normal. The cabinets still sagged, the trash still overflowed with takeout containers, and the sink was still useless.

Darek's gaze locked on the small window above the counter. The trees shifted and waived unsettlingly. He shook his head, trying to make sense of their movements. The trunks seemed to bend and curve like snakes.

Count to five.

Darek closed his eyes, counting slowly with each breath. Once his eyes reopened the trees no longer moved. He moved over to the counter, intent on forcing himself to stay grounded. Not even a summer breeze stirred the branches.

"It's fine." Darek looked around more, inspecting each tree and bush individually. The trees felt closer somehow, though he chalked it up to a trick of the lowering sun.

He stepped over to the fridge and pulled open the aging appliance. The idea of food turned his stomach, but Darek stood there anyway, reveling in the cool air of familiarity.

"Today should be the sink." He turned, examining the rusted kitchen faucet. Cold air flowed around his calves as he thought, goosebumps creeping up his legs.

With a slow breath out, Darek closed the fridge behind him and headed to the bedroom to get dressed.

Darek stood, buckling his belt, and pulled on a t-shirt. He fought to focus on the list of things needed to fix the cabinets. He drifted through the house in a daze, feeling drained and sluggish.

He carefully pulled the keys from their hook and stepped outside. Fresh pine air filled his nostrils again, bird song floating through the air. The walk from front porch to his car felt a lifelong journey as each step dragged on, draining what little energy he had left.

A small grin settled on his face regardless, the smell of clean air and the sounds of nature overwhelming the paranoia and anxiety of the morning. He slid into the driver's seat, calmly rolling down the driveway again, turning onto the road.

Warmth.

And the god damned sunlight again.

Darek shot up, his stomach aching from the movement. His skin felt tight almost as if it couldn't move with him. He leapt from the bed, mind locked on getting his pills before panic set in again.

Before he could take a step, his attention was grabbed by the open curtains. He always closed them before bed. Even having bought a house in the middle of the woods he worried about potentially being watched while he slept.

But they stood open today. Even with the fabric gone the trees blocked most light from coming in. The shadows felt darker this time, the trees seeming to reach out to him, limbs contorting into grasping claws. Darek shook his head hard and shot into the bathroom, his heart hammering harder with each moment.

He deliberately ignored the mirror and the ominous figure looking back from it, the shifting trees behind the figure, anything that wasn't his pills. Rummaging through the drawer yielded only more worry, the pill bottle was missing. Fumbling through the drawer again brought the same result. No meds.

"Okay. White knuckling today, it is." Darek gripped the edge of the counter tightly, squeezing his eyes shut tightly. "It's fine. I'm fine."

He opened his eyes, looking into the reflection. No dark figure, no evil grin. Just tired eyes and a sunburned face.

A sigh of relief escaped his lips, though the skin on his stomach was tugging again. A step back revealed more scars, intricate and flowing together in a terrifying calligraphy, spelling out a message.

Hello

Shadows flashed across his vision, filling his gaze as icy fingers dug through his body, grasping at every loose thread in his mind.

Warmth.

Light.

Panic.

Sobs wracked Darek's body as he refused to rise, to even roll away from the stinging light in his eyes. If he stayed in bed then he wouldn't have to face himself, real or shadow. He wouldn't have to acknowledge the new tugging on his torso, whatever message was now carved into his flesh.

If he didn't see it, it couldn't hurt him.

As he lay there, the sobs ebbed into a silent agony of the soul. The quiet of the cabin gave life to every demon that lay in wait in his mind.

A crouched beast glared from the darkest corner of the room. It's clawed feet tapped on the hardwood, echoing in his mind, yet no sound reached Darek's ears.

The dark walls shimmered and gave way to a never-ending sea of trees bathed in shadow. Black limbs reaching out, clawing at the air, waving to him. Glowing white eyes peered at him from around the evergreens and the remaining furniture in the room. Pictures floated in the nothingness as safe havens for creatures unimaginable.

Some winged monstrosity perched on the curtain rod, silently opening and closing its beak at his shivering form. Talons scratched at the brass, leaving deep gashes wherever they touched. The rod wept an inky blackness into the room from the open wounds, pooling and swirling ever closer to the bed.

Darek turned over, pulling the covers over his head to hide from the ever-growing crowd of creatures. Even in the complete darkness, he could see their fingers…claws…branches…elongated appendages pressing against the bedsheets. Digging at him. Feeling for his flesh to leave their next message. To bid him onward.

Why was this their game?

"No!" He wailed, weeping around the words. "This is my escape!" He shook violently under the covers, demanding control. Safety. Anything.

He withdrew the sheet, revealing an empty room. No beasts. No shadow creatures. No forest.

Darek cried freely, tears soaking into the pillow as he gave in to exhaustion and fell unconscious once more.

Darek opened his eyes slowly. No sunlight. No creatures as far as his aching eyes could tell. A shuddering breath brought the scent of pine.

He slowly sat up, peering around the room. The blinds were open. Very little light filtered in through the trees as the sun set low. Rich purple tendrils arced across the sky. The trees felt foreboding at this time of day, looming tall and dark.

He noticed the window open just a crack, just enough to allow the eerie silence to seep in with the soothing scent of pine. No bird songs, nor even the usual insect buzzing that signaled the start of night in the forest.

Darek stood, breathing in the scent of normalcy before closing the window as he strode to the bathroom. The drawer sat wide open, its contents torn apart and strewn across the counter. All except for a small orange bottle sitting in the drawer.

He chuckled, slowly letting it turn into a deep belly laugh as the stress and fear leeched from his pores.

"God fucking damn it." He laughed harder, doubling over, holding the counter for support.

"Hoooo…." Darek breathed out hard, getting control of himself again. "Okay." He grabbed the bottle, popping a few pills in his mouth.

A few extra couldn't hurt right now, he thought, popping a couple more in his mouth before suckling the sink for some help to swallow the mouthful.

He glanced at the mirror.

Tired, red streaked eyes looked back. His face thin and gaunt, like he hadn't eaten in weeks. Yellowed teeth sneered as his lips pulled back to see the graying gums that had sunk into themselves.

Panic rose again like the bile tickling the back of his throat. How long had he been locked in this house?

Bang.

Darek spun to face the open door, a darkened hallway lay beyond.

Bang.

Something was smacking into a window, the sound of glass rattling in its pane echoed through the house.

Bang.

Terror held Darek in place as the banging stopped. His breathing came in short gasps, his chest and stomach tightening with each one. He moved to face the mirror again, his body moving of its own accord. He stared in horror as his hands pulled up off the tank top again. More scars replaced the old ones, intricately, almost artistically carved into his flesh.

Answer the call.

A silent scream caught in his throat, mouth gaped wide as the scars shifted and changed. Darek could feel his skin changing. The memory of agony clawed at his mind as some unknown talon had carved his flesh, yet no actual pain came as the scars formed their next message.

You cannot ignore us.

More ghostly memories of pain as line after line was carved into his flesh, healing into a horrifically beautiful letter to his broken psyche.

You cannot hide from us.

Darek fought to stay awake. Darkness crept into his vision, shadowed fingers waving from his periphery. Teeth ground together tightly, threatening to crack each other apart as he battled for control of his own mind.

Darek swallowed hard. Panic built in his chest, fear clawing at the tattered edges of his mind, silent whispers filled his ears. Unseen eyes peered at him from ever corner. He knew it. He knew they were watching his every breath.

Bang.

Darek jumped at the sound, regaining control of his body. Jaw tight, he leaned around the doorway, peering into the dim bedroom.

A tree branch banged against the window again, its limb curled over itself, almost as a fist knocking on the window. Pulling back before slamming forward again. Each impact rattling the glass, threatening to shatter it.

"Stop." The word came out as a whisper.

Another hit, cracking the window.

"Stop!" Darek shouted, his voice booming louder than expected and startling himself.

The limb paused a moment. Carefully, the branches unfurled into their natural form again before retreating into the shadows beyond.

A shaky breath slipped from his quivering lips. Exhaustion tugged at him, begging him to lie down. Darek shook his head, looking back to the mirror. Dark eyes looked back at him, that wicked grin once again present, this time clear and burning into his mind.

The sound of glass shattering filled his ears, yet he dared not look away from the mirror again. He watched in a panicked stupor as the next message arose from his flesh.

Come dance with us in the dark.

SCARLET AND THE WOODSMAN

Carolyn Kay

Scarlet pulled her hood further over her head and settled in the shadowed corner, cradling her injured arm. The tavern was modest and poorly lit except for the center of the hall where a large antler chandelier hung from the ceiling. Dozens of stinking tallow candles dripped molten fat onto the table—and occasionally its occupants—below. The stench didn't seem to bother most of the patrons, but Scarlet found the burning tallow mixed with the scent of stale beer and even staler humans all but unbearable.

By the bar, a broad-chested young man, no more than twenty, regaled most of the village with a tale of heroic daring. At least that was the story his words conveyed. His green eyes said something different. They darted to the shadows, as if he were worried something lurked there.

The central table held a sizeable feast. All to celebrate the death of a horrible monster that'd been terrorizing the small hamlet. And by terrorizing, the villagers meant a few sheep had been killed and maybe a goat or three. It was terror only for the slain.

A sly orange tabby with most of an ear missing snagged a hand pie while no one was looking and ran off. It made a bee-line to Scarlet's corner, but pulled up short when it caught her scent. Fur rippling, it arched its back and fluffed its tail, hissing around its prize. Scarlet growled at the little thief, a deep rumbling at the back of her throat. She didn't think it was possible for the cat's tail to get bigger, but it doubled in size. She chuckled as the poor thing ran a zigzag into the far shadows, its dinner forgotten on the sticky floor.

A comely barmaid approached Scarlet's table with a pitcher of ale. She smelled of oat grass and goats. Scarlet waved her away. Her mug of ale sat untouched on the rough wood table. She didn't like ale; her tastes ran richer, but it was easier to listen in on conversations if the tavern folk thought you were just a drunk in a corner.

"The beast could have stood shoulder to shoulder with a horse," the young man said, "with teeth as long as my hand." He held up his hand for comparison and the small crowd around him gasped. "It had long black fur and a row of teats like a sow that leaked blood." The barmaid blanched at the description and hurried behind the bar.

Scarlet growled under her breath.

"It lunged at me and I fought it off with my axe. All the while, the first one, the one in the trap, growled and tried to free itself." The young woodsman puffed up his chest, trying to look brave.

Scarlet bet the people gathered around him couldn't smell the sour fear that still clung to him. She rubbed at the ache in her arm.

The man continued after a long pull from his mug. "At one point, I thought I was done for. The beast had me pinned. Its slavering jaws were going for my throat, but the other one barked, and suddenly I found myself free. I pushed to my feet in time to see the beast release its comrade. But that was its downfall."

He paused, looking around the crowd. Seemingly pleased with their rapt attention, he continued. "While it helped its friend, I raised my axe and brought it down upon the beast's head, splitting it like a melon." His fist hit the table with a resounding thud. Several in the crowd jumped. "I'm sad to say the other beast got away, but its leg was mangled in the trap, so it'll be easy hunting."

The crowd cheered and someone ordered another round of drinks.

Scarlet stood and pushed her way out of the tavern, tears streaming unbidden down her cheeks. She hated these humans. They didn't respect the order of the forest, always taking prime prey and more than they needed, never paying respect to other predators. And they were cutting down her forest to expand their village. More humans were coming. It would only get worse.

The moon was creeping up the horizon, its waxing light illuminating the trees surrounding the village. The pine-scented quiet called to her. Looking over her shoulder to see if she was being followed, Scarlet slipped into the trees and disappeared into the shadows.

The morning crept in on quiet feet. The fog hugging the forest floor glowed with the rising sun. Birds whispered to each other, unable or unwilling to disturb the quiet with loud song. Scarlet loved mornings like this. She stretched, wincing when the wound on her arm pulled.

Damn traps. A coward's way to hunt. She'd been careless when trying to disarm the one she'd found along a well-traveled path. It only firmed her resolve to rid the forest of traps and those who set them so that no one else would get hurt. If a hunter couldn't give their prey a quick death, they had no business hunting.

Shaking pine needles from her cloak, Scarlet stood. She scuffed out the rough hollow that had been her bed. No need to give away the location of a prime sleeping spot. Scents of cooking breakfasts wafted on the smoke from the village, and her stomach rumbled. She turned her back on the village and drifted further into the forest. Breakfast could wait.

Scarlet adjusted her grip on her basket and stepped onto the path. Her shadow stretched before her in the early afternoon sun. The clip-clop of horses' hooves approached from the village. She turned her back to the sound and started walking. When she judged the horse and rider close enough, she stepped off the track to let them pass.

As she expected, the rider moved his horse to the side of the track and slowed. "Ho there," the young man from the tavern said.

Scarlet nodded a greeting, looking up at the young man. The wind blew a lock of red-brown hair across her face and she tucked it behind her ear.

"This is a hunter's track, miss, and not well traveled. May I ask where you're going?"

It was an effort for Scarlet to keep the growl from her voice. "I'm traveling to my grandmother's house." She held up her gingham-covered basket. "She's not as spry as she once was, so I'm bringing her some treats from the village baker."

The young man smiled, showing a row of fine, white teeth, and his blue eyes brightened. "I didn't know anyone lived this deep in the woods. If you don't mind the company, I'll travel with you until I get to my traps."

The hair on Scarlet's neck stood up at the mention of traps, but she remained outwardly calm. "That's kind of you, but there's no need. My path will soon diverge from this track."

"Even more reason for an escort, miss. There are beasts in this wood that wouldn't hesitate to make you their dinner. In fact, I killed one just the other night."

Scarlet's lip started to pull back in a snarl, but she forced herself to smile instead. "Did you now? Well, that does make me more wary. I would welcome your company." The last part she nearly had to spit out, but pushing him away now would only defeat her purpose.

The young man pulled his horse to a stop and dismounted. The horse laid back his ears and danced, ill at ease, but his rider didn't notice. He came around and held out his hand. "Well met, I'm Peter."

Wincing as she switched her basket to her injured arm, she gripped his outstretched hand. "I'm Scarlet. Well met."

"Here, let me take that." Peter reached for the basket. "How did you injure your arm?"

Scarlet thought about not handing over the basket, then relented. Having both hands free could be advantageous. "Oh, it's nothing." She tugged her sleeve over the bandage. "Just a burn from brushing against a hot cooking pot."

"That's too bad." Peter peered into her hood. "Are you new to the village? I don't remember seeing you around."

Scarlet shook her head and started walking. She didn't want to tell Peter anything. Suppressing the urge to change and rip his throat out right then and there took all her self-control. But her grandmother had urged her to try a different way. She'd hold it together, if only out of respect for her elders.

"I live near my grandmother. I came to the village for a few things." Scarlet nodded toward the basket.

"I wasn't aware there was another village nearby," Peter replied. He tugged on his horse's reins to get it to follow. It hesitated, pulling back against Peter's tugs, before relenting and following its master.

"There's a lot of things about this forest that you don't know."

"What is there to know? It's a forest, and one filled with monsters." Peter patted the axe at his hip. "But we can take care of that."

Scarlet turned from him so he wouldn't see her eyes flash and growled softly. She didn't trust herself to respond, so she didn't. She increased her pace.

Peter hopped to keep up. He reached out a hand but drew it back at the look on her face. "Hey, I'm sorry if I scared you. But there are monsters in this wood. I'm surprised your family let you travel alone."

"My family knows I can take care of myself." Scarlet pointed to a faint track ahead on the right. "This is my path. Thank you for your companionship."

Peter raised a hand to stop her. "Are you sure that's the path to your grandma's house?"

Scarlet couldn't quite read his expression. It seemed like a mix between guilt and fear. "Of course I'm sure. Good day." She started down the path, knowing he'd follow despite her dismissal.

"Wait!" Peter squeaked, his voice cracking. He jogged after her, his long legs eating up the distance. "Let me go first. I thought this was a game trail and set out a few traps. I was hoping to catch the companion to the beast I killed the other day."

She stopped and turned to face him. She'd found the traps earlier that morning and disarmed them. Thankfully not in the same way as the day before. Her arm throbbed at the memory.

"Why do you want to trap that other beast? I've heard of no other attacks on the village."

"Why wouldn't I? We need to make the area safe for the loggers that will come soon. We need timber and cleared land to expand the village, but the loggers won't stick around if there are slavering beasts in the woods."

"Slavering—" Scarlet cut herself off. "Expand the village? Why?"

Peter stared at her, his head tilted like a wolf trying to pinpoint a sound. "Why? You really don't come into town often, do you?" He paused for a moment. "Well, aside from the drought to the south, a town that doesn't grow, dies. It's simple economics, really. And once we clear out this forest, there'll be plenty of land for an expanding town and the farms to support it."

Peter's tone grated on Scarlet's nerves. It was condescending, something she noticed men did a lot when talking to women.

They were coming up on one of Peter's traps. He stepped in front of her, nearly knocking her off balance. "Here, hold Dusty's reins. There's a trap up ahead. I need to move it." He thrust the reins and the basket into her hands and jogged up the trail.

Dusty didn't like being held by Scarlet and it was all she could do to keep him from bolting, so she let out the reins as much as she could without losing the animal and waited. She watched Peter kneel to examine the trap, and chuckled when he swore. Scarlet bit her lip to keep from smiling when he returned with the trap over his shoulder, its trigger pan bent at an extreme angle.

"I'm not very familiar with traps, but that doesn't look good." Scarlet did her best to sound sincere.

Peter stowed the trap in one of Dusty's saddle bags, then took the reins back from Scarlet. "Someone sabotaged it," he grumped.

"Not everything in the forest is a mindless animal, you know."

Peter rounded on Scarlet, his face red. "I'd accuse you of damaging my trap, but you're too small. Though I bet you know who did."

Scarlet stood her ground, barely holding back a growl. "Again, we're not the only beings in this forest. There are others who care if another creature gets hurt. Traps are a coward's way to hunt."

She might have gone too far with that statement. Peter's face turned magenta, and his hands clenched into fists. Had Dusty not been so fidgety, he might have come at her, but the horse kept Peter distracted. When she didn't back down, he turned his back on her and started walking.

"What do you know?" he muttered. "You're just a poor girl who lives in the forest with her grandmother."

Scarlet held her tongue until the silence grew uncomfortable. "There's more to this forest than just trees and some beast you keep talking about," she said.

"What, you mean like deer and rabbits?" Peter quipped.

"Yes, and no." She put a hand on his elbow and pointed to an enormous oak tree on their right. "That oak is the ancestral home of a family of dryads. If their tales are true, they've been here since before the mountains. When you cut down the forest, will you destroy their home too?"

Peter snorted. "If what you say is true, I should cut that tree down right now. Everyone knows dryads are evil seductresses."

"Says who? Your storybooks? Have you ever noticed those tales are always told from the human's perspective? Did you ever stop to think that the monsters in your tales might simply be defending their homes or trying to feed their families?" She and her kin had only ever taken the occasional sheep or goat when times were hard. It was an easy kill, but if done too often, would attract unwanted attention.

"Now you're talking nonsense," Peter said. "A monster is a monster. They're mindless beasts who want nothing but to kill and destroy. It's our job to rid this world of their kind."

"Says who?" This was going nowhere. She should just kill him now, but a nagging little voice urged her to wait a little longer. She kept walking, angling off the track.

"God." Peter followed her, too focused on the tree to notice anything else. "He gave mankind dominion over the earth and everything on it."

"That is certainly your opinion," Scarlet whispered.

"What was that?" Peter asked as he jogged a few steps to catch up to her.

"Aren't you afraid of being out here on your own, hunting

down fearsome beasts alone? What happens to the village if you should come to harm?"

Peter puffed out his chest. The gesture warred with the renewed scent of fear rolling off him. "I can take on whatever's out here. But if I should fail, there will be others. You can't stop progress."

Scarlet didn't reply but angled toward a small grove of apple trees. The apples were just starting to ripen. She picked a couple and tossed one to Peter.

"You really know your way around this forest." Peter took a bite of the apple, appearing to savor the taste. "These are wonderful!"

Scarlet picked a few more and tossed them to him. "Save the seeds and plant them in your village."

"Why? I'll just come back here and pick them."

She smiled. "You'd have to remember how to get here."

Peter opened his mouth to reply, then glanced around. His smile fell and was replaced with false bravado. "Well, you can lead me back here, show me the way."

"But you're going to cut down the forest, remember? Besides, wouldn't it be better to have apple trees right in town?" Scarlet liked taunting him. It was like chasing a mouse around a log. Eventually she'd pounce, but for now, the chase was fun.

"It will take some time to cut down this much forest, and time for the trees to grow and bear fruit. You'll just have to show me the way again, and I'll cut a path straight here."

Just like a human to order someone around. "You'll have to get out first," she said around a mouth full of apple.

"What?"

She swallowed, tossing the core onto a pile of scree. The brownie that lived there would appreciate the offering. "Nothing. We should go. It's getting late and we've still got some traveling to do."

She led Peter out of the apple grove. From the corner of her eye, she caught him grabbing a few more apples from the tree. They weren't ripe, but he wouldn't live long enough to find that out.

Shadows lengthened as Scarlet led Peter through the forest. She followed a deer track for a while, then angled off on a rabbit path, until she knew Peter was utterly lost. She watched him looking for landmarks and made sure that no one tree or rock outcrop was distinguishable from the other. Scent, and years living in the woods made it easy for Scarlet to get around, but Peter had no such tools to fall back on. All the while she tried to get him to realize the beauty and preciousness of the forest. But he was stubborn, like a lot of humans.

"We're taking a very random path to your grandmother's house." Peter picked his way across the shallow creek with care. He'd long since ceased to offer Scarlet a hand in difficult terrain. She wouldn't take it. Dusty followed, his head and ears up, still on the alert for danger. Peter didn't seem to notice.

"Roads and straight paths are not the way here." Scarlet replied. "This is an old forest, and those that live here respect its wildness and flow with it." They were getting close to her grandmother's house. She could smell the smoke from the central fire, though she doubted Peter could yet.

"But roads would make travel so much easier," Peter said. "Taming the forest is our duty. It is not for man to bow to nature, but for nature to bow to man."

"You keep saying that, and yet you fear the forest and those that live within her. If man is so destined to rule, then why are you afraid?"

Peter clenched his hand into a fist above the axe on his hip, as if he were resisting the urge to pull it. "Who said anything about being afraid?"

Scarlet just raised an eyebrow at him. He looked away.

"What will you do when the land, cleared of its forest, becomes barren? When there's no more forest to cut down for your progress, what then?"

Peter shrugged. "You speak of a far future. One that will

not impact either of us. But if I had to guess? Man will spread to other places, just like we do now."

Just like a human to make the future someone else's problem. Scarlet could think of no rejoinder and so said nothing.

They walked in silence for a space before Peter asked, "Why does your grandmother live so deep in the forest? Isn't she afraid folk will think she's a witch?"

They were close now. Scarlet could feel her cousins nearby in the twilight shadows of the trees. "Because this is where she's most powerful." She dropped back, letting Peter and Dusty go down the track several paces. Setting her basket down, she shrugged out of her coat and slipped out of her dress, letting her self-control go.

Bones lengthened, stretching her skin almost to transparency and popping her joints as they realigned. Her nose and teeth grew, while claws and dark fur sprouted from her skin. The transformation was a welcome relief, like a good morning stretch. Being human was so confining. The wound on her arm pulled, then healed. She sighed, glad to be rid of the pain.

Peter had turned at the sound of her joints popping and snapping back into place, but struggled to keep a hold of Dusty's reins. The horse was rearing and neighing, his ears pinned back to his head as he tried to keep all of the predators around him in view. Red eyes peered from the shadows, some low to the ground, many higher.

Dusty, eyes rolling in terror, lashed out at Peter, and when the boy reflexively covered his head, the horse bolted back down the path.

Scarlet heard one of her cousins run after it. It wouldn't do to have the horse return to town without its rider. That would only spur the villagers to come back into the forest. The rasp of Peter's axe leaving its ring on his belt brought her attention back to him. She stepped toward him, staying upright and licked her lips with a long tongue. Speaking like a human was hard in this form, but not impossible.

"You disappoint me, Peter, though I shouldn't be surprised. We talked for hours about the beauty of the forest, of the unique creatures that live here, and yet, you still don't see it. You insist that it's man's duty to tear all this down, to control the uncontrollable. You even bragged about killing my mother!" She couldn't hold back the growl that erupted from her throat. The pack howled in commiseration.

Peter brandished his axe, but Scarlet could smell the terror. She could almost feel his muscles frozen like a cornered rabbit. It made her mouth water. She shook her head to regain some control.

"I had hoped to change your mind. My grandmother made me promise to try, even though you took her only daughter from her and deprived the pack of its leader."

More howls. Wolves began to creep out from the shadows. Some on four feet, some on two. Peter seemed more focused on those who kept to four feet. Even after fighting one before, his brain couldn't come to terms with bipedal wolves.

"We've lived in this forest for generation upon generation. Since long before humans invaded the valley. And yet, even when you did, we let you be. But now you want to cut down our forest, destroy our homes, our civilization. We cannot let that happen."

Peter started backing away, looking around wildly for a way out. "Civilization? There's no civilization here; you don't even have roads!" Spittle flew from his mouth as his words came faster and faster. "Killing me won't stop the inevitable. More will come. There's too much wealth to be had here. You can't stop progress. You can't stop mankind!"

"Maybe not, but we can make them think twice about invading our lands." Scarlet leapt, twisting her hind legs at the last moment to avoid Peter's axe. She hit him broadside, her shoulder impacting his chest and knocking him to the ground. Her weight, and the force of the fall, knocked the breath from him.

As Peter gasped for breath, her fangs sank into his neck

with a satisfying gush of blood, and she shook her head hard. There was a snap, and Peter went limp. She ripped out his throat and spit the flesh to the side. She didn't like the taste, it was too sweet, almost rotten.

Scarlet turned her nose to the sky and howled, one long note to mourn her mother. Her pack joined in.

In the village, mothers ushered their children to bed, and fathers sharpened their axes as the forest erupted with howls and yips. They would not see another sunrise.

PARASITE

Robert Lewis

"Let's stop here for a minute," Jim Aldmann said, sliding his backpack off and leaning it against a massive tree's buttress roots. He peeled his shirt—damp and sticky from a combination of sweat, humidity, and rainwater dripping from the forest canopy—from his skin and fanned himself with the collar, smiling despite the uncomfortable state of his clothes. Without the interrupting sounds of their footsteps trampling through mud and rotting vegetation and the near constant clicking of his two graduate students' cameras, the buzzing of millions of insects sounded to Jim like a natural orchestra performing a rainforest symphony. He took a deep breath, enjoying the combined scents of pollinating flowers, decaying wood, and damp soil. The aroma of life.

Tom and Sara knelt in the small clearing—Jim's students had long since given up trying to keep their clothes off the damp and muddy forest floor—and started rummaging through their bags for snacks. After walking for hours, all three breathed a sigh of relief at the prospect of taking a break. But no self-respecting entomologist would waste any opportunities to collect specimens and study the marvels of the Amazon.

Insects of every variety scuttled and scurried about on their insect errands. Each and every one of them had some characteristic Jim found fascinating and admirable. Even the lowliest of ants, by far the most commonly seen inhabitants of the rainforest, merited study. But Jim wanted to find a more exotic specimen for his collection.

There! After just a moment of searching, he found something exciting. Tiny, noticeable only to a trained eye, stuck to the side of one of the nearby rubber trees.

"Look at this."

Both Sara and Tom followed their professor's gaze toward a nearby tree. Once he had their attention, he retrieved an empty jar from his pocket and carefully scraped the specimen into the container, holding it up for the students to see it better. Inside the jar was an ant carcass overgrown with fungus. Barely recognizable even when isolated from the visual noise of the rainforest.

"Never forget that nature is more horrible than you think. This is the *Ophiocordyceps unilateralis* fungus. It's nasty enough to not only parasitize the ant, but actually control its behavior to help spread the fungus."

Jim smiled as his students admired the dead ant with the mix of fascination and horror he'd come to expect from this particular lesson. Even if specimen collection was the primary purpose of this annual trip, he was always glad to teach young minds about the weird things nature dreamed up. These thoughts brought him back to his first trip to the Amazon as a young graduate student. He met his wife, Jessica, on that trip. She'd come with the parasitology department and they instantly bonded over a common interest in insect parasites. Bringing this specimen home would earn him some major points.

While his students studied the ant, Jim closed his eyes for a moment and listened to the sounds of the rainforest. Thousands of miles from his real home, the buzzing of all those insects, punctuated by calls from birds high in the canopy, made the rainforest his second home. As he listened, the indistinct buzzing of countless species gave way to the dominating sound of droning cicadas.

"Let's head back to camp," Jim said. If the cicadas were calling, evening was approaching.

Sunlight, already limited beneath the thick canopy of foliage, faded as the team made their way back to base. Walking by flashlight, they'd covered about a kilometer when Tom saw something to the side of the path they were on.

"Guys, stop," he said. "There's a nice web over here."

Jim took the lead as the group changed direction and saw what Tom was talking about. The three of them all pointed their flashlights in the direction Tom indicated. Almost glistening in the light was a large circular web spread between two trees. Jim estimated it was almost a meter across, but there didn't seem to be anyone home. He scanned his flashlight across the ground beneath the web and up and down the trees to its side, but didn't see anything of interest.

"Good eye, Tom," he said. "Let's take five and then look around and see if we can find its builder."

As soon as he sat down, he saw a small movement in the shadows at the edge of his flashlight's beam. He pointed the light toward the motion just in time to spot a large spider running toward Tom. It was one of the biggest he'd ever seen, with a leg span as wide as a dinner plate. As it neared his legs, Tom stumbled backward, trying to regain his footing and get out of its way. He cried out in pain, but the sudden movement seemed to scare the spider, as it turned around and ran in the opposite direction. Jim tried to follow it with his flashlight, eager to observe more of such an impressive specimen, but it was too fast.

After a few seconds of scanning with the light, Jim returned to tend to his student. Tom was hunched over at the foot of a tree, clutching his leg and rocking side to side. Sara stopped

Tom's movement and looked at his leg just as Jim bent down to look himself. As delicately as possible, he rotated Tom's ankle. The movement elicited a wince, but at least nothing seemed to be broken.

"It's just a sprain, Tom. I don't think anything's broken."

"Broken or not, it hurts like a motherfucker!"

Jim grunted in a mix of concern and frustration. He stood up and scanned around with his flashlight, still holding out some slight hope the spider might come back.

"Are you looking for the spider?" Tom asked. "Should we be worried about it?"

Jim shook his head.

"No, I'm pretty sure that was a goliath birdeater. Impressive as hell, but mostly harmless. I was just hoping to get another look, but I think it's gone. The web you found isn't its. The birdeater might have eaten whoever built that."

Jim sighed, wishing he could have seen more and wishing they had more time to look around. Arachnology might not have been his specialty, but animals like that would have excited *any* entomologist. Still, he forced his attention back to his students.

"Do we need to take him to a hospital?" Sara asked.

"No," Jim said. "We'll get him back to base and see one of the local medics. I don't think it's anything too serious."

He opened his mouth to say more but paused, looking around the forest again. Something seemed out of place, but he couldn't quite put his finger on what. Nothing would have pleased him more than to stay put and try to figure it out. Or even better, to figure it out *and* get another look at that tarantula. But as much as his scientific curiosity might have been the driving force behind the majority of his decisions in life, he was still responsible for his students' well-being when they were out doing field research.

Jim and Sara rushed to pack up their bags and help Tom to his feet. As he stood, Tom winced with pain. There was no way

Tom could walk back to base camp on his own. Resigned to the disappointing fact they couldn't keep collecting insects on the walk back, Jim shifted his bag of specimen jars to his left side so he could support his student on his right.

As they walked, Jim realized what had been amiss. The drone of the cicadas, the buzz of the insects, the tweeting and squawking of the birds, all the sounds of the rainforest had faded into the background. It wasn't completely silent—nothing was ever completely silent in the rainforest—but all the sounds he heard seemed more distant, as if everyone nearby decided at once to go into hiding. It was a disturbing thought. More importantly, it was a *curious* thought, but he couldn't afford to follow his natural curiosity until he got Tom back to their base camp. By the time they arrived, the sounds of life had resumed and Jim filed it away in his mind as just one more footnote for his research.

They got lucky. The trio arrived at the base just as the medic was leaving the next cabin over, and he helped them escort Tom into their own building. While the medic cleared a space on the sofa to tend to Tom's leg and Sara sat with her colleague, Jim carried their specimen bags back to his room. Little in the room offered any kind of homey touch, but it served its purpose well enough. It had a bed, a dresser, and a table below a small window. That was all he really needed. One by one, he extracted specimen jars from the bags, stacking them in neat rows on the table in front of his one decoration, a framed photograph of his wife and newborn daughter—Jessica and Elizabeth. Imagining the two of them admiring his specimens brought a smile to his face.

As he emptied the second backpack, something small and black dropped from the bag and skittered across the floor, vanishing beneath the dresser across the room.

"Shit," Jim said, crouching down and trying to catch sight of it again. Whatever it was, it had disappeared. He glanced back over the specimen jars to see if anything important had escaped, but all his treasures were present. This, apparently, had been a stowaway.

"Professor," Sara called as he opened the third bag. "The medic's finished."

He stepped out into the common room to greet the medic.

"You were right," the medic said in perfect English but with one of the thickest accents Jim had heard this entire trip, forcing him to stop thinking about his specimens and pay attention. "Nothing is broken, but the sprain is bad. Nothing much to do for it except wait. I will leave him some pain killers and you need to make sure he stays off his feet for several days."

With the medic's assistance, Jim helped Tom to his bunk. Once Tom was resting, he decided to call it an early night himself. He retired to his own room and moved the final backpack to the foot of his bed so he could sort through it after he got some sleep.

A sudden pain ripped Jim from his sleep. Disoriented, he looked around the room for Jessica. Everything was out of place, but he soon remembered where he was and why he was alone as his mind found its way back to full consciousness. A sharp stinging in his leg faded to a burning sensation before he figured out what was going on. He threw off the blankets to see why his leg hurt. As soon as the blanket moved, a small spider crawled between his legs. No bigger than a quarter with its legs fully extended, it was the deepest black in color—almost as if there were a spider-shaped hole in the world—except for two bright green bands on each leg, and it moved with startling speed. Reflexively, Jim tossed his blanket toward the spider in an attempt to capture the arachnid, but it darted off the side of the bed and out of sight faster than Jim could respond. Grimacing against the pain in his leg, he knelt on the bed and peered over the edge, trying to see where the creature had gone, but it was nowhere in sight. Jim wondered if it was the same thing that had dropped out of the specimen bag earlier.

Trying to ignore the leg pain, he slid from his bed to the floor, lowering himself down to search under the bed, around the floor, below the dresser. From that brief glance, he was certain it was a species he didn't recognize and, while he wouldn't quite allow himself to hope it was genuinely an undiscovered species, he still wanted—needed—to find it.

"Sara," he shouted. "Get in here!" Part of him felt a little bad about shouting for his students at...whatever time this was. Scientific curiosity, though, trumped common etiquette, and he assumed the kinds of grad students who volunteered to accompany their professors into the rainforest to search for insects would agree with him.

Mere seconds later, Sara burst through the door, her hair tangled either from sleep or from humidity, her eyes wide with an expression somewhere between curiosity and panic.

"What is it?"

"Nothing to worry about." Jim tried to calm her down before her state of mind shifted the rest of the way into true panic. "A spider woke me up and I'm trying to find it. Shut the door and stand guard to make sure it doesn't slip out under."

Sara took a second or two to process what her professor had said, during which time Jim shuffled over to one of the backpacks and retrieved a flashlight and an empty specimen jar.

"A spider...woke you up?"

Jim pointed the flashlight under the dresser and scanned from left to right, desperately looking for any signs of his eight-legged visitor. Nothing there except some dust. The cabin's floor was unfinished hardwood, but the boards fit tightly together. No way for the spider to have slipped through the cracks as far as Jim saw.

"Bit me on the leg," he said, shifting his search to the floor around the table.

"Are you serious?" Sara's voice increased in both volume and pitch. "Are you okay? Should I call the medic? Do we need to go to the hospital? Should I—"

"Relax," Jim said, abandoning his search just long enough to wave his hands in a *settle down* motion and give his student a comforting look. "I'm fine. I've been bit by spiders before and almost none of them are ever worse than a bee sting."

Sara nodded, but retained the concerned expression on her face.

"What's going on?" a male voice called from somewhere outside the room. Tom.

"Nothing," Jim called back. "Just trying to catch a spider."

Without moving from her assigned post by the door, Sara crouched down and joined her mentor's search of the floor.

"Why are we so interested in finding this one? Is this about science or revenge?"

Jim chuckled. "Always science. It got away before I got a great look, but I didn't recognize the species."

Finding nothing under or around the table, Jim shifted his attention back toward the bed, checking both for the spider itself and for any possible route through which it might have escaped.

"Leave it to Dr. Jim Aldmann to discover a new species by getting bit by it," Sara said. Her voice had returned to a normal register and Jim was glad she was returning to a calmer state of mind. He genuinely wanted to help and support his students, but he was always better with insects than people and he had no idea what he would do if he had to tend to one injured student and one panicked one.

"Shit," he said, pushing himself off the ground to sit on the bed. "Can't find it."

Now that the adrenaline was starting to wear off, he realized his leg hurt more than he initially thought. He examined the limb more closely. A tiny bump rose at the point of the bite itself. If he hadn't known exactly what he was looking for, it would have easily blended in with the assorted other bumps, scrapes, and mosquito bites covering his skin. The slightest hint of redness extended beyond the raised bite. By appearances, though, it didn't seem like anything to worry about.

"Do me a favor," he said. "Hand me that bag by the foot of the bed."

Sara did as she was asked but kept her eye on the floor by the door the whole time. Still looking for the spider to try to escape. Jim smiled. He'd trained her well to always keep at least one eye on the science. After rifling through the bag for a moment, he extracted a bottle of pain killers and a nearly-empty bottle of water. He took the pills and dropped both bottles haphazardly back into the bag, then paused for a second and slid back to the floor with the bag.

"I wonder," he said. "Help me keep an eye on this."

In a single motion, he shook the contents of the bag onto the floor and scanned over the entire pile, looking for any sign of the spider. Empty specimen jars, cans of insect repellent spray, a couple of pill bottles, and miscellaneous other field gear rolled around the floor, but there was no spider to be seen. Frowning, he shook the bag again then looked inside with his flashlight, then carefully inverted each of its external pockets. No spider in sight.

With a sigh, he scooped the miscellaneous gear back into the bag, then repeated the process with the other backpacks, obtaining similar results. The longer he searched, the more his leg began to throb. For as long as was tolerable, he pushed it from his mind, but eventually he had to take a break. Sighing heavily, he sat back on the bed and stared at his leg again. Visually, nothing had changed, but the bite definitely hurt more than it had a few minutes before.

"Are you sure you're okay?" Sara asked. "I could call the hospital for you."

Jim shook his head. "Dangerous spider bites are too rare for all that. No need to go anywhere or do anything unless it develops severe symptoms. I do want to rest for a bit, though."

Repeating his heavy sigh, he glanced around the room again, wondering where the spider might have possibly slipped off to. He couldn't find it nor any obvious route of escape. Even after a lifetime of studying insects and arachnids, he was still amazed at how they could just appear and disappear without any apparent explanation.

Before lying down, he rolled up his blanket and tossed it to Sara. The evening was too hot for him to want any bed covers anyway.

"Do me a favor and shove this under the door on your way out," he said. "Just in case."

After his student left, he closed his eyes, trying not to focus on the intensifying pain in his leg. Instead, he focused on his mental checklist of symptoms of medically significant spider bites: no nausea or headache, no significant swelling or discoloration, no chills. No need to do anything but take some pain killers and rest.

When Jim awoke, not having realized he'd even fallen asleep, daylight poured through the small window across the room. Audible through the closed window, birds and beasts and insects went about the noisy business of the rainforest. With the window shut and a blanket still stuffed under the door, the room was like a sauna.

Pain in his leg yanked Jim's attention away from any other source of discomfort. That was surprising. He'd expected to already be well on the road to recovery by now. Still, looking at the bite itself revealed no particular cause for concern, and he hadn't yet manifested any of the symptoms he knew would necessitate medical attention, so he tried to force it from his mind and instead focus on making a plan for the day.

As he reached for the door, he caught himself and instead stepped back and completed one more survey of the room to make sure the spider wasn't hiding out somewhere, waiting for him to open the door so it could make its escape. But no such luck. With a bit of effort, he pushed the door past the bunched-up blanket and stepped out, replacing the cloth barrier behind him. Just in case, though his hope of finding the spider again faded by the minute.

Limping from the pain in his leg, he hobbled to the common area where he found Tom resting on the couch with his leg elevated and Sara sitting cross-legged on the floor. The former seemed immersed in some fantasy novel while the latter passed the time by writing notes about one of their specimens. Both looked up as Jim entered.

"Morning, Prof," Tom said.

"Morning," Sara echoed. "Feeling any better?"

Jim shook his head. "About the same. Stings like hell, but nothing to worry about."

Sara frowned. "If it still hurts that bad, I'm calling for a medevac. We're getting you to a hospital."

"No," Jim said, a bit more sharply than he intended. "Even if it happened to be a dangerous spider, they almost never require medical attention. And even if it did, there's not a whole lot they could do without knowing what species it is. Plus, Tom's supposed to stay off his feet for a while. So unless the symptoms themselves require medical attention, we stay put. If we're lucky, maybe we can either find the spider around the cabin or find another of its species back in the forest."

Honestly, Jim had to admit at least part of the reason he insisted on staying here was that he wanted desperately to identify a potentially new species. If he had to get bit by something, he should at least get scientific credit for it. But he also knew his logic was sound. Almost no spiders were dangerous, and the real dangers were often exaggerated. Here in the Amazon, the most dangerous one anyone had ever seen was the Brazilian wandering spider, and even those rarely killed anyone. And this thing—whatever it was—looked nothing like the Brazilian wandering spider.

Sara stood up, but neither left nor said anything. Jim could tell she was trying to decide whether it was worth arguing with him. But she'd come around. Sara might be a bit on the nervous side at times, but she was also arguably his most promising and attentive student. And he gave the same lecture every year before taking students on these trips: spiders are scary, but almost always harmless. Back home, he always told his students that there were only two species to watch out for: the black widow and the brown recluse. And neither of those were aggressive. During the flight out for this trip, he warned his students that Amazonian spiders could be more aggressive and more dangerous, but he also reminded them they'd be more likely to suffer from an infected mosquito bite than any spider bite.

Before Sara said anything else on the subject, Jim decided to distract her with some minor errands.

"Will you call the medics and ask them to bring more pain killers? Between Tom and I, I think we're going to deplete our stash pretty quick."

After Sara left, shutting the door behind her, Jim checked in with Tom's own injury. Satisfied they were both doing well enough, but not quite up to wandering around, he went back to his room, intent on finishing his specimen-sorting from yesterday. Instead, he decided to lie down on his bed for a few minutes, a bit too distracted by his pain to get any real work done. His leg throbbed, but the pain medication, limited as it was, took the edge off. He took another pill and summoned his motivation. With a bit of a struggle, he sat up and swung his legs over the edge of his bed. He couldn't stand lying in place, much less lying in an uncomfortable pool of sweat, wondering if it was because of the heat and humidity or the throbbing leg. Even if he didn't feel up to moving about, he could at least find something to occupy his mind and keep himself out of bed.

He tried to think of what to do but couldn't make any sense of his thoughts. He knew the rules of field work. When to worry and when not to worry about injuries. Spider bites were almost always harmless, but he couldn't shake his doubts. Serious bites were rare, true, but the pain didn't usually get progressively worse, and he was sure his leg hurt more now than it did the night before. Should he cut the trip short and bring his students back to the United States? Should he visit a local hospital? Should he wait it out here and keep trying to find that spider? What was that spider anyway? Nightmarish images of his attacker flashed through his mind. Its tiny black and green legs carrying it toward him faster than any such animal should be able to move. But in this image, it didn't bite him. It crawled up his chest and stared him in the face, as if its alien gaze could penetrate his thoughts.

A piercing headache suddenly coursed through Jim's head, shutting out all other thoughts. He closed his eyes and gritted his teeth, groaning in pain. As the pain peaked, he blacked out, falling backward onto his bed. He didn't wake for the rest of the day. As he slept, he began to dream.

In his dream, Jim felt like he was dying. But it wasn't because of the spider bite. He was dying because he was alone in this room, locked in and forgotten. It had been days since anyone came to visit; days since anyone brought food or water. This cabin wasn't a research station anymore. It was a prison. It was a grave.

"Don't be so dramatic, Jim." That voice. That soothing voice. It was his wife. It was Jessica. But where was she? She wasn't on this trip. She was back home taking care of their new daughter.

"Everything will be fine," she said again. "Elizabeth and I

are waiting to see you again."

With every word she spoke, Jim's heart rate slowed. With every sentence, his pain subsided.

He looked around the room to see where his wife was, but she wasn't with him. He was alone in this room. This empty room, with just a bed, dresser, and table. A clock appeared on the wall, its hands spinning faster than they ought. Seconds became hours. Days wound by as he stared at that damned clock. Why couldn't he go home yet? How long had it been? Was Jessica still waiting? Was Elizabeth going to grow up while he wasted away in this room?

"Jessica?" he called.

"I'm here, Jim," Jessica replied.

Jim tried to pinpoint the direction from which her voice came, but it seemed to come from every direction at once. Or more like it came from inside his own head.

"Where are you?" he asked.

"I'm waiting for you. Elizabeth is waiting for you."

"I understand," he said. "I'm coming home to you."

Even as he spoke, the pain in his leg faded to nothing, replaced by thoughts of home and family.

He awoke soaking wet from sweat, and with pain still throbbing in his leg, worsening again since the pain medication was wearing off. He wasn't sure how long he'd been asleep, but daylight had yielded again to darkness. And what the hell was that dream about? He figured it must be either fever or a side effect of the pain medication making his brain play tricks on him. With nothing else to do, he tried to go back to sleep.

Sara gently shook Jim's shoulder until his eyes opened. For a few seconds, he alternately squinted and widened his eyes as he acclimated to the daylight. He tried to sit up but a sharp pain in his leg kept him from doing so.

"Don't get up," Sara said. "You still need to rest. Does it feel any better?"

It was hard for Jim to answer that question. At the moment he awoke, the pain had all but disappeared, but in those few seconds, the burning and stinging built itself back up to how it had been earlier. At least the headache had faded. Trying to compare levels of pain under those circumstances seemed futile.

"It's about the same," he said.

Sara held out a couple of pills and a glass of water.

"Take these and then try to get some more rest," she said.

Jim took the pills and rested his head back against the pillow, but he didn't close his eyes.

"Probably not what you expected when you signed up for field research, right?"

Sara smiled—one of the only times, Jim realized, that she'd done so since their walk through the forest—as she shook her head.

"No, not really. But of the two of us, I don't think I'm the one to complain."

Jim returned the smile and closed his eyes while he remembered past trips.

"I met my wife on one of these trips," he said. "Did I ever tell you that? I was a grad student in entomology and Jessica was working in the parasitology department. We bonded over studying insect parasites."

"Is that why you still make these trips every year?"

"That and the science. Usually, Jessica would be here with me. We've spent a lot of years studying the impact of parasites on insect populations together. This is actually the first time I've taken one of these trips without her with me, but she had to stay back and watch the baby."

"I didn't know you had a baby," Sara said. "Is it a boy or a girl?"

"Girl. Elizabeth."

"Lovely name. Why didn't you just postpone the trip,

though? Wouldn't you rather be home with your family?"

Jim nodded. "Right now, I'd much rather be home with my family. But that's the thing with me and Jessica. The science has always come first. We met in the field. Had our wedding at a museum. We even collected data on our honeymoon. Jessica wouldn't…."

Jim paused, trying to collect his thoughts. As soon as he opened his mouth to speak, the words seemed to leave his brain. For a moment, he couldn't remember where he was or why he was talking to Sara instead of his wife. Even the pain in his leg receded from his consciousness, forced into the shadows behind the thought of Jessica.

"Sorry," he said. "My mind just wandered. I think I should get some more rest. The sooner I recover, the sooner I can finish our research and get back home."

Sara nodded and left her professor to sleep for the rest of the afternoon. As he lay in bed, the pain crept back to the front of his mind, accompanied by another piercing headache.

By the next day, Jim was back on his feet again. His head still ached and his leg still throbbed. Indeed, the throbbing now spread further, as if every pulse of his heartbeat hammered through his entire body. And this headache wasn't merely a headache. It was a piercing headache, and in the background, he heard a phantom buzzing just distinct enough from the background buzzing of the rainforest to constantly distract him from his thoughts. But at least he could stay awake now, and at least he could limp around without help. Everyone else was leaving him alone for the most part. He figured Sara was trying to let him rest and Tom had his own resting to do, but the solitude was beginning to bother him more than he thought it would after only a couple nights. There was no point in being alone with his thoughts if his headache kept him from thinking.

He hobbled down the hall and found his students in the common room playing cards. Sara had set up an extra chair for Tom to rest his leg, and a small table between them. Tom looked up as he entered.

"Professor," he said with some surprise. "Are you sure you should be up?"

"I can't stand to be alone anymore."

Jim walked over and took a chair near his students.

"How are you feeling?" Sara asked.

"Like I've been run over by an eight-legged truck. But better than I was yesterday."

Surprisingly, he realized that was partly true. His leg was absolutely better. This headache was something unlike anything he'd ever experienced, though. Every thought had to fight through the pulsing, piercing pain at the front of his head.

"Can I get you some pain killers?" Sara asked. "The medics said they could bring some stronger ones for us tomorrow."

"No," Jim said. "But you can figure out what it'll take to get home early. I just want to go home."

Tom shook his head. "Do you think that's a good idea? We already have a medic on his way in from the city to bring us better drugs. Shouldn't we wait to hear what he has to say? Isn't that how you always said to handle these situations?"

"No!" Jim almost yelled, surprising himself with the forcefulness of his response. "I appreciate everything you're doing, but I feel too alone here. I need to get back to my family. If I need a doctor, there are plenty of them back home. I just…."

He let his voice trail off. He couldn't think of anything else to say. Thoughts of home dominated his mind. It probably would be a better idea to wait for the medic, but he couldn't shake the feeling that if this bite was going to be anything more serious, it already would be. And even if he did happen to make a turn for the worse, it would be better to be at home, in America, with Jessica and Elizabeth. Home, Jessica, Elizabeth—the thought of them pushed the pain to the back of his mind.

"I just need to get home," he said, standing up. "Let's pack up and get a ride back to the airport when the medic comes."

He wandered off to pack his bags, thinking of nothing but getting back to his family. It was the only thought powerful enough to burst through the constant buzzing silencing his other thoughts. As he packed his fungus-riddled ant specimen, a smile began to form. Jessica would love that one.

It was nearly a full day of travel before Jim got on the airplane. Tom leaned on Sara and Jim leaned on a baggage cart as they took the ATV to the bus, the bus to the taxi in the city, then the taxi to the airport. As Jim boarded the plane, his mounting exhaustion gave way to a sense of euphoria to which nothing he'd ever experienced could compare. The throbbing sensation and headache felt physically like they were going stronger, but they were dwarfed mentally by the sensation of overwhelming relief that he was finally going home.

Taking his seat on the plane, he dry-swallowed another pain killer and closed his eyes, hoping sleep would bring him dreams of home that might transition seamlessly into the reality of home after the long flight. In his dreams, he saw his family. He saw his house. Jessica stood in the doorway, holding Elizabeth in her arms, smiling at him. He saw his office at the university, its walls lined with his favorite books and specimens he'd brought back on previous trips. All the people and places that made him happy. Soon, his wife and daughter would greet him at the airport and all would be right with the world again. He smiled as he slept.

Several hours into the flight, he awoke with a start, in so much pain he couldn't even manage a moan or a scream. His insides were on fire, all through his body. His headache worsened to the point it felt like someone was driving an ice pick into his skull. He clutched at his chest with his right hand and gripped his armrest as tightly as possible with his left. His legs curled under his seat as his muscles tightened. A disembodied voice on the overhead speakers said something about remaining seated during their final descent. Several passengers, both of his students among them, left their seats regardless to try to do whatever they could to help him.

Something moved inside of his chest. As the pain behind his ribcage continued to worsen, as if something was ripping him apart from the inside, his headache faded. Through the pain, his thoughts began to clarify. He remembered his favorite lesson about *Cordyceps* and the carpenter ants. Suddenly, everything began to make sense.

What if, he thought, but cut his own thought short before he formulated it into words. *What if it really is…and I fly it back to….*

The pain in his chest migrated upwards in a manner unlike anything Jim had ever experienced, moving from his chest through his neck and settling in the back of his head.

The students and a couple strangers tried to attract his attention, but before anyone could begin to formulate a plan of action, his grimacing and twitching stopped as fast as it began. He whispered, "Jessica." His arms fell limp to his sides. His head rolled onto his shoulder with his mouth still hanging open, an expression of pure agony frozen on his face.

"Oh my god," Sara said, holding her hand to her mouth as one of the other passengers checked for a pulse. After the disturbance, the entire plane felt eerily silent.

As Sara looked on, uncertain what to do, something small and black pushed its way from behind her professor's eyelid. At first, she thought it was just an errant eyelash, but as it pushed its way further out, a green band emerged, followed by the rest of a spindly structure she recognized as a spider leg. After an unbearable second or two, the silence was broken by Sara's scream as the spider pushed the rest of the way out, dragging a trail of blood behind it and leaving Jim's eye bulging from its socket and apparently held in place only by the eyelids. As Sarah watched in horror, a trickle of blood dribbled from each of Jim's nostrils, followed by two more spiders.

Sara's screams were quickly joined by others as dozens of black and green spiders burst from Jim's lifeless mouth. Cries of terror filled the doomed craft as it gently landed as if nothing were wrong, carrying its deadly cargo to the airport where Jessica and Elizabeth waited.

EARS

Charli Cowan

Kylie darted down the high school hallway, avoiding eye contact with every classmate she saw. When one group got tired of staring, a new group of ogling eyes arrived to fill the void. It was never-ending. Her ears burned as students whispered amongst themselves. She knew she wasn't meant to hear the comments, but her hearing was keen.

She's so weird!

Why is she like that?

They were familiar questions to Kylie. Doctors had always declared her medically sound and healthy. It didn't stop the wide-spread curiosity. Even news stations had approached her family about her strange condition over the years. Being a minor had saved her from being in the press, at least. But high school was a different beast.

She slid into her first period class meekly, passing two tall boys. Luckily, they didn't notice. They were the guys who picked on her the most. Kylie knew they would have something snide to say once they did spot her.

That day, it seemed that there were some students she'd never seen before. That wasn't abnormal; it was the beginning of the school year. One was a boy wearing a grey hoodie. He watched quietly and offered a smile. She knew that wouldn't last.

Kylie took the usual seat in the back corner of the room and made herself as comfortable as possible. She touched the white hat on her head gingerly. Her maternal grandmother had made it for her years ago and she'd worn it every day since. She tried not to think about her grandmother….

Her hat fit snugly and kept hidden what she hated the most about herself. But there was a strict no-hat policy at school. Kylie reveled in her momentary peace, knowing it would be over as soon as Mrs. Spencer walked in.

She peered out the window next to her, as usual, and studied the tree line at the edge of the football field. There had always been something alluring about it. It was her favorite place to be—out in the woods, away from gossiping observers. That patch behind the school was where she'd gone every afternoon before she'd started walking home from school, a nearby haven to hide in while she waited for her mother to pick her up.

"Hey," someone said, yanking her from her thoughts. She didn't want to look. It was one of the bullies. His name was Chad. "Hey, Jane Doe." The insults were never very bright, but they still stung.

His friend Brandon, the other boy she'd passed, snickered. He was slightly shorter than Chad, with dark brown hair. He was quieter and seemed a bit more intelligent, though she wasn't sure how she got that impression.

Kylie didn't respond to Chad. She sucked her lips into her mouth and stared at one specific pine tree outside. Her breathing was jagged.

"Oh, deer," Chad murmured, his breath fanning her neck. One of her ears twitched, and she shivered. He smelled like B.O. and some sort of greasy food. Kylie held her breath so she wouldn't have to smell him.

"Alright, everybody. Pull out a pencil and put everything else away," Mrs. Spencer chimed as she entered the classroom. "Quiz time."

Kylie glanced over at her, hoping she would notice Chad's proximity to her. Both her tormentors had turned forward in their desks, feigning innocence. She sighed, relieved that they'd stopped. For now, anyway.

Mrs. Spencer looked at Kylie somberly and gave her a tiny smile. That was the sign.

Kylie took a deep breath and reached towards her head. Many of her classmates were focused on the upcoming quiz. A couple did turn to watch. Chad and Brandon ogled her, of course. But she noticed something new: a soft green stare from the boy in the hoodie.

Great, she thought. In a moment he'll be traumatized.

She always tucked her real ears into the faux white ones on the hat. The only indication that she was abnormal arose when one of those ears moved. She pinched a fake ear and tugged off her hat, revealing the two large deer ears. They were the same color as her hair, and sat slightly above where human ears would have been. If they would obey Kylie and lie flat against her hair, she thought they may not be noticeable. But standing upright the way they did, if the shape wasn't apparent, the cream-white fur lining the inside of the pinna would be.

Kylie tucked her hat in her lap and looked at the students who had watched. Some girls turned away in disgust, Chad and Brandon sniggered, but the boy…he gave her another smile. Kylie couldn't tell if that was a good sign or a bad omen.

Her ears twitched, scanning for any ill-mannered murmurs. There were none. She took the quiz from Mrs. Spencer as she walked by, and then focused all her attention on her work. At least she excelled in the academic side of school. Although it wasn't as rewarding as the social side of it, of course.

At the end of the day, Kylie sauntered home, ears tucked into her hat and her heart hanging low in her stomach. She lived close to her high school, and by some strange stroke of luck, none of her classmates had discovered her address. Of course, that was probably due to her practically sneaking into the house every day after school, but she was still relieved. It had always been a fear that someone would follow her home, but so far, it hadn't happened.

Kylie walked into the house and leaned against the front door for a moment, trying to compose herself. She decided the day hadn't been entirely horrible, took a deep breath and went into the kitchen for a snack, leaving her backpack and her hat by the front door. She never wore her hat at home. She was in her den now.

Her mother popped her head out of the pantry with a box of crackers, and she grinned at Kylie. A motherly smile that looked past any deformity. "Hey, sweetie. How was school?" she asked, her hazel eyes examining Kylie carefully.

"Not the worst." Kylie shrugged as she gave her mother a quick hug. She smelled the same as she always did: a soft perfume she'd worn for as long as Kylie could remember. The scent calmed her nerves.

Her mother seemed appeased with her answer. "Great! That's a good way of looking at it. I rinsed off some grapes. They're by the sink," she said, stacking a box of crackers onto a high shelf in the pantry.

Kylie decided that yes, grapes were enough. She sat down and popped them into her mouth, playing a game on her phone. As she ate, the worries from the day dissipated. Once she'd had her fill, she discarded the stems and exited the kitchen. Her mother was still putting away groceries.

"I'm gonna take a bath," Kylie called as she headed up the stairs.

"'Kay. Your dad's getting a pizza on the way home," Mom

replied.

The thought of pizza made Kylie smile.

As Kylie waited for the bath to fill, she avoided the bathroom mirror as if it would strangle her. She had always begged her parents to cover the mirrors in the house so she wouldn't have to see her dreadful deer ears. Of course, they'd blatantly refused, insisting that she needed to see her own beauty.

She tried not to look, but her eyes wandered masochistically until she regarded the appendages she so despised. There they were. Staring at her like fuzzy little monsters. She tried not to cry. She grabbed her ears and tucked them against her hair. Finally, with her ears covered, she was normal. She calmed herself and examined the rest of her face.

She had soft, light brown hair and large baby blue eyes. There was a freckle here and there on her cheeks, and her skin was fair. Her mother always told her she was pretty, as mothers do, but Kylie only saw it with her ears out of the picture. Kylie released them and they rose timidly. She examined them—the left one twitching from being restrained. They were long and thick—the same shade as her locks. The inner hairs were a snow white that almost passed as lovely.

The ears would be pretty if they were on an animal and not a seventeen-year-old girl. Kylie huffed and turned away from the bathroom mirror, hugging herself like she was freezing. She checked the bath water and slipped into the tub, wishing her ears would dissolve into the water with the soap suds.

As the water rose around her shoulders, she found herself thinking about her grandmother again. The thoughts bubbled here and there—memories rising from the depths—but what settled to stay was the perpetual question that haunted her family. Where was her grandmother now? No one had seen her since Kylie was twelve years old.

It was something she normally shied from, but in quiet moments, it arose on its own.

Kylie dunked her head beneath the bath water, rinsing the pondering from her brain.

When Kylie got to her first period class the next morning, she moped to her desk and dropped into the attached seat like a sack of rocks. She hadn't slept very well with all the worries poisoning her mind. Everything seemed so much heavier this school year. She rubbed her temples, ears twitching involuntarily as students entered the room. It was a quiet morning. Quiet, that is, until someone flopped into the desk in front of her, jostling her.

She blinked at the person's back. It wasn't the girl who usually sat there. After a moment, Kylie realized that it was the boy who had smiled at her the day before—the one who'd seemed so kind.

Not kind. You don't know him, she corrected, shaking her head slightly.

Today, he wore a white hoodie. She also noticed that he smelled very nice, though she couldn't place the cologne. The scent calmed her, despite her instincts telling her not to let her guard down. The boy's hair was shaggy and black, falling in waves over his broad shoulders. She thought he looked like a boulder. But he didn't seem coarse or rude.

You don't know him, she reminded herself. What was with her?

She fished a notebook out of her backpack and started doodling, feeling too animated to sit and look out the window like usual. She began sketching a non-descript flower.

Her calm demeanor shattered when Chad and Brandon entered the classroom, jabbering on about some video game. They crashed into their desks, radiating almost tangible energy. Their scents filled the air, almost electric because of their moods.

Kylie felt her pulse quicken. Why did they have to get there so early? She checked the wall clock. Mrs. Spencer would still be a few minutes, she was sure. Unless she was running late. Then it might be ten or fifteen minutes.

She could already feel Chad and Brandon staring at her once they'd quieted. She had no cover—nothing to shelter her from the predators.

"Hey, Kylie," Chad purred.

Brandon snorted. It was the same old routine. When would they tire of her?

And of course, Kylie began to hold her breath. She didn't move.

"I'm trying to talk to you," Chad said, his voice full of malice. Without warning, he wrapped his hand over hers on her desk and she whipped around, wide-eyed. His skin was hot and dry. "Finally, some recognition. Was that so difficult?" Chad looked at Brandon as if Kylie were being unreasonable.

Brandon shrugged.

"So I've got a question for you, deer. Do you, uh," he looked her over in a way that made her insides wriggle, "have a cute lil deer tail to go with them ears?" He released her hand only to yank off her hat.

Kylie gasped, her face burning and her stomach spinning. She grabbed her ears and held them down, glancing around the room. A few students were watching. Some seemed sympathetic. But no one said anything.

Chad stuck his fingers in the fake ears on her hat and wiggled them around. Then he and Brandon nearly fell out of their desks laughing.

The room was spinning. Kylie couldn't catch her breath. Tears readied themselves at the corners of her eyes. Her head started to throb.

"Hey, shitheads," the boy in front of her interjected, swiveling in his desk.

Chad and Brandon glanced at each other and then at the boy. Kylie also stared at him. The air stilled.

"You got a problem?" Brandon asked, glancing at Chad like he wanted approval.

The new boy glanced at Kylie, and she swallowed dryly. "How about you shut up before I—"

"Sorry I'm late, guys," Mrs. Spencer said as she blew into the classroom with an armful of papers. She spilled them onto her desk and pursed her lips as soon as she looked up. She noticed Chad holding Kylie's hat in his grimy hands and eyeballed both guys, mouth closing in a firm line. Her prior train of thought barreled out of the station. "It seems to me that you two had a lot of the same answers on yesterday's quiz," she said.

Chad pursed his lips and started to protest. Brandon glowered at her.

"Chad." She pointed to a desk in the opposite corner of Kylie's. "Brandon." She summoned him forward to the front row. "Questions?"

Chad sighed and got up, dropping Kylie's hat on the floor. Brandon got his things together wordlessly. Once they had both relocated, Kylie reached for her hat only to find the boy holding it out to her gently in his big, tan hand.

"Jackasses," he whispered when she took it. "Garrett."

She brushed her hat off carefully. "Huh?"

"My name's Garrett."

"O-oh. Kylie."

"I know," Garrett said before turning around in his chair.

She blinked to herself and squeezed her hat between her hands, unsure of what to make of Garrett, the new boy.

Kind? she wondered tentatively.

She didn't get a chance to interact with him much more during class. Once the bell rang, he disappeared out the door right after Chad and Brandon did. She found herself wondering if he'd say something else to them—if he'd beat them to a pulp. But when she raced out into the hallway, she saw Chad and Brandon heading in the opposite direction. Garrett turned a corner long before she could even form his name on her lips.

She didn't see him for the rest of the day, but she couldn't get him off her mind.

The rest of that week, Garrett continued to sit in front of her. They didn't interact much, except for a passing look or smile, but she couldn't deny that she felt some warmth emanating from him. She was letting her guard down, as much as she didn't want to. But she was still a bit cautious. When she remembered to be.

Brandon and Chad left her alone when Garrett was near. It didn't take long for Kylie to notice the correlation. That, and the healing black eye that Chad was nursing. She tried not to stare, but found herself looking between the wound and Garrett. Was there a connection there, as well? Either way, Kylie was happy to be left alone.

On a warm fall day a few weeks later, as Kylie was heading home, she heard something moving behind her. She paused and glanced back, wondering whether it was human or animal. Her heart raced. She considered running home—it wasn't that far and her legs were long and strong—but she didn't want to be a coward. If anything, she wanted to be tough and take care of herself. She thought her father would be proud of that. She mustered together any courage she had and shoved her ears forward, feeling for any and all sounds.

A leaf crunched.

"What do you want?" she barked, trying to ignore the tremble in her voice. There was no response, but she kept listening.

Finally, someone stepped out from behind a bush. Not the most creative of hiding places, but he'd had her fooled. It was Garrett.

Kylie felt a rush of emotions, but the most prominent were

confusion, terror, and excitement. In that order. "What do you want?" she asked again, even more perplexed.

He blinked at her—was he embarrassed? A wide, sheepish grin spread across his face. He held out his hands. "You caught me."

"Well, obviously. What were you doing?"

"Following you?" Garrett mumbled.

"Why?"

He sighed and glanced around. "Those creeps were watching you leave the school. I was worried they'd try to pull something."

Chad and Brandon, of course. "Creeps? Says the guy stalking me?" Kylie blurted, surprised by her own sass.

He stared at her. "Yeah," he decided after a moment. "That's fair. Can I walk you home?"

She studied him for a moment longer. Her heart was racing, but it wasn't from fear. She looked him over and caught her breath. "Now you ask?" she muttered.

"Is that a yes?"

"I guess." She shrugged, her eyebrows sailing into her hairline. "But you better not try anything funny because my dad should be home and he's always carrying," she lied. The house would probably be empty and the most dangerous item in the house was a kitchen knife.

That could still do the job, she thought, nodding discreetly to herself as she turned. She heard him walk up next to her and they continued down the sidewalk together.

"Do you always walk home?" Garrett asked.

"Do you always follow girls home?" she retorted.

"Only when they want me to," he said. When she peered over at him, he looked just about as weirded out by his statement as she felt. "Sorry. That was dumb."

"Horrendous. Anyway, yeah. We can't afford another car and I don't really go a lot of places."

"Why not?" he asked.

She gave him a hard stare. "Hard to leave the house when it's always hunting season."

He didn't say anything, just stared at the sidewalk and any leaf that crossed his path. After a moment, he glanced at her.

"Do you always watch Brandon and Chad?" Kylie asked apprehensively. She wanted to hear it from him. Maybe she wanted him to know how much her school life had improved without the harassment.

Garrett looked her straight in the eye and said, "Just when they're around you. And…maybe I've bumped into them a couple of times."

Kylie studied him quietly. That was all she needed. "Thank you."

He nodded with a smile.

They walked in silence for the next block, but it wasn't uncomfortable. It was easy, being next to him. Easy to talk to him, too. Kylie tried to tell herself to be careful and that she shouldn't be acting so carefree, but she couldn't help herself. Being with him just felt…normal. And normal was a luxury she wouldn't pass up.

They reached her house and she considered lying about it being a few blocks down. She wanted to prolong their walk. She wasn't sure why—they weren't even talking. Maybe it was just because she was curious about him. But she sighed and halted in the middle of the sidewalk.

"You okay?" Garrett asked her, blinking those jade eyes inquisitively.

"This is me," she said, hooking a thumb over her shoulder.

"Ah," he nodded. Was he as disappointed as she was? She couldn't be sure.

"Well, thanks for having my back," she said coyly, walking up to the front door. "Although I don't really know why you do. Hopefully you don't have any ulterior motives?" She stuck her key in the lock and turned it.

He chuckled at that. "No. No ulterior motives. Though, I

wouldn't tell you if I did," he assured her.

She stared at him.

"I'm really not good at this—"

"No, you're not." She giggled, shaking her head. "I guess I'll see you tomorrow?"

He bit his lip like he had something else on his mind. That made Kylie antsy. "Well, I wanted to show you something."

She watched him carefully. "What?"

"Well…your ears—"

"What about them?" she asked. She felt her ears twitch.

"I, uh…."

She waited for him to continue. Her mind was spinning scenarios—he hated her ears; he thought she was a science experiment; he had some weird kink. The list grew every second he didn't finish. He smiled out of nowhere, and she feared that he was about to make fun of her. Instincts kicked in and she rushed into the house.

"Wait!" He threw himself into the door, pushing it open. "Relax, look—"

"Get away from me!" She shoved him away from her.

"Kylie," he huffed, sounding exasperated. He caught her wrist and shoved his hair back with his other hand.

Kylie stared at him incredulously. It took her several seconds to process what she was seeing.

There were two fuzzy black ears poking out of his shaggy locks.

"That's not possible—"

"Obviously it's possible," he retorted.

She felt like she couldn't breathe. Everything was spinning. Garrett's mouth was moving, but the words were muted. Kylie managed to close the door and lock it, and everything fell away.

The front door smacked into Kylie's back and she fell forward on her hands. It took a moment to become aware of her surroundings. Her cheeks were streaked with drying tears and her breathing was slow. Thoughts ambled through her brain. A voice shook her from her trance. Abruptly, she became aware of two things: she'd been in front of the door lost in her own thoughts, and someone had just opened it.

"Kylie? What're you doing, sweetie?" Her father crouched beside her. His pale blue eyes were wide and concerned.

Kylie cleared her throat and looked around. It took her a moment to recollect herself. Then, everything flooded back into her memory and she gasped. "Ears! He has ears!"

"Um…what?" her father inquired, pushing her hair out of her face. "Who has ears?"

She didn't respond. All she did was rush up the stairs to her bedroom.

The next day, Kylie decided that she wasn't going to speak to Garrett until he apologized for everything—following her, barging into her house, causing her panic attack.

He was sitting at his desk when she walked into the classroom. She held her breath as she approached her desk.

"Do you like pie?" he suddenly asked, turning.

Kylie looked up, dumbfounded. "What?"

"Pie. You and me. Tonight?" he grinned.

She scoffed and glared at him. She didn't know how to take that response. What confused her even more than his weirdness was her abrupt response: "Fine. Pick me up at six."

Around 5:45, Kylie's mother caught onto her daughter's plans when she walked past Kylie's bedroom to see her eyeballing a blue dress and a pink blouse on her bed. Her mother com-

mented that she'd go with the blue dress and then pounced once Kylie agreed. "What's this for?"

Kylie looked up at her with wide eyes. Her ears went back shyly. "Nothing."

"Do you have a date?" Mom asked. Her eyes widened so much they looked like they'd burst from her face. Kylie thought she'd spontaneously combust, she was so excited. Her mother rushed out of the bedroom giggling about getting her phone.

"No, no! He'll be here soon!" Kylie cried, chasing her mother down the stairs. She didn't want to get her hopes up. She was still skeptical about Garrett. Maybe she even thought he was temporary—a blip in her lifetime. A momentary chance at happiness. Even normalcy, if that could be achieved. She sighed and shook her head. "No pictures."

"Second date, then," Mom grinned. "I'm so excited; you never go out!"

Kylie scoffed. "You're ridiculous. I have to get ready." She went back into her bedroom and slipped into the blue dress and thick black leggings. Then she completed the outfit with her usual brown boots. She stared at herself in the vanity her parents had stuck in her bedroom when she was ten and nibbled on her lip. She tucked her ears into her hat and gave them a few testing wiggles. The hat didn't mesh well with the outfit, unfortunately.

Kylie wished her hair was as fluffy as Garrett's. She wished her abhorrent ears were as small as his. But when she thought of his ears, she found herself smiling. She thought they were cute. If only she felt that way about her own ears.

The doorbell rang, shattering her thoughts completely. She raced down the stairs but she wasn't quicker than her mother, who was already pulling the front door open. "Oh my goodness, hello. Michelle," she blurted, throwing her hand into Garrett's face.

He glanced over at Kylie once she was at the bottom of the stairs and blinked. He was holding white roses and had on a light green button-down shirt with black pants. "You look nice," he commented with a smile. Then he turned to her mother and took her hand. "It's good to meet you, Michelle. I'm Garrett."

Kylie walked up awkwardly, unsure of where to look. Garrett was still staring at her.

Kylie's mother looked him over excitedly as she shook his hand. "Well, you two have fun. Stay out late. It is a Friday, after all. Toodles!" She shoved Kylie out the door and locked it behind her.

Kylie stood there in disbelief, shivering slightly. It was a bit chillier than she expected. But maybe that was nerves.

"The flowers…" Garrett mumbled, peering down at them.

Kylie looked over at the bouquet, still in his hand, and up to his eyes. "You didn't have to," she told him.

He glanced at her and smirked. "I wanted to." He tipped them down towards her nose and she took a whiff.

"Mmm," she smiled.

"Let's go," he beckoned, walking towards his little red car. He opened the door and she got in slowly, still shy. That didn't change when he got into the car and headed down the street towards a restaurant by her house.

She commented on how big he looked, bulging in his small car, and that was all they said. It was a short drive.

Garrett opened her car door once they arrived and then the restaurant door. He got them a table and Kylie slipped into the booth across from him, a quiet smile on her face. She liked being pampered. He was a genuine gentleman. At least he seemed to be.

Cautious, she reminded herself.

"You're a quiet one," he commented, holding a menu up to his face.

"Yes," she shrugged. "Is that a problem?"

He set the menu flat on the table and snorted. "Why would that be a problem?" he wondered. He looked her over, his eyes lingering on her hat. "I figured you just wore that at school," he commented.

She shook her head.

"Why do you always wear it?"

"I get sick of people staring," she shrugged, noting that he didn't seem to mind. Of course, his weren't obvious like hers.

Suddenly, his hair parted and his ears poked out. He touched one carefully and "hmmed" to himself. She laughed at that. He was so casual about them—so natural. But why wouldn't he be? He was comfortable with himself—that much was obvious.

A few people noticed, but he didn't seem to mind.

"What are they?" she asked, pointing with her chin at his head.

"Black bear. Take your hat off," he urged.

"No, I can't."

He stared at her for a moment. "Give me a chance," he said softly.

When she didn't budge, he reached across the table and pinched her hat between two fingers. She held her breath but she didn't fight it. He slid it off and laid it on the table. Her ears shook back and forth, freeing themselves from their captivity. It was more comfortable than having them tucked into the hat; the restaurant was cramped and toasty. She peeked around as people gasped and pointed. A few children cried out in excitement or horror. She wasn't sure. She shuddered.

"Kylie," Garrett said, reaching across the table and scooping up her hand. He was warm and soft. "Let's get some food. The world isn't going to explode," he smiled.

She blinked a few times and tried to ignore the gossiping whispers around them. Her ears twitched, then settled. She took a deep breath. "Okay," she murmured.

Over dinner and pie, they discussed all sorts of topics she'd never been able to share with anyone outside her family. They talked about their favorite subjects, celebrities, movies, different music they listened to. She was surprised to find they had more than just their peculiar ears in common.

One thing they didn't have in common was their relationship with their families. While Kylie's parents had always loved and accepted her, Garrett's parents regarded their son as an abomination. She couldn't stop thinking about the horror stories he told her over dinner—when his mother locked him in the basement as a child, his sisters calling him names and shaving the fur off his ears while he slept. Kylie felt guilty and astonished at her own feelings. She began to feel lucky—a sensation she'd never experienced, especially regarding her ears.

They talked long into the night, until the restaurant was getting ready to close. Then Garrett paid for their dinner and they strolled out, each full of food and laughs. Gently, he slid his large hand around hers and smiled down at her. Her heart raced in her chest, pounding against her ribs like it was about to explode. She tried to calm her quivering breath.

When Kylie got to the car, Garrett opened the door for her and she slid in, excited and disappointed at the same time. He'd be taking her home soon.

She plucked the flowers out of the back seat and held them against her chest, hiding her frown when he got into the car. He turned on some music from a band they both liked before he got onto the road and gave her a smile. That eased her sorrow for the drive home.

He pulled alongside the curb and got out of the car without a word. Kylie wracked her brain for something to prolong their evening. She couldn't think of anything, and she ran out of time when the car door opened. Garrett helped her to her feet, then closed the door behind her and held her hand all the way up to her front door.

Kylie's mother peeped through the curtains beside the front door. Garrett didn't seem to notice, but Kylie was filled with such nervousness and embarrassment, she paused.

"What's wrong?" Garrett asked, turning towards her. He was tall and tan and kind—so kind. Her stomach filled with butterflies. She couldn't even remember why she'd been mad at him before. His ears poked through his hair again, panning towards her curiously.

She figured this was her chance. "I don't want it to end," she admitted.

"What?" he blinked.

"Tonight."

He smiled and took a step closer. "Then I guess we'll have to do this more often." He tilted her face up with a finger beneath her chin.

Her heart raced again. She could feel her whole body burning. She wanted him closer—she couldn't bear the distance between them.

Garrett examined her ears with a soft smile and touched one between his thumb and forefinger. Kylie shivered, but it wasn't a bad feeling. She smiled bashfully. Then he leaned down and pressed his lips to hers.

She couldn't move, couldn't even breathe. She didn't want to do something wrong. All too suddenly, Garrett pulled away and kissed her forehead.

"Goodnight," he told her, walking backwards towards his car.

"G-goodnight," Kylie breathed, waving shyly.

He got into the car and watched her until she went inside the house.

As soon as the door closed behind her, Kylie was being interrogated by her parents.

"What did you talk about? What food did you order?" her mother burst.

"Did you have a good time?" her father inquired.

Kylie couldn't function, much less articulate herself. "I like him," was all she could muster. That silenced both of her parents. Her mother beamed and her father studied her.

The next couple of months were busy for Kylie—especially in her mind. She had never thought about someone as much as she thought about Garrett. When she was with him, when she was without him. It didn't matter; her brain was on an endless repeating cycle of Garrett. It was maddening.

He continued to sit in front of her in history class and take her on dates. He became her personal bodyguard at school. Outside of school, they were the perfect pair. They went to movies, hiked, and even went ice skating. She loved every second of it. But the stares and murmurs of the people around them still put her on edge. Some days, Garrett couldn't convince her to even consider taking her hat off.

As winter thawed, though, it was harder for her to justify wearing her hat. Pants gave way to leggings and skirts, sweaters moved aside for tees. Warm, fuzzy hats wouldn't survive the season much longer.

One spring night, they were sitting on her couch watching a new superhero movie. They didn't go to his house often, as his family regarded her with the same judgment they did him.

Garrett had his arm around her and she was curled up with a blanket, her cheek on his shoulder.

"Do you wanna go to the woods with me this weekend?" Garrett asked suddenly.

"That sounds fun. Where do you want to go?" she replied, looking up at him while her ear batted his hair away.

He chuckled at that, but it wasn't very joyful. He caught her ear in his hand and examined it, rubbing the white fur on the inside. "No…I mean," he hesitated. Then he breathed the last two words, "to stay."

Kylie regarded him for a minute. "What?" she laughed incredulously.

But he was serious. "We could just leave all this behind,"

he continued.

She knew he meant his family just as much as the class-mates who terrorized her and the people who studied them when they were out and about.

"I don't know," she said, considering her parents. For some reason, her grandmother popped into her mind, as well. She shook that thought away. There was no time to ask that question now.

"We can just get some stuff and leave," Garrett continued, sounding like he was musing to himself rather than Kylie.

"I don't know, Garrett," she mumbled. "My parents… school…."

He sighed and shook his head. "Okay…I just thought… you might be feeling it, too," he murmured, giving her ear a gentle kiss.

"Feeling what?" she asked cautiously.

He paused, considering his words. "Ready," he finally said.

"Are you… ashamed of yourself? With your family, I mean?" Kylie asked softly.

Garrett sighed. "Always with my family. Never with you. I haven't felt ashamed for a while, though." He kissed her forehead and rubbed her arm. "I feel a lot more comfortable these days."

Kylie fidgeted with the edge of Garrett's T-shirt and considered his words for a while. He returned his focus to the movie.

Once Garrett had gone home and Kylie was lying in bed, staring at her ceiling, she turned their interaction over in her mind. She thought about what it would be like, leaving her world. About being with her favorite person in their favorite place—the woods. Was he really worth losing her family over? Could she honestly run away with him and be happy without her parents? She was only seventeen. She thought it would be romantic and daring, but she was also wiser than that. Surely, she couldn't go through with it. Questions and worries filled her mind. Her stomach churned.

A quiet knock echoed through her room. The door opened and her mother peeked in at Kylie. "Hey," she smiled. "I was going to make some hot fudge sundaes. You want one?"

Kylie swallowed dryly. "I'm not very hungry."

"What's wrong?" Mom questioned, coming up to the side of the bed. She sat down and touched Kylie's ear. It shivered beneath her fingers.

"I don't know…I guess I'm feeling kind of uneasy lately."

"About what, honey?"

Kylie bit her lip and gathered her thoughts. "Garrett?"

Her mother sighed and looked away from Kylie. "You know, your grandmother was a lot like him towards the end. Happy with herself. Comfortable. Maybe you should work on your confidence and see if it helps?" Her voice was quiet, like she was thinking about something she wasn't saying.

"I miss her," Kylie murmured, staring up at the ceiling. A tear ran down her cheek and she swiped it away.

Her mother looked over at her. "I know, sweetie. But she's happy…."

Kylie met her mother's eyes. She glanced at the wall above Kylie's head. There was something there in her eyes. A thought she was failing to mask. Like she knew something she wasn't talking about.

Kylie pursed her lips but hesitated just before she could form any words. Her mother sat with her for a while longer before kissing her forehead and disappearing from the room without another word.

New, frightening questions arose in Kylie's thoughts. She shook them off and closed her eyes. She just needed some sleep. That would ease everything. In the morning, she'd figure something out.

The next day was a Saturday. Kylie felt compelled to see Garrett—to make sure he was alright. He'd seemed so off, so vague the night before. She wanted to do something grand for him—something more than just a phone call or a text. So she went to the store and got him a box of blueberries (his favorite) and headed over to his house on the edge of town. It was the starting point of all their hikes, just a few hundred feet from an expanse of wilderness. She'd loved it since she'd first seen it, despite the tension from his parents and two sisters.

Kylie went to the front door and knocked, but there was no answer. His car was parked out front, where it always was. His parents' van was gone, though. She wiggled the doorknob. It was unlocked, as it usually was. His parents and sisters usually went out on weekends, so she wasn't confused by their absence. What did confuse her was when he didn't respond to her calling his name.

She tried again. "Garrett? Where are you?" She didn't allow herself to worry, but concern still planted itself in her brain like some kind of weed. She went to the back of the house, where his bedroom was, and caught hold of the doorknob. "I brought berries," she cooed, smiling softly as she pushed the door open.

She dropped the plastic box immediately. Blueberries spilled across the carpet.

Sitting in front of her was a large black bear. He did not move or look away, he only stared at Kylie. He had soft green eyes, and even softer, shaggy fur. She could feel herself starting to shake, but it wasn't out of fear.

"Garrett?" she whispered. She fell to her knees and stared at him, baffled. "What happened to you?"

He made a small noise, like a groan, and got to his paws. Then he rummaged through the berries on the floor and looked at her gratefully. Despite his altered appearance and animal sense, he seemed…happy.

Kylie reached out towards him and cradled his face in her hands. "Are you okay?" she whispered, a few tears slipping down her cheeks. She wasn't sure why she was crying. Then it dawned on her. Garrett was slipping away. She was losing him. She started crying more and he leaned the side of his head against hers. He moaned again, speaking bear-talk in her ear. Her ears twitched. They burned.

Suddenly, he stood up and rambled out of the room.

"Where are you going?" she cried as he made his way through the house. She followed him to the back door and watched as he got on his hind legs and nudged the door open, cracking the wood as he went. "Garrett!"

He barreled out the back door and into the trees at the edge of the property.

"Garrett!" she screamed, running after him. She looked in all directions, but she couldn't see him. She listened, but he made no sounds.

He was gone.

After wandering around aimlessly for over an hour, Kylie realized he'd left the area. She picked her way through the foliage and got back to the yard just as the sun was setting. The house was still vacant. She wasn't sure if they would care, but she left a note for his family anyway. They would probably rejoice at his absence. She didn't want to think about it. So she went home, unable to halt her tears.

Once she got home, she hurried into her bedroom, not bothering to hide her damp cheeks.

"Kylie?" her mother called. She came into her bedroom gently, looking Kylie over with a mother's sadness. "Baby?"

"He's gone," Kylie bawled. She explained through gasps what had happened. How he was there—how she knew it was him, and he'd run away from her and into the woods. She wasn't sure if her mother believed her. Why would she? It wasn't a normal thing for a daughter to come home crying because her boyfriend had turned into a bear. But then again, that daughter also had animal ears.

Kylie felt like she was losing her mind.

She paced all around her room, avoiding her reflection in the vanity. She felt like she was about to break. Like she would crack into a million pieces and her mother would never be able to mend her.

"There's nothing you could've done, sweetie," her mother said once Kylie had quieted. She coaxed Kylie onto the bed, sat her down beside her, and stroked her hair. Then she rubbed her ears. It had soothed Kylie since she was small, but now the ear rubbing left her feeling even more distraught.

She lurched away from her mother and scrambled towards the vanity. She glared into her reflected eyes. "Why do I have to be like this? They're so ugly!" she screamed, yanking on her ears.

"They're unique and I love them. So did your grandmother. So does Garrett," her mother replied coolly, folding her hands in her lap.

Kylie covered her face with her hands, sobbing. "Why do you keep bringing up Grandma?" Then she fell to the floor and leaned her forehead against the vanity drawer.

"Kylie," her mother sighed. But she didn't answer Kylie's question.

"Maybe if I was normal, he wouldn't have left," Kylie grumbled. She could feel her mother staring at her.

"You know that's not true. Why would he feel that way?"

"Because he can hide his ears and I can't?" Kylie tested.

Her mother crossed the room and sat cross-legged on the floor next to Kylie.

"He wanted to leave. He wanted to go to the woods," Kylie whispered. "He left because I didn't want to go with him."

"Just give him some time. He'll come back. He loves you,"

her mother said. "I'm sure he'll find a way to turn back."

"Why would he want to? He's normal now," Kylie sniffed.

"Or maybe he's just accepted himself for who he is," her mother offered. "That's what he wanted you to do, right?"

Kylie glowered at the floor. Her mother wrapped her arms around her. When she started crying again, she rocked her back and forth until she was calm enough to go to bed. It wasn't a restful night.

The next day, she didn't leave her bedroom. She sat waiting for Garrett to appear somewhere. She checked her windows constantly to see if he was in the back yard or on the side of the house. She was exasperated, almost too drained to cry. All she did was lie in bed and watch TV. Occasionally she would stare at the ceiling, tiny tears trickling out of the corners of her eyes. She wondered where he was, what he was doing, if he missed her. If he was completely empty without her.

Her father checked on her in the afternoon. It was around lunchtime, so he offered Kylie a sandwich. He didn't speak, just held up a plate cautiously.

Kylie sat up and muted her TV. Her father came in without a word and then sat on the edge of her bed. "PB and J," he said with a quiet smile.

"Thank you," Kylie mumbled, taking a bite of the food.

Her father sat for a while longer and then sighed. "I'm sorry about what happened."

Kylie didn't meet his gaze. She just chewed in silence, watching the muted images on the TV screen.

"He probably could've stayed, instead of just disappearing," he said suddenly. He seemed…angry.

"Why do you say that?" Kylie asked after swallowing.

Her father blinked at her and then touched his chin thoughtfully. "Well…people don't think about the impact it has when they just vanish…what it does to their loved ones. Your mother was a wreck when your grandmother disappeared…. We all were."

Kylie studied him for a moment. What he said…. It seemed like her grandmother had made a choice. What if…? "Why do you say that? Like you know something about Grandma? Why does everyone keep talking about her?"

Her grandmother had been normal. Right? Kylie couldn't remember seeing her grandmother's ears. Had they always been beneath her hair? What if she'd hidden animal ears beneath her locks just like Garrett had? When she disappeared, did she…?

Her father straightened up sheepishly. Then he got to his feet and shook his head. "I was just…. I'm sorry, sweetheart. I know Garrett didn't have a choice. But he's happy now, at least." And with that, he left the room and Kylie spinning with even more questions. What did her parents know?

That night, her head hollow and her heart swollen, Kylie sat in front of her vanity after she finished her shower. She studied her horrid ears. She looked for any beauty, any cuteness. Anything that Garrett saw. She was determined to see it; she had to know where it was. She moved them back and forth, trying to spot anything appealing.

Then she thought of how ridiculous she felt, fanning her ears around like satellites, and a giggle escaped her chest. Maybe it was because it was so unexpected or she was so distraught, but she kept snickering. It did seem to help a little bit. She giggled some more and played with her deer ears. They were soft, she realized. And somehow, they seemed to add brightness to her eyes. She thought of Garrett and his ears and beamed to herself. She felt like she would see him again. Somehow. She wanted more than anything to see him.

Before she crawled into bed, she combed her hair around

her ears and braided it. She didn't like to braid her hair since that meant showing the sides of her head, where human ears should've been. But that night, she made herself comfortable with the ears she had. She thought of Garrett stroking them and all the love he'd poured into them—through his words, his kisses, his hands. He had so much love for them, just as Kylie was full of love for his unorthodox ears. There had to be something in that.

She touched the tip of her ear one last time and then curled up beneath the blankets, relieved to feel some sort of wholeness—even if she still missed him. She had a part of him with her ears. And she wouldn't trade that for anything—even human ears.

I'm okay, she told herself as she closed her eyes. It's alright.

When she fell asleep, it was long and soft, and filled with dreams of Garrett. She saw him as a human and as a bear, always happy regardless of his form. She followed him everywhere he went, ducking under tree branches, tiptoeing through creeks. It was paradise.

The next morning, she awoke feeling groggier than usual. When she rolled out of bed, she flopped to the floor. She made a small peep, but it didn't sound right. As she stood, she caught sight of her ear in the vanity and thought nothing of it. Until she saw the rest of her body. She froze, her ears going forward in astonishment. She looked herself over—her whole, furry body. A fluffy white tail flicked behind her as she stepped forward, trying out her slender legs.

After seventeen years, she finally matched her ears.

She expected to be mortified and waited for sorrow. But all she felt was joy. She knew where she would go. She was sad at the thought of not being with her parents, but her relief at finally being herself outweighed that sorrow.

When Mom popped her head in to wake Kylie for the day, her eyes grew wide. Kylie stared at her mother, unmoving.

What will she think? she thought, her heart racing. She'll be horrified!

Her mother came into the room and examined her daughter. She reached out and touched her ear first, then trailed her fingertips over her neck and sighed. "You kept those pretty blue eyes," she said. "I'm so proud of you, baby." She leaned down and hugged Kylie's neck, burying her face into her fur. "You're so beautiful."

For the first time, Kylie believed her mother's words.

Dad came up saying something about pancakes being ready. When he saw Kylie, she was filled with dread once again. He planted a solemn kiss on her forehead and stroked her ears. "Look at you, sweet girl," he sniffled. A tear rushed down his cheek and Kylie's mother hugged him tightly, comfortingly. That was the only indication that he was sad.

Kylie suspected that her parents were trying to keep a strong face for her sake. It filled her with a worry and a sadness. But when her mother looked at her again, she was beaming. She knew, then. Her mother had been through this before.

This is what happened to Grandma, Kylie realized. She thought maybe in the very back of her mind, she'd pieced that much together. But it was something she had buried. Perhaps it was too painful to consider until it happened to her. Now all she felt was peace.

After a little while, Dad glanced at the window. "You have a visitor," he declared, pointing with his chin.

Kylie and Mom made their way to the window and peered out. Kylie almost danced on her hooves.

Sitting at the edge of the tree line was Garrett. He pawed at one ear and glanced around. He was probably keeping an eye out for passersby. After all, people usually panic when they see bears.

"It's only right, sweetie," Kylie's mother comforted, patting

Kylie's back. Then she went to her bedroom door and waved her over with a smile. "Let's go."

Dad went over to stand by his wife. They exchanged a look. Then, they both regarded her joyfully and that was that. They guided her down the stairs, making sure she didn't fall with her lanky limbs, and then they walked her to the front door. Hooves were surprisingly slippery on a wood floor. But Kylie took it slow, and once the front door was open, she scampered out into the sunlight and rested her feet in the grass. Nothing had ever felt better.

Except seeing Garrett.

Without a thought, she raced across the yard and they touched noses. He made one of his small bear noises and pressed his cheek to hers for a moment. Just being able to feel his warmth was amazing. She leaned back and looked him over. He was beautiful in his black fur—strong and broad. She wanted to jump around him in circles and show off her new body—sleek and graceful. He tilted his head slightly at her.

Kylie paused and glanced back at her parents. She gave them a slow, solemn nod and they smiled back at her. She'd never been happier. She was ready. But were her parents?

"Be safe," Dad called.

"We love you," Mom added.

Garrett moved around Kylie and nudged her shoulder with his, encouraging her to go. She took a few steps and looked back at the house—her old life, her family. They watched her as she did. But she didn't question it.

This was where she was meant to be. She knew that now. So she turned forward and followed Garrett into the trees.

OLDEN'S WOOD

Henry Snider

Olden's Wood grew again.

Cheri Addison pressed her cheek against the bedroom's cool window frame and watched the afternoon's fiasco unfold two blocks away. Police, volunteers, even a military division worked tirelessly to contain what was once simply twenty square acres of undeveloped property. Now, like spring gone insane, the entire wood throbbed with life, pulsing larger with each passing minute, and turning suburbia into a jungle.

"I...see...you," she chimed, looking at trees which usually took decades, in some cases centuries, to grow. As of late, trees emerged overnight, reaching ever skyward. Grass grew to waist-high thickets even the best bush hog would have trouble cutting.

Her fingers stroked the window frame, caressing its swollen paint. Individual flakes fell and Cheri watched as they fluttered to the floor.

The neighboring lawn grew shaggy before her eyes, transforming from an immaculate manicure into a dandelion-infested mop. Leafy green shoots thrust through sidewalk cracks, forcing gaps larger and forcing concrete to jut up at awkward angles.

A news crew, led by the local favorite reporter everyone in the city seemed to fawn over, gave an account at an intersection two doors down. Cheri took a step back into the bedroom hoping she wasn't spotted.

Cra-pop!

One block over, a roof split as an oak, already in full bloom, burst forth, sending shingles frisbeeing out in every direction. Several flew with enough force to embed themselves into the house she hid in, one connecting right by the window.

Screams echoed through suburbia-gone-mad. Both officers and military used bull horns calling for people to evacuate to the south where decontamination crews were waiting.

Thwahhhhhhhh!

A multi-toned musical note reverberated throughout the neighborhood and synced in time with a cloudy expulsion from the Wood…something that could easily bring down the walls of Jericho, thrumming bones as if at a concert The resulting haze hung heavy above treetops before drifting slowly south.

"Tick-tock, tick-tock, Mother Nature's tired of your world-of-rock." Cheri repeated the rhyme and wandered through the abandoned house. Smells of burnt wood and burst combustibles wafted, scents in such sharp contrast they tickled her senses. Wine bottles bearing paper labels now sported mossy growth, the pressed wood striving to return to what nature intended.

Nature worked to reclaim what man wrought. Panes split as branches sprang anew from treated lumber. Glass shattered as an ashtray fell from a decorative hall table as healthy branches pushed through the table's painted finish, leaves unfurling as the handful of branches grew nearly a foot high in the span of a single breath. Plank floors actively shifted underfoot, looking for an easy exit from wall-to-wall carpet. The grandfather clock now sported, to Cheri's amusement, a leafy beard worthy of its name.

Boom!

Another explosion rocked the neighborhood. Air

whooshed out, telegraphing the blast's force.

Silence.

Meandering steps led her downstairs to the kitchen where she'd first discovered the pot. A simple miniature rose contained in a clay pot rested on the windowsill. She picked up what could only be considered yet another of mankind's prisoners and marveled at what growth already occurred during her half-an-hour's stay here. Once a simple, four-inch plant now bloomed at well over ten inches. Deep red petals yawned toward life-giving light.

Thwahhhhhhhh!

Sound ripped through the house, bringing tears of both joy and pain to Cheri. So loud. So very loud.

Walls shook and splintered under the stress. Drywall swelled and split, releasing fresh branches from studs.

Cheri lost her foothold and fell, sliding gracelessly against a wall beside the home's back door. Her grip on the pot tightened. Another window shattered, shards twinkling like starlight as glass flew in every direction.

Scents of decaying matter filled the kitchen, followed by a light haze Cheri saw once on a vacation to the Everglades. Recognition took a moment.

Spores.

Her Wood was growing.

Thwahhhhhhhh!

Though sounds from Mother Nature's trumpet still sounded, the mixture of foliage and construction masked its full volume.

Cheri pushed herself upright and looked at the remains of the typical 90's era kitchen. Eggshell white paint flaked off walls in palm-sized chunks. The ceiling buckled in two places, giving an unexpected upper story view. Movement in the gap between stories caught her attention.

A snake slithered across the open gap.

Twenty seconds passed and this single reptile continued to cross, apparently without end.

"Ah," Cheri breathed, recognition brought a smile to her face.

The root, now recognizable as one, spanned the ceiling's gap. A second joined, followed by a third.

Wetness ran down her cheek, breaking the hypnotic vision of nature in motion. Cheri wiped a droplet away with the back of one hand.

It came away smeared with sweaty blood.

Cheri touched her cheek and winced at the rose's thorn's intrusion.

Cradling her charge, she examined the plant. The end of one stalk bore a long thorn, hooked in a barb inspired by a scorpion's tail. No blood dripped from the barb, yet the stem's end offered a crimson hue instead of typical green. It swayed slow, testing the air.

Kitchen tiles shattered without warning, forced up by aggressive rooting matter. Memories of some half-forgotten horror movie surfaced, some desert cow-town movie about giant worms and a handful of forgettable performances. She pitied that handful of poor worms searching in vain for sustenance.

Other explosions echoed, followed by urban responses of shouts, screams, horns, and the grating sound of tires against pavement. A cacophony worthy of city life rang over roof and treetops.

The entire house shifted, walls tipping southward, mimicking that of airborne spore's direction.

"Time to go."

Ten careful steps brought Cheri back into the living room's entrance. A grove of thickly packed aspen filled the room, new shoots crossing both floor and furniture. She couldn't help but to stop and stare at veins of root pushing forth virgin growth every foot or so.

The living room's orange couch puked foam in response to a cluster of gray saplings that recently burst free.

A loud thud echoed from the door.

"Get away from there," a man's voice outside shouted. "The place is about to fall in!"

She placed her palm against painted pine and felt reverberations as someone rattled the doorknob from outside.

"There's someone in there," a feminine voice said. "I saw them."

The reporter.

A volley of small pops emanated from the door. Five branches, each over an inch long, sprouted from the varnished carpentry. Cheri stroked one. The caress drew new growth toward her ministering fingertips.

Heels clicked against pavement, signaling the pair's retreat.

"Bye-bye," Cheri whispered, amazed that a woman would wear heels in the first place, but doubly baffled at the concept that the woman wore them here, in a warzone.

A groan confirmed what the reporter's comrade said. This house was, in fact, coming apart.

"From the ashes, new life emerges." Thoughts of the phoenix myths and their promise of new life sprouting from death proved true within this place. All around her life burst anew from death, and reclaimed what man should never have harvested.

Thwahhhhhhhh!

She pulled on the doorknob and her grip slipped a bit on the pot.

No access.

The house's awkward angle jammed the door in place. More pencil-thin branches pulled free of sealants and stretched out, striving to explore the hallway. Light was now in short supply. Growth of every kind clogged windows, pushed against clear prison boundaries and left Cheri in shadow.

Noises behind the walls distracted her.

Rattling. Popping. Slithering.

Cheri retraced her path back to the kitchen, footfalls sure due to the floor's concrete pad. Glass crunched with each sandal-clad step. The back door appeared more jammed than its mate and light broke through a small gap at the top.

Her attention fell to the green-rimmed hole that once served as a kitchen bay window. With skirt hiked up, she crested the Formica counter and pushed out into bright afternoon daylight, still cradling the rose like a child.

Waist-high grass cushioned the fall, blades folded around her like a mother's embrace. Temptation to lay there pushed into the forefront of her mind.

"No," Cheri said out loud. Not in suburbia. Rest would be granted in the Wood. She rolled over and pushed onto her knees. Grass tangled into her braid and snapped as she pulled free. Reaching up, she pulled a blade free of her hair. It writhed in a lazy zigzag, similar to an earthworm searching for soil.

With the rose pot clutched in one hand and windowsill in the other, Cheri stood and viewed the birth of this new world.

The enclosed backyard looked nothing like when she'd ventured here just over an hour ago. This lawn now sported grass threatening to swallow both her and the landscape someone once carved from Tennessee clay. A wooden playset bore little resemblance to a child's imaginary escape, its visage now more that of a giant root cluster.

Somewhere in front of the house Cheri heard the news van's engine roar to life. Tires peeled as the van sped away.

The house continued to remake itself. Every natural part of the home stretched with life. From siding to doorframes, all wooden elements sprouted branches…all reached for sunlight's graces. Even the window she extricated herself from looked more a part of some demented Chia-Pet's mouth than part of a tract home.

Cheri surveyed the yard and contemplated the puzzle of escape. Odd how a thing so simple as leaving a yard grew into a difficult challenge. Remembering side gates were commonplace, she kicked her way through grasses and checked for an exit. As luck graced, the gate was not only there, but left ajar before Olden's Wood declared war on its urban oppressor.

Wooden slats making up the hinged access rooted themselves solid to the ground, branches intermingled with those from the fence and created its own form of barrier. A space of a foot remained between reborn trunks.

"I can do this." She stepped forward into the branches. They didn't give way as expected, rather responding as any other tree would. Even the thinnest branches resisted, pushing back against this sudden intrusion. Flower and pot shifted as Cheri wormed between trunks. Her breasts compressed painfully as she forced her torso through the narrow passage. Just past the cluster of trunks, more knee-high grass and a vague outline of a birdfeeder fell into view. Minor depressions along the grass line foretold where the homeowners placed slabs of slate to accent the passage between homes.

Crack.

The pot split.

Cheri stepped free of the backyard and returned to cradling the pot with both hands. "Easy now. We'll get you to a new home." With her left hand still gripping the pot's bottom, she set out for the Wood. Within two steps a shard stabbed into her palm.

Thwahhhhhhhh!

Cheri looked in the direction of Olden's Wood, a view blocked by the house she'd just exited. The intense noise came in a harmonic cluster of tones, similar to a group of flutists in disagreement about which note to play.

She kicked her way from between the two homes and out into the front yard. Her skirt hung in tatters below the knee, exposing a multitude of minor scratches on her legs—gifts from the grass now bearing edges that weren't there when she made her way into the confinement zone.

Cheri stopped, awestruck.

A carpet of life blanketed all she surveyed. Clapboard houses no longer appeared hewn by the hands of man. Now the structures healed into massive trunks that sprouted leafy hair through crumbled remnants of roof. Where brick was chosen as the material of choice, vines worked, climbing and destroying walls with equal fury. The single stucco home, which stood out as a monstrosity among monstrosities, crumbled into a skeletal heap before her. Support beams jutted from the ruins like skeletal fingers in a final act of defiance.

Along the entire street, trees multiplied by the minute. Air hung heavy with spore and gave everything an eerie dreamlike glow.

"Heavenly-haze." Cheri inhaled, savoring the thick smells of nature. An aspen fuzz, at least she thought it was aspen, lodged in a nostril and she sneezed it free.

Another thirty feet brought her to the puzzle-piece remnants of the sidewalk.

Boom!

An explosion less than two feet to her left rocked Cheri off balance and she staggered to stay upright.

Boom! Boom!

Tires burst all around the block as probing foliage penetrated rubber. Initial shock now gone. Cheri smiled.

"Final, futile shots in a war lost," she murmured, reminded of what a tottering old grandfather once said about conflict, "are always in vain."

Blood scabbed from a dozen scratches and her hand throbbed in time with each heartbeat. "Damnation," escaped Cheri's lips and she shifted the pot, yet succeeded in somehow digging the shard in further.

The asphalt stood against nature's onslaught and stood as a black river through the suburban jungle. Grass and seedlings encroached on the thirty-foot expanse between curbs. Tar-bound gravel held better than any of the other manufactured materials.

Shrubbery bled across sidewalks and masked what couldn't be easily reclaimed. Colors more vibrant than any child's art box burst forth in a bloom of pinks, reds and blues so strong Cheri felt the need to blink several times.

Opting for the path of least resistance, Cheri stepped from the curb between two cars and out into the street.

She sneezed again. Sweat dripped from every pore. My gods, she thought, the temperature must have jumped ten degrees in the last few minutes. Humidity and luscious layers of green promised the dog days of August were well at hand.

A grey mass thumped against the pavement to the right. Curiosity drove her to investigate the disturbance. Feathers stuck out at odd angles from a magpie's body.

Pain shot through her hand again. "Gods damn it." Embarrassed by the second curse in a single day, Cheri moved on.

Another mass fell on her right and Cheri chanced a wary glance skyward. Intensely bright haze barred sight beyond a creamy canvas of gray with the sun little more than a brighter shade of white. Squinting didn't help spot any potential avian bombs. Spore clogged their beaks and sprouted from ever-open eyes.

"Just as long as one doesn't fall *on* me."

A late model car, draped in leafy canopy and cape, rattled by. Its engine sounded ready to take passengers nowhere but the nearest junkyard. The driver concentrated on the road, oblivious to her scrutiny. Cheri watched as the woman occupying the passenger seat pointed and said something lost behind glass windows.

Then they were gone, black smoke spat out a final insult to what nature wrought.

Grasses swayed as vines snaked their way to higher ground. Any semblance of wind was non-existent in the afternoon sun. Cheri panted, unable to easily get her breath. She wiped away an itchy drop of sweat from her nose, hand coming away pasty.

"More fuzz."

Cheri walked to the center of the intersection and surveyed as much of the neighborhood as possible, basking in the emerald tide appearing to throb with new life every moment or two. Waves of growth undulated everywhere in the neighborhood, moving as a breeze that's more sensed than felt, blowing eastward. To the west, yet another barricade blocked an intersection eight blocks up. Emergency lights blinked red and blue through the fog. A vine worked to envelope a stop signpost, tendrils reached ever skyward and masked the letter "S," thus changing the word to a proclamation of herbal achievement instead of a vehicular command.

Cheri smiled at the irony and turned to walk the three hundred yards to Olden's Wood.

Homes on the next block proved even less recognizable than their predecessors, nothing more than dense growth and perfectly spaced hills. More birds fell from the sky and struck with barely a thud before being overtaken by the living carpet surrounding her. Runnels of sweat traced their way southward from Cheri's armpits, breasts and thighs.

Her pace quickened; anticipation drove away all thoughts except those of getting to the Wood.

Spore haze hung heavier here.

Thwahhhhhhhh!

Louder this time, Cheri heard the Wood's call. Repetitious thumps sounded all around and foretold of new feathered fatalities. Plumage vanished in seconds under leafy attention.

A grove of trees spired above the others, standing as a grand maternal castle to the simple subjects of the plant realm. She passed the first block with nary another glance and headed into Olden Wood's lush outer expanse.

Camouflaged cars, doubly hidden now with leafy growth, lined the road and blocked easy access. Cheri frowned, not wanting to walk up and over another block just to return on the other side of this wreckage.

"Besides," she said out loud. "How do I know it's not just as bad up there?"

In response, the pot slipped again and thorns dug into her skirt's waistband. The shard dug deeper into her upturned palm.

"Damn." The word barely escaped her lips before more guilt washed in. That wasn't language Cheri the Wood Nymph would use—that was language best left for Cheri the burnt-out waitress with decades-dead dreams of escaping this hell-hole for Hollywood.

"Best to be rid of it." Several deep sighs escaped, taking with them, Cheri decided, all desire to express herself with vulgarity.

More greenery spread past her on either side of the street. New cracks formed in the pavement with each step as asphalt finally surrendered its battle. A nearby news van now served as a hothouse, foliage pressed firm against the windshield's interior.

Cheri saw the locked grip from a pair of pale hands on the van's steering wheel. Light glinted off the left hand's gold band.

"All…wars," she forced the words around a sob, "have… casualties."

Reality turned to horror as the hands convulsed against a rubberized grip.

Instinct urged her to flee, to run from this place, to return to a world which made sense. Desire screamed for her to stay. The latter won and continued to pull her toward a fantastic dream, a fanciful place where fairies lived, elves were prevalent, and Mother Nature was a physical being able to grant a woman's deepest desires if only she dared to brave the journey. Desire placed one foot in front of another, driving forward at a steady pace.

A final glance in the van's direction showed hands still gripping the wheel. Did other vehicles contain similar displays, visual stories with no beginning or middle, rather only the end for an audience of one to fathom?

A familiar sound, alien in this environment, caught her attention. An engine somewhere in this mass whined. It wasn't just running, it revved. Someone else still survived through the Wood's onslaught.

Cheri picked her way through hulkish masses, careful not

to crush more greenery than necessary. Honeysuckle bloomed here; its sweet smell so harsh in the windless heat that nausea threatened to overtake her.

"It's a test." An onslaught of sneezes followed the statement.

More pops echoed throughout the neighborhood.

A military Hummer sat wedged between two vehicles, one a HazMat truck and the other a troop transport. Inside, an enlisted man worked to keep the vehicle running. Flattened tires, perforated and stitched to the ground with vines, strained against the engine's pull.

Their eyes locked.

"Get out of here," he yelled.

Cheri walked the handful of steps to the truck's side. "It's okay," she said. "I belong."

"Don't you understand?" He screamed, forcing Cheri to wince as a headache began to throb. "We've lost our perimeter. The plants are spreading! It's not safe! Get in!"

"The Wood," she corrected, "is taking back what belonged to it in the first place."

Both recognized the other as beyond salvation and each returned to their respective tasks.

Cheri walked past the Hummer's rear and saw a fist-sized cluster of vines probe at the vehicle's exhaust pipe. Other clusters, vaguely man-shaped, dotted sibling yards. One HazMat suit stood out against the blanket of life, reflective orange and yellows appeared as an obnoxious bloom on life's beauty.

The figure rested on its knees; arms hung limp. A silent, skyward scream craned the head back, action frozen by growth entangled into the woman's dark ponytail. Growth frothed from both eye sockets, bushy life sprouting in the form of nail-sized leaf clusters.

Cheri stopped, transfixed by the Wood's gruesome statuary.

"Gnaaaaaaaaaaah."

Cheri's mouth dropped open.

The statue became animate, thrashing against rope-thick binds and shook its facial mass with the vigor of a cheerleader's pompom. Vines tightened, strapping the victim more securely against the ground.

"Gufaaaaaaaaaach." The woman stiffened once more.

Horns and sirens continued to blare in the distance. Overhead, a helicopter thumped, hidden by a legion of seed. A loudspeaker boomed, slicing through a symphony of natural processes gone wild.

"Attention. All remaining personnel are ordered to pull back to the twelve-hundred-yard barricade."

Cheri pulled the rose in close and cradled it. Two stems already worked their way into her blouse's fabric, forcing a button free. The sharp thorn which scratched her a short time ago wavered before her face, swinging to and fro with deliberate menace.

"Easy, baby. We're almost there."

New growth clustered so close Cheri couldn't see into the Wood beyond the tree line, which shifted before her eyes as this amazing spring tide came in.

"A tide of life."

Glass shattered to the right, nature's quest for support too much for windows to bear. A curtain of vines fell in the house. A residential mouth now yawned in a morbidly humorous pose which reminded her of a Monty Python skit she'd seen years before.

Cheri continued the journey, her steps shifting toward the street's center to avoid crushing the leafy masses. Skyward, well-defined stroke patterns in the blanket of spore defined wind patterns—patterns denied to those on the ground.

Thwahhhhhhhh!

Between the noise and reverberations from such a powerful expulsion of spore, Cheri stumbled again and fell against a car. Leafy stems set to work entangling themselves in a sleeve.

She stepped back, draped in a vine blanket still anchored to the car. Two forceful tugs allowed release, though now she lacked a fist-sized swatch of fabric.

Thwahhhhhhhh!

Olden's Wood pulsed and another expulsion shot high into the air. This time a blow-back of air hit her in time with its skyward release. It hit as a wave, the pressure physically resisting advance.

Ahead, leaves pressed against each other as branches realigned to fill in gaps. The Wood's border effectively closed to prying eyes.

Thwahhhhhhhh!

This third blast struck with an unexpected breeze and, as if with a backhanded compliment, pelted her with a barrage of fuzz and other airborne matter. The storm lasted a handful of seconds, yet was enough to thoroughly coat her left side, the substance turning to glue against damp skin and garments.

Cheri stepped forward and searched for any access to the new kingdom…*her* kingdom. Thorns bit at the skirt and entangled themselves.

"Just a bit further."

A tinny volley of snaps and cracks sounded from ahead on the right.

"Don't move."

She continued, command unheeded.

"You're in a restricted area," the tense voice continued. "This location is off-limits. You must immediately…." The speaker clicked off for a handful of seconds. When it returned another voice spoke. "This is Colonel Huff. You *must* come toward this speaker now. Soldiers will assist you. It's not safe here."

Cheri bit her lip and steered each step as far to the left as possible.

"Miss!"

In response, Cheri shook her head and walked with purpose rather than care. Vines crunched underfoot, threatening to upend her as they pulled back.

Gunshots sounded from the barricade several blocks behind her.

Thwahhhhhhhh!

A whir came from the speaker's direction twenty yards distant. Vines folded back and exposed electronics worthy of any science fiction movie to the elements. Two orange-clad shapes exited a trailer before it closed.

Cheri's pace quickened.

"Miss!" The man's HazMat suit muffled communications as he shouted.

She glanced around, feeling rabbitty and ready to bolt.

"No way in." Tears cascaded. "There's no way—"

"Lady!" A second man called out as they closed the distance between her and them. "Come with us *now*!" He reached out and tried to knock the rose from her grasp. One stalk buckled under his might.

"No!" Cheri shook free and darted into the nearest yard, hurdling susurrating barriers every few steps.

"Get her," the trailer's only remaining speaker bellowed.

She ran into the yard which bordered the Wood's expanding outer perimeter. Vines lay haphazard against a ranch-style home covered with a plastic tent. Streaks of yellow "Do Not Cross" tape lined the mid-yard point, barely visible. Cheri crossed with nary a thought.

"Stop," someone yelled.

Cheri looked for a way into the Wood. "It has to be here!"

Olden's Wood's outer edge covered a third of the house before rising cliff-like for all to see. Leaves pressed together and formed a scaly skin offering no visible access.

"Damn it, lady!"

Cheri leapt over a knotted mass of roots, slid through plastic and into the front doorway. Where a standard front door normally blocked access, the military chose to place a second curtain of plastic, it's opaque style blurring reality into vague impressions of furnished shadows standing out against white walls. She shouldered her way through the barrier and entered the living room.

Outside, rustling announced her pursuers' arrival.

At first the general impression was a mudslide had occurred, with brown masses puked forth from down the hall, cascading through the living room before they disappeared into a once stylish kitchen. A second look told Cheri these were even more roots, clustered masses of naked anchors expelling themselves via this house.

The outer layer of plastic shifted.

Cheri pushed into the hall where wooden anchors webbed in every direction. Working past the bathroom, she couldn't help but notice a network of roots taking residence in the faucets and, of all places, the toilet. A single root, thick as an arm, snaked into the waste receptacle and appeared somehow obscene. Then the view was gone, replaced with a photograph-covered wall as she pressed on.

"Lady," the lead man said while he carefully picked his way through an ankle-breaking maze making up the living room floor. "You need to come with us. It's not safe here. Nuts," he muttered loud enough to be heard. "She's fucking nuts."

Cheri moved faster. The need for access urged her uncomfortably close to a photo of a rather bland looking family of four. Cardboard matting bubbled against glass and strained to free itself from a prison of metal and glass.

"Damn it, Ed," the latter man said, "Like you said—she's nuts! Let's get back."

"Move your ass, soldier," the one in front retorted.

Cheri ducked underneath a canopy allowed entry to the end of the hall and proceeded to the garage which now appeared as nothing more than a cavern of mushrooms.

A hand locked onto her ankle.

"Easy now," Ed said. "You're going to be okay."

Cheri dove forward, pulling her ankle free and rolled into

the garage. Both arms wrapped around the rosebush.

Fleshy mushroom caps broke under her weight, and she tumbled down the three steps to a concrete floor. Smells of mildew—sickeningly putrid—wafted up. Moisture soaked through already-drenched summer fabric and cooled her backside. Splinters of sunlight segmented the room, spearing in where rafters grew anew and parted shingles to gain sunny access.

"Let her go," the man in back said. "She's not worth it."

"Lady," Ed continued, "You don't know what you're doing. We've gotta get you out of here."

"Ed!"

"We will retrieve her, *Private*." Cheri heard venom in the man's words. This man of war was not going to give up until he accomplished his goal.

Cheri rolled onto her side, a handful of painful stabs pricking at her exposed upper chest and neck as the rosebush's thorny stems groped for their own purchase. Her head shook with purpose, chin dislodging her ward's grasp.

"Just a little farther."

The side door window remained intact, though plastered with unfurling leaves which blocked nearly all the sunshine.

"No more time."

She looked for an exit, feeling the same rush of adrenaline as any other quarry sure of its capture. Cheri bolted to the window and dove. High school memories of pole-vaulting guided a much older body into a spin as her head and shoulders broke through the transparent barrier.

White-hot pain sliced down the small of her back as glass cut into the meat of her left buttock. An Escheresque knotwork of roots made for a winded landing. The rose scraped against exposed flesh in time with the sudden stop.

Cheri forced herself to stand. Warm wetness replaced cool along her posterior. She reached back, hand coming away red… dark red. The kind of red calling for a trip to the hospital.

Curses echoed from within the garage, followed by a series of crashes.

Cheri looked for an easy route to freedom.

A shadowy landscape.

Roots.

Leafy barriers blocked all except the most indirect light.

She'd done it. She was past the barrier and actually *in* the Wood. Dirt caked her once floral dress, further scabbing the multitude of injuries endured along this two-block journey.

"Where is *the grove?*" Cheri'd dreamt it—a place deep in the Wood's heart. Open to the sun, this grove of the gods opened to sprites, fairies and nymphs who danced through grasses and basked in eternal sunshine…a place where the worthy could rest.

Summerland.

Looks in every direction offered naught to the question. Undergrowth proved minimal in the dim light, mosses and toadstools making up the majority of the wooded carpet. Oaks with diameters nearing those of Washington's redwoods towered. Roots for the behemoths weaved amongst peers, using each other as added support.

Air pressure increased and Cheri pinched her nose to equalize pressure. The breeze shifted, forced suddenly past.

Thwahhhhhhhh!

Her ears popped as the neighborhood reverberated with release.

An over-the-shoulder glance bore witness to a soldier, she couldn't tell which one, working at a fevered pace to extricate himself from the door's window in a pitiful imitation of their quarry. Branches had grown as much as a foot since her exit only a moment before, further clogging the hole.

Outer branches, tips thrust up in a mini cavalcade of spires, stabbed at the man's resistant suit.

The gust ended, slowing to a gentle breeze.

Cheri looked around and picked the path least clogged by slippery undergrowth. Progress proved difficult, her leg stiffened with each stride taken and Cheri limped on the other in compensation.

"Soon," she crooned through gritted teeth which sounded more like a stressful moan than soothing. The bush, beyond what any plant lover would call pot-bound, continued to bloom in accelerated beauty.

A barrage of thuds echoed on the route just taken and foretold of the second man's efforts to free himself and take her from the Wood.

Cheri's pace increased, all conscious effort willed toward the simple goal to reach Olden's Wood's heart. Intricate patterns of ankle-breaking roots netted the ground, lazy movements stretched in every direction. She stared at the physical expression of nature reclaimed. A wooden picnic table grew heavy branches from all ends before they reached skyward. The sight gave the impression of leafy horns. The table's bench blossomed similarly, thus adding to the effect of a great horned face.

"Pan," she murmured, staring at the green face.

"Hello," a voice called out behind her.

"There," another voice replied in excitement. "Lady!" A barrage of heavy footfalls replaced voices.

Thwahhhhhhhh!

This time the rush of air was audible before it arrived and Cheri grabbed onto a nearby trunk, cradling the rose. Wind whipped by moving all the underbrush in undulating waves of green growth. Soldiers toppled, another string of curses carried away by their formless aggressor.

Cheri gripped the plant tighter and continued, teeth gritted against an insistent dull throb of pain from her posterior. Blood clotted, solidifying warm wetness into a tight, sticky discomfort. Each step pulled at the wound.

Ahead, gloom gave way to sunlight. Bare roots, rather than burrowing underground as usual, worked their way higher, creating an insane jungle gym. Tree anchors coiled and entangled themselves into a knot-work only a lumberjack could undo. She slowed, unsure of where to gain access.

"Gods, it's hot." The thought expressed itself orally. Hearing her voice in this place sounded somehow wrong—alien amidst the natural. Between two trees, a few beams of direct sunlight shone, slicing through a forest full of shadow.

Footfalls fell nearby.

Cheri quickly chose a passage into the root cluster, stepped with one foot and dragged its mate.

"Stop!" One voice echoed with such authority Cheri hesitated. A lifetime of conditioning screamed to obey the commands of this authoritative figure. Then the tone was gone, replaced by something else, something weaker. "Come *this* way. *Please!*"

Shuffling noises began again. The soldiers were on the move.

Cheri resumed the quest's final leg and pushed herself faster. The scabbed wound pulled open and wept red once more.

Six feet.

Three.

The root-work maze stopped as quickly as it rose, rimming a steep moss-covered incline. Seeds of all kinds drifted by. Aspen, Russian olive and a multitude of plant seeds floated about, their sire unseen in the Wood. Miniscule spores darted in different directions with unknown purpose. Two steps up the slope, she slipped, misjudging the foot-thick growth that reflected such a dark green that it appeared more a hole than root. Spiny material resembling ground-up glass covered the mosses surface and she itched coming in contact with it.

Then it burned.

Cheri retreated, stepping free and back onto the dirt, ankles and shins bright red from an instant allergic reaction.

Another sneezing fit doubled her over, forcing an expulsion of snot larger than she felt her head capable of containing. Feeling nothing like Cheri the Wood Nymph, she blew and forced free the last wet clump of mucus. Slime akin to that of a sea cucumber went from clear to red as it fell free, landing with a plop in the dirt.

Something—Cheri couldn't make out what—moved in the mass.

She took a handful of steps north and looked for safer ridge access.

Thwahhhhhhhh!

Cheri braced for the toppling blast of wind. It came, but without the intensity expected. Looking back showed the wind by the debris it carried, racing over the top of the root system she'd navigated. A tremendous tone burst from the mound's crest, musically firing its own addition into the escaping masses. Fuzz shot up and flew free of Olden's Wood in much the same way the overabundance of mucus escaped Cheri's nose seconds before.

Light blinked yellow. Cheri caught it out of the corner of her eye. A box, camouflaged to blend into the natural environment, flashed, showing man's involvement in nature's revolt. Still behind her, the two soldiers worked their way through the root windbreak, proving by their grunts of difficulty that men weren't overgrown boys always looking for an excuse to go outside and play.

In front of her something pressing over the roots, reflected dully.

A plank leading to the Wood's heart.

The metal walkway, half covered with moss, lay the rise's length, its surface coated with a gritty substance to offer better purchase. Not daring another walk in the moss, especially with footwear as simple as sandals, Cheri walked onto the plank. Childhood flashbacks rushed to a time when she was Wendy, standing at the brink of impending doom and waiting for Peter Pan to come to the rescue.

"Pan." Cheri said the name out loud; recognition brought the childhood fantasy into adulthood's worship of the woodland god. Guide to weary travelers. A trickster damned into a demonic persona by modern-day religion. "Lord of the Wood," she voiced. Surely, *he* was here…teasing her…testing her resolve… waiting to see if *she* was worthy of *his* home.

A second step put Cheri onto the plank, her weight sinking the aluminum slab over six inches into a mossy, emerald mass. Steps fell carefully as she refused to be deterred by the springy response to each step.

Brightly colored forms climbed free of the windbreak and navigated their last few feet on hands and knees. She rose above the ridge's crest, head above the Wood's highest earthen point.

Six bulbous forms rested atop the mound, scattered in no particular pattern, each waist-high and familiar. Arm sized spires rose from the mound in every direction, changing angles in time with the mound, flexing at knee height. Earth shifted as the mound swelled. Rapid movements came from two of the growths.

"Not growths," but something—

A covered hand broke free from one shape and flailed. Woven vines braided the extremity's length, working to once again secure the masculine arm.

Cheri stepped onto the second plank, its path led her past one of the people and ultimately to the mound's summit. Her ankles throbbed. Both soldiers stopped and were involved in an unheard, but heated, exchange.

"This is not your wood," she whispered, then with more confidence and volume, "This is not your wood!"

The soldiers stared at her.

Six forms threw their heads back, yawning mouths little more than black orifices.

"This is not—"

Thwahhhhhhhh!

Cheri's words were lost in the mound's sudden expulsion of spore, thrust skyward by the earthen contraction. A great geyser of fertile material shot past treetops in another massive exhalation, thrust forth from six yawning mouths. She fell forward, landing half on the catwalk and smashing the rose pot between herself and an unforgiving metal plank. Thorns picked at her exposed flesh, digging in where opportunity and angle proved advantageous.

Dirt fell from between her fingers, leaving a rat's nest of roots to hold. Cheri went to set her charge down, but the plant didn't fall free. The act of opening her hands shot pain up each arm. A repeated action offered a duplicate result.

No release.

Cheri grabbed the bush with her free hand and pulled to release the shrub-sized beauty from its entanglement. Pain, white-hot, shot the length of her farm, emanating from deep within. Tears welled.

The mound sank as the Wood's lung ran low of air.

Six heads fell forward once more.

Overlapping voices spoke.

"Dear God, kill…."

Sobbing.

"Mamma. Mamma," rasped a man, judging by how deep the voice was.

Laughter, maniacal in its intensity.

Other words followed, mostly unintelligible, spilling themselves with such consistency a single lungful of air would never allow.

Hoarse screams.

"Nonononononononono…."

Voices fell silent and the mound swelled once more.

Six figures shook, each straining against the unyielding process of life.

Cheri looked from the nearest form to her upraised palm. Roots from the rose pierced flesh in a multitude of places, bloodlessly splitting the skin to complete an unwelcome marriage and forcing a nature-blessed stigmata. Knotted clusters bulged, running from wrist to elbow, showing the extent of her violation.

Cheri cradled her extended appendage without intimacy, now mustering only revulsion. A handful of stems intermingled with the moss, seeking an earthen purchase as well. One broke as she jerked the bush free. Another wave of pain shot up her arm, pain not felt since tripping on the stairs at work and breaking two fingers during the subsequent fall.

Both orange-clad men stared at her but stayed well away from the embankment.

"I don't understand."

Warm wetness tickled her upper lip, then lower. Cheri licked them, tasting copper. A second wave of nausea swelled, the tang of blood cramping vegetarian innards.

She stood, shaky on the rising mound.

The two orange forms retreated, backing in the direction originally navigated.

"Hel…help!"

They kept moving away.

One of the engulfed bodies called out, "Don't leave me."

Cheri stepped off the plank, her only remaining desire to navigate the shortest distance between them. Moss pressed against both feet, itching in a way poison ivy never could. Ground shifted and pitched her forward. Instinct took over and Cheri the would-be nymph pistoned her arms in an effort to stay upright. The rose bush flailed in her hand and forced her to overcompensate and stumble.

One of the men took a step in her direction.

"Help," she sobbed. Tears fell. "This wasn't how it was supposed to be. I'm one of *them*."

Vines wound around her legs and worked higher, coils tightening around calves, above knees, belting a natural corset around her waist. Restrictions ensued, pulling Cheri toward the ground. She strained against the unnatural crouch, failing to resist falling to her knees.

Something solid scraped the inside of one thigh, snaking toward where legs met hips. *That* place—her most private place.

"No!"

Her knees buckled and the world went black.

Bloated.

Cheri nodded slowly; thoughts jumbled as if waking from a dream. Her belly hurt and felt distended. With effort, her tongue drug across both lips, the sensation akin to dragging a finger across the surface of bark.

She opened weary eyes.

The rosebush rested upright, having nested itself, and her hand, firmly to the mound. Cheri's other hand, the right, lay free. Neither leg registered to her touch, nor anything below the ribcage for that matter. Half her body lay numb. Nervous fingers worked higher up her leg, driven by fear of what fingers might encounter.

The bloated sensation grew worse, visibly swelling her torso beyond that of pregnancy. Organs pressed up and strained against the ribcage's confinement.

"Ow," she croaked. "It hurts. Help."

The military men were gone.

How long had she been there?

Vibrations shook the mound and jarred everything with equal intensity.

"Nononononono," floated across the mound. The sob played melody to the word's rhythmic repetition.

Lungs collapsed. More air escaped in a belch. It spewed from her stomach, pushing up first as a burp, fired through the esophageal sphincter in quick repetition, then as a long blast, drying what little moisture had returned to her mouth.

The mound forced wind through her penetrating spire, making passage through Cheri and out into open air. Her head snapped back allowing faster passage for the immense exhalation.

A new voice, an alto, joined the sextant's choir.

And Olden's Wood grew.

KEEPER OF THE WOODS

Shiloh Silveira

It was fitting that I should die in the forest I dedicated my life to. The creek with its border of mossy rocks, the old creaking bridge Granddad built—now sunken beneath the surface—and the miles of trees and shrubs had been the setting of the greatest memories of my life. These guardian trees witnessed epic battles of war as my siblings and I charged, barefoot and dirt-smeared with our wooden swords, against the invisible armies of Gamorordia. Rotted remains of our fort with the pallet board swinging door still lay in a heap not far from the creek. The voices of laughing children had long faded from the forest. My own voice had grown hoarse with old age, but this place still held the same joy for me. Even in death, I'm mesmerized by its beauty.

I slipped on a loose stone, my balance not what it once was. My world momentarily turned black. When I opened my eyes, the birds still fluttered from tree to tree and a fiery throb spread through the back of my skull. For a moment, instinct told me to cry out for help. I opened my mouth and then closed it. Even if my soft voice had been strong, who would come? The farm that had been in my family for generations no longer housed my loved ones. Ma and Pops died years ago. Our Dutch Colonial style farmhouse, along with its two hundred accompanying acres, were now a historic landmark. The only people to frequent it were tourists, and that was between noon to four. Judging by the low position of the sun, everyone had packed up and gone home.

The hot blood pooling from the back of my head painted the rock beneath me crimson and seeped into the soil. From where I lay, limbs bent at awkward angles from my fall, the treetops came in and out of focus. I'd planted many of these trees with my own hands. This forest, and my family's farm that it bordered, had been my home for eighty-five years. It belonged to my grandparents, and great-grandparents before that. I planted hundreds of trees over my lifetime, and built countless gardens. I dreamed of rich dark soil everywhere.

There were no accolades for a lifetime of farm work, but that never mattered to me. In town they called me crazy. Some called me a witch. I was neither. I preferred nature and my books to keep me company. My fingers twitched a few times before they ceased to obey my commands all together. The thumping of my heart began to slow, and a great fog clouded my mind. Soon the blood, sweat, and tears for this land would all be spent.

The tree branches above me waved in the breeze, and wind flowed through their leaves, forming a whispering sound like the rush of voices.

"He's coming," they seemed to chant all around me. "He's coming."

My lips parted in the weakest of smiles.

I must be hallucinating, to think that the trees are talking.

" Wh—Who's coming?" I asked. My voice was weak and ragged.

The trees whispered to me, "The Keeper of the Woods."

I chuckled. Silly trees. Didn't they know that I was the keeper of these woods? A sudden updraft of wind brought a cloud of leaves that swirled in the air before condensing into a solid humanoid form. A tall figure drifted down from the treetop. His cloak made of interwoven leaves billowed around him. His green-tinted bare feet sunk into the soil. He knelt inches from my face. Huge deer-like eyes surveyed my broken body. His face was long, hollow-cheeked, and framed by a thick red beard tangled with leaves. Broad moss-covered antlers protruded from his skull. He sniffed the air, before gently tracing his fingers in my bloodied hair.

My grip between reality and dreams seemed to be slipping. He looked as real as anything I had ever seen.

"What have you done, Arna?" He asked me.

"Slipped," I gasped. "Rock was loose.... Hit my head."

The Keeper of the Woods shook his head. "There's no one coming, is there?"

I licked my lips feebly. Soon everything would go black. I knew this was it.

"No one. I have no one."

"You have me," the creature said. "You have the trees you planted, and the animals that find shelter in them."

If I could nod, I would have. "I…I'm ready to die."

"I will let you go, if that is your wish." The Keeper drew closer. "I can give you life in this forest, Arna. For all that you have given me, I can give you another chance to continue on, but you won't be human anymore, and you cannot return to the life you had. Do you wish to become a part of this?" The Keeper gestured to the tall trees that had grown still and silent as we spoke, hushed, waiting for my answer.

"A thousand times, yes," I said without hesitation. My last human words.

The Keeper of The Woods nodded solemnly and bent down to kiss my wrinkled lips. How few kisses had been given to these lips in my lifetime. The pain in my skull faded away. As I drifted off, the last thing I saw was the Keeper wave his hand

and the soil rushed up over me. My life as Arna, daughter of Bill and Nancy, mother to no one, and friend of few, was over.

My body imploded into something miniscule. There were no physical sensations of hands or feet, only a vague awareness of darkness. As if in a sleep, I was vaguely aware of a light in the distance above me. Slowly, I started to move towards the light. Breaking through the layer of soil that had covered me, I did not gasp for breath. No longer human, I didn't need to breathe. At least not in the same way. There were voices around me, and movement, and the temperature changed from time to time, but still I remained dormant, with little sense of the passing time. Finally, I awoke.

I had no eyes to see, but the forest was still evident. Towering over the creek I had played in as a child during hot summer evenings, I braced for the wave of fear that would come from being at such heights, but it never came. The trees greeted me with immense joy.

"Arna is awake," they whispered in anticipation.

"I am?" My words formed from the rustle of leaves. My leaves. The shadow of a tall tree mimicked my movements as I swayed branches back and forth. There were no aches and pains, no weakness, just beauty and strength.

Beside me sat the Keeper of the Woods, cross legged, and leaning against my trunk. "Good morning, Arna. How do you feel?"

"How do I feel? I don't know."

"Focus on your body," The Keeper said. "Try to feel everything. From your branch tips to your roots. You need to adjust to these new sensations."

My roots sunk deep into the earth and stretched out far from me. The soil felt cold and damp underneath me and incredibly soothing. Millions of stringy hairs of mycelium attached to my roots, stretched out to all the other trees and entwining us together, like many gentle hands connecting. In an instant I felt the rush of many emotions from the trees. For one panicked second, I wished to disconnect. Then comforting images came to me. One tree, named Strom, recalled my youth. Like a ghost from the past, my childhood self sat at Strom's Trunk reading a fairy tale out loud. I felt the tree's happiness as it had looked down on me. The image faded, quickly being replaced by another. A gangly teenager in tattered overalls pushing a wheelbarrow of manure and leaves out to lay at the tree's trunk. I felt its gratitude and love, and my former self patted its trunk and then vanished. If I could cry, I would have. They welcomed me as one of them. As an old friend.

The Keeper of the Woods lay his cheek against me and listened to my communication with my friends. "Are you happy, Arna?"

"I am," I whispered. "I finally belong. Thank you."

My first morning as a tree began with a particularly alarming discovery. My arm had fallen off. That is, one of my many arms. I looked to the floor to see the piece of me laying abandoned. Sensing my feelings through our root connections Strom said to me, "Do not panic, Arna. You are thinking with the old human ways. It does not hurt does it?" I turned my attention to my spot where sap was already beginning to seep out.

"It stung for a moment," I said. "But that branch had felt disconnected somehow. Not quite as strong as the others. I suppose I feel…."

"Relief?" Strom asked.

"Yes, relief!"

Strom chuckled. "This life will take some getting used to for you. Don't worry, my friend. We look out for each other. When a real injury happens, I can send you sugars."

This was something I remembered from my books in my former life. Trees can send each other sugars through their roots and will even send sugars to a tree stump for years after it's been cut down. I focused on my feeling of gratitude and sent it through our root system.

Strom waved a branch in acknowledgement. "I sense you will catch on quickly."

During my first rainfall, I felt the heaviness of the earth underneath me and greedily drew the water up through my roots where my xylem transported it all the way to my crest. As thousands of droplets tickled my leaves, and those of all my friends, creatures all around us scurried for shelter.

"You're welcome to join me," I said to a little family of squirrels far down below. The mother scampered up my trunk, and her babies followed. Their feet felt light and ticklish. I shifted a particularly leafy branch to cover their heads. We waited out the storm together. From then on, she and her children frequently visited my branches and played games, racing up my trunk or leaping between my friends and I. Being a host for birds and squirrels brought more joy than I'd experienced in years. They always shared news of the surrounding forest: the movements of bears, humans, and the occasional cougar. I quickly grew to feel pride over how much comfort I could bring to others. I even carried a nest in one of my branches for a sparrow and her eggs. There was great excitement amongst my friends when her hatchlings were born, and she sang a lovely song to celebrate.

Fall frost soon gave way to a carpet of glittering snow. Grateful that my bark protected me from the elements, I surveyed my friends. A family of snow-white bunnies played around Maple's trunk, and she was deeply entertained by their antics. Douglas had lost more branches in the night and felt bashful about his lack of covering. Strom conversed with an owl who seemed to be telling him some distressing news. We all listened quietly as Strom's thoughts entered our shared network. A fox had been killed by a cougar in the night half a mile away, and if I wasn't mistaken, he was a fox that had kept shelter under my branches. A wave of sorrow swept over me.

"Take heart, Arna," Strom said, picking up on my feelings.

"This is the way of things. The cougar needs to eat."

"I don't have to like it," I grumbled.

"Even the fox killed the mouse," Maple added.

"And the mice eat invertebrates. I get it," I added.

"But for every death, there are countless more lives being added to the forest," Douglas added, sending me the equivalent affection of a hug. "Just you wait until springtime comes, Arna."

So it was, when springtime came, and the last drops of snow melted. The air filled with the chorus of singing birds and croaking frogs. Animals scurried everywhere under branches once again heavy with leaves. The forest was alive with the whisperings of thousands of trees, as news spread of the births of deer, rabbits, birds, mice and countless more living things. Every so often, the Keeper of the Woods himself would show up and walk serenely among his family. Though the forest was a never-ending cycle of death and life, its rhythm was somehow beautiful. It was fitting that I died in the forest that I had lived my life caring for, and an honor to live in it again.

BEYOND THE FLOODWALL

Kari J. Wolfe

The light blue two-story house on the corner loomed over me as I slid out of the rental car. If my brother Ricky wasn't missing, I don't think I'd have ever come back to West Virginia, much less to this particular house.

In the past eleven years, someone had cut down Mom's holly bushes and left her old cigarette patch bare in front of the porch. The yard was stripped, unusual for summertime, tan dusty dirt where green grass used to be. The sidewalk leading to the porch steps was broken in pieces. There wasn't even a dandelion growing from the cracks to prove that any life remained.

The floorboards creaked as I stepped up to the front door. The door shook with each knock. I didn't expect anyone to be home, but I couldn't barge in as if I owned the place. I hadn't lived here in years.

"It's Janey," I said, knocking again. No response.

The key from the package I received a month ago slid into the lock easily. I turned it and the door opened, a musty smell emanating from within.

A week ago, I was content in my Colorado apartment, attending classes for my bachelor's degree and ghostwriting articles for Internet content providers in whatever spare time I had. The big question of the moment was when my fiancé, Dave, and I were going to be married. Dave and I had met freshman year, both of us in the same Philosophy class that semester. At the end, he popped the question and there we were.

He, of course, thought the package was a wedding gift when UPS dropped it off. I almost didn't open it because of the return address: Hunton, West Virginia. I had left West Virginia when I was young and never wanted to go back. Not even for Ricky. A couple of years behind me, he and I had grown closer after Jonathan, our older brother, disappeared the summer before I was sent away, but we lost touch in the decade that followed.

I tossed the package in a corner of my office and forgot about it.

The interior of the house hadn't changed much, an eclectic mix of '70s and '80s styles never updated. Dark wood paneling on the walls, a tan and brown couch with printed flowers, and threadbare green carpeting. A staircase with a black wooden railing and balusters led to the bedrooms and the only bathroom.

Each step I took inside caused the floor to groan and complain. I felt lost, confused as to what I should do.

Before I left, Dave asked me several times to explain why I had to go back. Each time I had deferred to the phone call we received from Ricky's girlfriend Leah. Digging out the UPS package from West Virginia, I quickly opened it to discover a notebook and a key. No note explaining why they were sent to me. The package was postmarked a few days before Leah brought the police in. Ricky must have sent this to me before he disappeared. But why?

I sat down on the edge of the couch, the cluttered coffee table a reminder that someone once lived here. I picked up the remote for the TV. Pressing the button didn't work so I tossed it back on the table where it landed between a half-empty beer bottle, a mostly empty pack of menthol cigarettes, and a full ashtray. I slid a cigarette out of the pack and placed it under my nose. The smell of unburned tobacco was one of my favorite smells, but the menthol reminded me of something medicinal.

A few envelopes on the table caught my eye, but looking through them, I saw nothing recent. It had been a week since Leah called to give me the news and, according to the postage date, the envelopes were from way before that.

Maybe if we'd been more careful as children and watched the dog better, nothing would have ever happened. Jonathan wouldn't have disappeared, and I would still be sitting in my apartment, watching TV or knitting an afghan. Ricky might still be around, but I wouldn't be here, trying to figure out where he was while putting together pieces of his life.

Fuzzy hung out with whoever would play with her. She'd chase tennis balls all day and we rewarded her with treats. But, at night, she was still my dog and she'd curl up on the blanket near my feet, keeping them warm.

I heard a loud thump, but I didn't know what it was until Rick started screaming that someone had hit Fuzzy. My stomach dropped. Then the shrill squeal of rubber on pavement cut through the neighborhood. I was in the backyard, climbing our large maple tree, and climbed down as quickly as I could.

By the time I ran to the front of the house, it was too

late. Fuzzy was dead, laying on her side on a blanket that Mom brought out of the house. Someone—probably Jonathan—had placed her on the lowered tailgate of our station wagon. Her yellow-white fur was matted with blood, one glassy black eye staring at me. I couldn't help but stare back. A lump developed in my throat, and I swallowed hard, eyes stinging through the tears.

Ricky grabbed me around my waist and whispered what had happened through sobs into the security blanket he always carried. The van's driver must have sped off once he realized what the noise was.

"Jonathan, I'm going to need you to bury her." Mom blew cigarette smoke out through her pursed lips. She was looking out over the top of the car, searching for something. Probably for whatever vehicle did this to our poor dog. "I can't carry her over the floodwall and into the woods."

Jonathan nodded. He was the one Mom depended on. Jonathan had become her rock, the man of the house once Daddy left. "I can do that. Hey Ricky, go get a big black trash bag from under the sink, okay?"

Ricky ran inside, his security blanket trailing behind him.

I felt numb. Fuzzy was my birthday present when I started school. She was the first to greet me when I woke up, with big sloppy kisses, and the last I saw when going to bed at night. When I whispered my deepest secrets to her in the darkness, she would curl up next to me as I cried, licking the tears off my cheeks with her soft doggy tongue.

When Ricky came back out, Jonathan and Mom together placed Fuzzy and the blanket into the bag. He had a hold of the neck of the bag and was getting ready to go.

"Hey, uh, can I go?" I asked Mom, pointing toward Jonathan. She nodded and took another drag on her cigarette. "Thanks."

"You ready to do this?" Jonathan asked me.

"Not really, but…." I paused for a moment, wiping my eyes clear. "I have to do this. She was my dog."

He studied my face for a minute and whatever he saw was enough for him to nod and say, "Okay, let's go."

As we walked down the alley leading to the floodwall, I looked back over my shoulder and Mom and Ricky were standing there, watching us. I wondered what they were thinking.

Behind our house was the floodwall, a giant pyramidic wall of hay and dirt as tall as the first hill on a roller coaster. It was created by the Army Corps of Engineers to keep the flat residential land from the floodwaters of the Ohio River. It dominated the end of the alley and was cordoned off by four iron posts with a chain strung across them like a single strand of spiderweb.

I only had a few memories of being on the floodwall. One summer, Jonathan and I raced down the grassy hill, sliding on cardboard boxes while our parents laughed. Ricky was a baby in Mom's arms. Looking back, that memory was one of the only times I saw Mom and Dad genuinely happy together. Other times, they were distant, never showing affection to each other, only occasionally holding hands while us kids were in the room.

My dad left when I was young. He just didn't come home one night. Mom tried to find him for months. Every evening for dinner, she set an extra place at the table, hoping he might show up one day as if nothing happened. The three of us kids tried to help her around the house, to take Dad's place in the only way we could, but she never accepted that he was gone.

Walking up the side was a feat. The floodwall was essentially a large field of uncut grass up to my crotch, laid over a hill. We waded through the long fingers of grass while they slid by, their sides sharp enough to leave small cuts on my bare legs. As I got closer to the top, pain shot through my calves until I couldn't bear it anymore and tried to sprint the rest of the way. My side developed a stitch, and I collapsed when I got to the top, panting like my poor puppy should have been, then I rolled over and looked up at the sky. White and overcast, just like it was the rest of the fall and winters here.

"Come on," Jonathan said, moving the black bag from one shoulder to the other as he reached the top. "I don't want to be out here longer than we have to be."

On the other side was an identical steep slope with long slick grass; only this time, it ended in a long stretch of dark woods and heavy undergrowth along the riverbank. I couldn't see where the trees ended and the water began. Some of the leaves on the trees had already changed colors to reds, oranges, and yellows. Branches waved in the wind that had just started to pick up and the hair on the back of my neck prickled.

"Wait, we're going there?" I asked. I didn't see a break in the undergrowth for us to enter but I smelled the Ohio, a wet, dead fish chemical smell.

"Yeah. The ground will be soft and wet. We can bury Fuzzy there," Jonathan said as he started walking down the other side.

Dark gray clouds rolled in from the west as I began my descent, scanning the woods at the bottom for any sign of life beyond the plants. The further into the darkness under the trees I tried to see, the more I began to think I saw a hint of something right out of view.

"Janey!" a man's voice said nearby. The voice sounded familiar, but who would be in this place? I glanced around, but I didn't see anyone nor was there anywhere to hide. Except the woods.

"Hello?" I called out. My next step was into a hole. There was a loud snap and a sharp pain shot up my leg. Gasping, I collapsed onto the grass, unable to support myself.

At the base of the floodwall, Jonathan turned to see what was wrong, then he peered back into the brush. He said something, but I couldn't make out the words over the wind rushing in my ears. An alabaster white hand extended from the dark and clutched Jonathan's empty hand. He looked back at me, waving at me as he took Fuzzy and shuffled forward.

I waved back at him, wanting to tell him what had happened. He could bury Fuzzy without me, but why did he look so happy?

A weathered grimy face peered out of the woods. The face was far paler than I remembered. I remembered a darker complexion, one covered in grease and grime from working all day. With a sly wink and a toothy grin, it withdrew into the greenery.

"Dad?" I yelled then shook my head. Surely it couldn't have been. "Jonathan?" I wanted Jonathan to turn back around, to remember I had followed him. If that really was Dad with him, maybe we were saved. We'd take Dad back to the house and everything would go back to the way it was. Back to normal. A cold wind howled as the tree branches danced and I knew something was wrong.

It couldn't have been...could it?

I sat still, trying to ignore the pain in my ankle and wishing I had long sleeves or pants to keep myself warm. I didn't want to think about what I just saw. Or who. The smell of rain was thick and with the thunder in the distance, I needed to get my ass up and back to the house. I looked along the edge of the woods, trying to see if my brother was coming back, but nothing stood out. Everything was as quiet as it could be before a storm.

Jonathan's ear-piercing scream filled the air from the darkness beyond the woods.

Wide-eyed and with my heart trying to pound its way out of my chest, I stood, lifting my foot from the hole, and on all fours, I hobbled over the floodwall to my house before the rain started.

Sometime later, apparently babbling things about Jonathan and Dad all the while, I was taken to the hospital where my ankle and leg were placed into a cast. Once my leg was taken care of and the pain dampened by meds, I was able to sleep. When I woke up, I didn't remember anything I had been saying in my delirium.

Mom finally reported Jonathan as missing. Two policemen showed up at the house and asked me a bunch of questions about that day beyond the floodwall. Reclining on the couch, my cast propped up on a few pillows, I told them about Jonathan disappearing into the woods, but I left out the part about Dad. I didn't want to raise Mom's hopes without a good enough reason.

When Jonathan left, Mom's extra plate at the table every evening became two extra plates. She would sit at the table across from what would have been Dad's plate, glare at both empty plates, and stew in her anger. She blamed me for Jonathan's disappearance. After all, I had been the last person to see him as he carried the trash bag with my dear sweet Fuzzy over the floodwall, right? I must have known something.

For weeks afterwards, even after the police interviewed me, Mom continued to ask if I knew where Jonathan was. She left work early in order to be home after school to make sure I didn't sneak out to see him. As if I knew where he was. Her new boyfriend placed a recording device on our home phone to listen to my conversations. Except for school, I stayed in my room, day in and day out, and ate dinner alone with my books.

My father's pale thin face haunted me everywhere I looked, peering out at me from any darkened spot or shadow. I became jumpy. Anything could scare me. My heart raced, my skin tingled, and I'd scream as loud as I could. The girls at school thought it was hilarious to sneak up behind me in the hallways and tap on one shoulder, then walk off as though nothing happened. When I punched one of them for doing just that, I was sent home and suspended for three days.

During my three-day suspension, Mom apparently had enough and decided to send me away to Happy Trails Juvenile Correction Facility, a Kansas-based home for incorrigible children. It was at Happy Trails, on the vast open prairie, that I learned to forgive and forget. Mom never tried to contact me again.

Ricky would call on occasion. He called and told me what his grades were, who his first girlfriend was, all the different types of things a teenage boy would tell his sister. Ricky kept me sane during the months between Fuzzy's death and Kansas. He would sit at my closed bedroom door and talk to me, keeping me company or playing games. Ricky brought me notes from what friends I had left and surreptitiously slid them under the door. We'd talk about Jonathan, sharing our memories of him. For us, talking about him was a way to keep him around.

When I graduated from Happy Trails, I left my phone number with Ricky, thinking we'd keep in touch. But then life interfered. College led to homework and needing a part-time job then a fiancé and my time became scarcer and scarcer.

Earlier this year, Ricky called and told me Mom died from a brain aneurysm. There was a small funeral. Only Ricky, Leah, and a few of the people Mom knew from church attended. I stayed in Colorado and didn't even light a candle.

I never kept a journal when I lived at home. I was petrified Mom would read what I wrote and kick me out of the house. At Happy Trails, I discovered I loved to write and from there, I began keeping the journals that ultimately lead to working toward my English degree.

But I waited until I was home in West Virgina to read Ricky's journal. In Colorado, I had flipped through its pages, looking for anything that might stand out. Dave tried to convince me it might be good for me to read it before I left, but I wasn't ready.

Night finally arrived. I tucked myself in Ricky's old bed and curled up with the book, looking for something, anything, to give me even a hint of where he was.

The beginning was from right before Mom died. The last child living at home, it fell on Ricky to take care of Mom in her senior years. There was no money to place her in a nursing home, even though she probably needed to be in one, and the only way she could afford medical treatment was through government services.

A few months before she died, she began accusing him of sleeping with all the women in town. No home health care nurse would work with her. The first nurse ran out of the house crying half an hour after she arrived. Mom berated her and accused her of lying, saying that she recognized the nurse from the grocery store. Mom claimed that the nurse only wanted to be there because she wanted to sleep with Ricky. The second one stayed three days but then left suddenly and never came back.

About the time the second nurse left, while looking through his bedroom window, Ricky saw Jonathan standing on the top of the floodwall. Jonathan wore his favorite Mötley Crüe t-shirt, the one he wore when he disappeared, and waved at him. It had been twelve years since Jonathan's disappearance, but he looked the same as he ever did. Ricky ran outside and into the alley leading to the floodwall, but stopped when he didn't see Jonathan at the top anymore.

That wasn't the only time Ricky saw Jonathan. His writing became a bit more sporadic, yet excited, the further I read into the book. He saw Jonathan a total of three times.

The second time, as he was walking into the house, a bark came from his left. When he turned, he saw Jonathan's back as he walked toward the end of the alley, a whitish-gray dog next to him. As he reached the base of the floodwall, Jonathan turned around, smiled, and waved for him to follow. Ricky couldn't move. If he hadn't been sure of whether it was Jonathan before, he was convinced it was this time.

The third and final time, Ricky woke up to Jonathan standing over him in his room, at the foot of his bed. Jonathan tried to speak, but nothing came out. He pointed out the window to the floodwall and Ricky nodded.

The last line in the journal read, "I will meet you there."

I closed the book, placed it on the nightstand, and took a look out his window. The floodwall seemed to glow in the light of the full moon.

My boots crushed the long green grass with each step I took. They weren't the best shoes to be climbing up a steep grassy hill, but they were what I had. It was probably stupid of me to be climbing at night, but I was too impatient. I needed to do something. The moonlight illuminated my way forward, but I would face the darkness on the other side. I pulled my jacket closer to me as the wind picked up and the swaying grass created waves of dark shadow that sounded like the static on a television screen.

At the top of the hill, the scent of the Ohio river hit me, the smell of dead rotting fish and brackish water laced the air currents, joined by pungent chemicals. Nothing had changed from the last time I was up here. I could make out the shape of the houses across the river, butting up next to it with broken-down docks and moorings where boats should have been.

On the dark side of the floodwall, the woods stood, black and shadowy, the moonlight unable to penetrate the tree cover. Something white came into view through the brush, but disappeared a moment later. My mind tried to convince me it was Dad's pale face.

Time to go down. I stepped down the hill sideways, careful to avoid any holes this time, the slick soles of my boots wanting to slide on the grass. At the base, I looked back up. Bright moonlight hid all the stars from me. These woods haunted my dreams. Ivy and holly bushes with prickly leaves blocked my way into the woods and I didn't know whether I should have been grateful for that or not. I needed to go in, to see what I could see. To find that Dad's face peered out at me.

Was my father in there? Why had he looked so terrible?

"Hello Janey," a male voice said behind me. My stomach dropped and I spun around.

Ricky stood between me and the floodwall. He wore a pair of dirty jeans, the kind of dirt that would never get out of the denim, and a dark t-shirt. It had been at least a decade or more since I had seen him. Uneven scruff had grown on his face, a thin mustache and a patchy beard, and his dark eyes squinted at me under a mop of hair combed over the bald spot he hid since his mid-teens.

"Ricky! Where have you been? Leah's been worried to death," I said, my heart rapid-firing in my chest. Seeing him here, in person, in front of me, I was unsure of what to do. Was I rescuing him? Trying to find out if he'd actually found Jonathan?

"Well, I've been…here," Ricky said. His demeanor was different, quiet, much quieter than the Ricky in his journal. "Why?"

"Leah…she called me and said you were missing."

Ricky tilted his head to one side as if he were a dog. "Missing?"

"You've been gone for over a month, Ricky!"

"I've been here. I finally found him." He turned away from me, glancing around the wooded area.

"What? Found who?" I knew what he was going to say. I was just scared to hear him say it.

He turned back around, a twinkle in his eye. "Jonathan."

"What? No, Jonathan's gone. He's dead." I sounded like a whining dog. Jonathan never came out of these woods. I knew that. I was sure of that.

Ricky's head tilted again. "What do you mean?"

"It's been twelve years since he went missing," I said, holding my hands out. "Don't you think he would have come back by now if he were able?"

"What if he found some place…different? Some place new? Where he could be with Dad again." Something in Ricky's voice gave me chills.

"What? What are you talking about?"

Ricky stepped towards me and I scooted backward, a holly leaf pricking my back as I held my hands out in front of me. "Stop it!"

He took another step towards me. "I can take you to him."

He waved his hand, and the holly leaf scratched my back as the bushes and brush gave way behind me, creating an entrance to go deeper the woods. I stepped aside as he moved forward along the path he created. As he went into the woods, a cold shiver came over me. If I followed him, I didn't know what was going to happen. I thought about Jonathan, and wondered if this was what he had seen before entering the woods. Did Dad open the woods up for him? My mouth was dry, and I could hardly swallow, but I made my decision.

With a deep breath, I followed him along the path, into the darkness.

Ricky walked effortlessly down the path while I stumbled over branches and tree roots as I followed, even as I tried to keep steady. We walked out onto the riverbank then a bit further. I had been told as a kid, there was a drop off somewhere, where the river met the bank, but I wasn't sure where it was. Every step, I prayed I wouldn't step off into the water. As we kept walking, the ground squished beneath my feet. There were no large puddles of water. Only dead fallen leaves and branches, ivy and undergrowth from the trees.

Darkness gave way to shadowed stippling on the mud before us then Ricky came to a stop. In front of us was a pile of sticks and branches cemented in place with mud, rock, and ivy. In a way, it looked like a beaver's den. Not that there were beavers in this part of the woods.

"Here, stay." Ricky said. I walked over to the den to get a closer look at it. There was a stone sticking out, like a headstone, from one end. Scratched into the rock was the word "Fuzzy."

There was a squelching, sucking sound and I spun around to look at Ricky. His face started to bubble as though it was boiling. I opened my mouth to scream, then clapped my hand over it before anyone could hear. Not that anyone else could have heard me. Just like no one else had heard Jonathan when he screamed. I was out here on my own, by myself, and there was no one to help me.

Big fat boils erupted on his melting face and everything about him morphed. His hair lengthened in the back while the sides shortened into a mullet, his face covered with his hands. Now he wore a Mötley Crüe t-shirt.

He finally uncovered his face and Jonathan peered out at me, looking me up and down. His voice, the same as when we were children: "Janey, is that you?"

He looked exactly the way he looked the day he disappeared into the woods. No sign of Ricky remained. This couldn't have been my older brother. My older brother would have been in his late twenties, yet here he stood, not a day over fifteen.

In a small voice, I said, "Yes."

"Why are you here?"

"I didn't forget you. Ever. Or Ricky," I murmured. My eyes teared up. I wiped them quickly with my hands. "I loved you both so much."

"Why didn't you follow me into the woods, Janey?" The creature who looked like Jonathan stepped toward me, his arms outstretched. "This is what happened."

I bolted from where I stood next to the den, rushing to get out of reach from this thing that looked like my brother. My boots slid on the leaves and the mud and I plopped down on my ass in the middle of the small clearing.

Why, oh why, did I follow Ricky—or whatever it was that had turned into Ricky?

Before I could scramble to my feet, a slimy scaled appendage shot out and caught me by the neck, turning me around to face the creature. The creature had changed its face again, revealing the pale thin face of my dad. Only it was angry. Very angry. I scrabbled against him, trying to get free, but the more I struggled, the tighter the tentacle became until I didn't have the energy to do it anymore. I didn't have the energy to do anything anymore.

The creature growled. "He found me, Janey. Daddy found me and now he's found you too."

Dave bolted awake from his nap. He was surprised that the nightmares had been so intense during the day. Janey had only been gone a week, but these dreams just wouldn't stop. He kept seeing her buried in mud near a riverbed, the river washing over her from time to time, her blue eyes being bleached white by the sunlight.

He grabbed the package that arrived earlier that day. The return address said, "Hunton, WV." Ripping the packaging off, he opened the box.

Inside was a book, a key, and a note.

"Come find me!"

ROAN'S PILGRIMAGE

Christophe Maso

The witch peered down upon piebald earth, as he soared across the naked sky.

From his height, all depth perception vanished. The land presented itself as a sloppy patchwork quilt of yellowish cream, reddish pink, blueish gray, and all shades of green. It almost looked close enough to stretch out his hand, grab it up, and wrap it around himself as a cloak.

The thinning air above the clouds always made him feel beautifully drunk. He closed his eyes, grinned, and gloried in the moment, silently reciting a verse from one of his favorite poems.

> *The children of the wild rejoice*
> *And peasants weep for their crucified god*
> *As the moon announces in silvery voice*
> *"On broomsticks witches are flying abroad!"*

The DHC-6 Twin Otter fishtailed slightly as the plane passed through a momentary crosswind. The witch grasped the inboard handrail above the open side door to steady himself.

Getting to his intended drop zone was going to be tricky enough as it was, and he didn't want to exit the plane prematurely.

He stuck his head out the door, gazed straight down, and waited a few more seconds for the landmark to line up directly below, a split in the river whose shape reminded him of the Eye of Horus. Out of habit, he glanced at his wrist altimeter (yep, still at 13,500 feet), then he took a breath and jumped sideways out of the plane into empty sky.

As he plunged into freefall, he was met by a frigid, disorienting blast of wind that seemed to hit him from all directions. Truth told, this was always Roan's favorite part of a skydive, those first few seconds where the wind thrusted him this way and that, like a lover who'd lost all restraint caught in the throes of passion. There was nothing he could do in those wild moments except hold a firm, arched-back position, and trust that it would grant him aerodynamic control soon enough.

The landing zone of the Wild Blue Skydiving Center lay to the northwest, in the direction of the prevailing winds. That was where all the plane's skydivers were supposed to be headed, and normally Roan would have been headed there as well, for a smooth, running landing in a wide open grass field. Head into the hangar to re-pack his canopy, inspect his rig, take a quick shot of THC oil off the vape pen, and if the skies were still blue, head right back up for another jump.

Today, however, was much more than just another jump.

After spending a year and a day as a prospect of Coven Hawthorn, he'd finally begun the coven's initiation process, a series of tasks which would end with his ritual induction into the coven as a full-fledged member. No more weekly classes, no more keeping the covenstead clean and tidy. No more exclusion from the coven's full moon rituals, hanging out with his fellow prospects in someone's living room watching *American Horror Story* and trading tarot card readings while the "real" witches worked magick together in circle somewhere else. No more watered down, training-wheels witchcraft…and it was about damn time.

Contrary to what the average Bible-thumping book-burner was taught to believe, witches didn't worship the Christians' devil, or even have much to do with their whole guilt-ridden, woman-fearing, sin-oriented cosmology, really. Witches worshiped the natural world, to the extent that they worshiped anything—the lush earth, the teeming greenery, all the creatures of feather, fur, fin, and chitin that wove the endless dance of life—and that's what this jump was all about. The final task before his initiation, a lone "pilgrimage to nature."

Roan and the other prospects who'd been invited to join the coven had been tasked by Epona, Coven Hawthorn's High Priestess, to plan their individual pilgrimages, subject to her approval. Some of them had planned epic camping trips, canoeing or hiking for days through wild backcountry, seeking natural temples for communing with the land and its spirits. Two prospects had pledged to participate in an upcoming "Earth First" protest, where they would chain themselves to trees and use their own bodies to block heavy equipment, in order to protect old-growth forest from the cutting operations of a multi-billion dollar timber company. A dangerous affair, and one which Roan couldn't help but respect for its boldness and dedication. But his own proposed pilgrimage was the only one which the high priestess had reckoned so dangerous that she rejected it outright.

"No, hon," Epona had admonished him in her homespun Baltimorean accent. "You aren't spending a night alone in the Patuxent River Forest. Not now, not ever."

She'd narrowed her dark eyes and bared her teeth slightly, the way she did when she was about to lay down the law for her two kids. "In fact, you're going to give me your solemn word, right here and now, that you won't step into those woods as long as you're affiliated with this coven."

Roan flashed her his best pretty-boy smile. "Wow. This from the proud enchantress who taught us not to fear haints or anything else that goes bump in the night? The Powers of the Sphinx, which you drilled into us—to Know, to Will, to Dare, to Keep Silent. I guess the 'dare' part of that isn't so important after all. So, what…I'm supposed to be afraid of the ghosts of a few dead motorists?"

Patuxent River Forest had earned a reputation as the most haunted wood in Maryland, infamous for the number of souls who'd been killed in car accidents—particularly on rainy nights, and particularly on one bend of Brock Bridge Road that often flooded, causing many an unwary driver to collide head-on and wrap their ride around the trunk of a thick and ancient oak dubbed by local lore as the "Crash Test Oak."

Epona smiled. "It's not the spirits of all those poor people, Roan. It's the river. It's the spirit of the land itself. It desires life. It *consumes* life. It doesn't care if you honor it or hold it as sacred. Some places are just like that, the same way some *people* are just like that."

Despite his respect for her, Roan didn't relent. "*Or*, that's a total cop-out—a lazy, easy conclusion that no one's ever bothered to test! Maybe the land there's just wounded and poisoned, like the human race has done to most of the Earth. Maybe instead of allowing it to suffer, someone should find the balls to walk in there and offer the land healing. *That's* the pilgrimage *I* want to make."

Epona sighed and rested her hand on his cheek. "And that's exactly how I'd expect a true son or daughter of the moon to think, hon. But one day you'll understand. Not everything can be, or wants to be, healed. Not everything in the world, seen or unseen, responds to respect, reason, or love. And as far as those woods are concerned, I'm not willing to risk your life to find out."

"Oh really?" he pressed, "Because last I checked, *my* life is *mine* to risk as *I* see fit, and not any—"

"Enough!" she bristled, her hands upon her waist and her gaze practically pinning him down. "Yes, your path is your own, but if you want to be considered for membership in *this* coven, you'll do me the respect of giving your word as I've asked!"

Roan tried not to roll his eyes. "Of course, *my lady*. I, Roan of Laurel, Maryland, who doth humbly seek entry into your coven, giveth thee my word, and swear by all the goddesses, and all the gods, and all the witches murdered in the Burning Times, and by the yawning yoni of Sheela Na Gig herself, that I will never step into Patuxent River Forest. So mote it be."

His sarcasm raised more than a few eyebrows in the covenstead, and Epona gracefully opted to ignore him rather than smack him upside his head, but that was that. A witch's word was a witch's bond. In the Craft, breaking an oath could get one summarily ejected from a coven, and known oathbreakers could always count on sideways glances in the company of fellow witches. More importantly, words had power, and nothing could render one's personal magick so impotent as knowing, in one's heart of hearts, that one's promises and one's words lacked truth.

But then, he thought with a rakish grin as his freefall stabilized and positioned his washboard stomach toward the ground, he'd found the perfect loophole. After all, he wasn't stepping into that forbidden forest. He wasn't actually *stepping* into anywhere now, was he?

At that moment, Epona was waiting for him to come back to her with an alternate idea for his pilgrimage. Sure, she'd have his guts for garters when she learned that he'd defied her and stuck with his original plan. But she'd forgive him eventually. Of all Coven Harthorn's prospects, he ranked as her favorite, and not just because of how he excelled at his lessons. He noticed how her gaze lingered on him when she thought he wasn't looking—and how it lingered on him sometimes even when he *was* looking. A little bit of her getting her Mrs. Robinson on maybe, her being a mom (albeit a fairly hot mom) of two, but Roan didn't mind so much. There was something to be said for a faith that didn't shame its members for their sexuality, women especially.

Besides all of that, hadn't he heard her say, more than once, that willfulness wasn't the worst trait for a witch to possess?

Of course, he had to get there first, and getting there was far from guaranteed. He'd jumped out of the plane at a far from ideal spot for reaching the forest, and that couldn't be helped. Short of hijacking the plane, it was the closest he'd ever get to it from the air. The winds blew in his favor that day—an auspicious sign, to be sure—but his best chance would have been to pop his canopy right after exiting, and then to ride the prevailing winds to the forest while drifting down at a leisurely fifteen miles per hour. But he needed an excuse for putting down near the forest instead of the usual landing zone, and that meant making it look like his canopy had malfunctioned on him and forced him to find an alternate landing site. If he popped his canopy early, it would be tough to explain why he hadn't just cruised to the designated drop zone. Landing anywhere on purpose other than the designated drop zone was a huge no-no—the kind that could get you banned from a skydiving site, or even get your A license revoked. So he'd have to fall and pull low enough that the plane couldn't see him.

Every horizontal foot he could travel before he hit the ground counted. Looking down to get his bearings, he lowered his right arm and raised his left to pivot clockwise, then straightened his legs out and brought his arms down to his thighs, tracking westward toward his destination.

There was something deeply mythical about skydiving: the tragic archetype of the beloved youth hurling towards Earth from the heavens. Icarus flying too close to the sun. Phaethon and his doomed attempt to pilot the sun god's chariot. Hephaestus thrown from Olympus by Zeus, for the crime of trying to protect his mother, Hera. Milton's Lucifer, who rebelled against a cruel and tyrannical God, hungry to live "free and to none accountable, preferring hard liberty before the easy yoke of servile pomp."

In his case, Roan liked to frame the whole ritual as an aerial courting dance. The Earth as his goddess lover, hungry to pull him down from the sky and into her naked, loving embrace. For this jump, though, she felt a little more eager than he would have preferred. The ground seemed to be rising toward him twice as fast as usual. Already, he could make out individual cars and pickups driving the few two-lane roads below. A bundle of cotton ball clouds that had seemed to hover right above the ground when he jumped out of the plane now drifted well above his head.

He checked his wrist altimeter, which read 7,461 feet. His plan called for him to pop his canopy at seven thousand feet, then turn west-southwest. He'd reduce his horizontal drag as much as possible, then ride the westerly tail winds that started at six thousand feet, and coast to a clearing about the size of a baseball diamond that lay in the heart of Patuxent River Forest.

Stupid hurts. This simple sentence figured prominently in skydivers' colorful vernacular, and for this jump, the forest's sheer density all but ensured any stupid would hurt a lot. Other than power lines and busy highways, the very last thing a skydiver wanted to come down on was tree cover, of *any* density. Even if you managed to avoid getting skewered by sharp branches, you could still fall through the foliage and get cut up on the way down, and then break or sprain something (or several somethings) once you finally hit the ground.

Or you could end up hanging tangled high above, waiting hours for rescue—if you happened to have your phone on you, or if you were within earshot of another human being, that is. If not, you could probably look forward to a long day or two just hanging around. During which time, even if you managed not to get cut, you'd likely end up having to piss or shit your pants at least once.

If Roan couldn't make it all the way to the clearing, an abandoned farm served as his backup landing zone, but it lay outside the forest proper. If he had to put down there, he couldn't enter the forest without breaking his word to Epona, that he would never step into it, and then his entire pilgrimage was a bust.

He counted silently, *one one thousand, two one thousand,* then he reached into the small of his back and pulled on the deployment handle. He relaxed in anticipation of his fall slowing to a float, ready to look back and up for the obligatory canopy check once it opened completely. Two seconds later, some giant, invisible puppeteer seemed to yank him upward, causing both of his feet to kick chest-high. The horizon began spinning like a runaway merry-go-round, as a surge of panic tore through his insides like a flaming shot of grain alcohol.

His canopy flapped like an enraged unkindness of ravens. Straining his neck to look, Roan saw that several of the canopy's leftmost suspension lines had broken, and its two leftmost cells had collapsed as a result, creating a rapid downward spiral. For a terrifying split second, he blanked on how to react to the malfunction, but luckily his left hand was way ahead of him. All on its own, his hand reached across his chest and pulled the rig's reserve canopy handle.

The wind rushed up from below as his main canopy cut away, and he began to hurl toward the ground again. Then the reserve canopy deployed, this time gently slowing his descent. Roan looked back and up to make sure it had deployed correctly, and once satisfied, tried his best to shrug off the pain caused by his main's malfunction. Stars shot in all directions within his field of vision, and he gagged a couple times, nearly heaving up his lunch of miso soup and poke. He managed to keep it down as he got his bearings and reached up to grip his canopy toggles. He turned toward the forest, a beetling carpet of green ahead, and now a thousand or so feet closer to the soles of his boots than they should have been.

First time that fucking thing ever malfunctioned on me, he thought to himself. *I thought I inspected that canopy before I packed it! Twice! Gods!* All things considered, he gave himself a solid A-minus for how he'd reacted, but still, that main canopy had cost him around twenty-five hundred dollars. *Stupid hurts.*

Like his main, the reserve was designed to drop at about fifteen miles per hour and move forward fifteen miles per hour in still wind. With a tail wind of fifteen miles per hour, that put his forward directional speed at thirty. To make it to the clearing now, he'd need every bit of forward speed he could squeeze out, and that meant eliminating as much drag as he could. He rolled up the cloth slider above his head and brought his knees up to his chest. He sucked in a breath and centered himself. Man, what he wouldn't have done for an extra five miles per hour of wind at his back.

Unlike in the movies and fantasy roleplaying games, magick didn't work on the physical world so much. Not from anything he'd ever observed, at least. No shooting fireballs from one's fingers or summoning of whirlwinds and lightning. It worked much more quietly and subtly than that. Magick wasn't a super-hero power; it was the art of creating coincidence, of altering perception, of gently tapping the odds in one's favor. Trying to witch himself some more wind was a bad bet.

Even so, he found himself chanting a spell for any extra bit of wind to carry him. He grit his teeth, and envisioned a safe landing for himself in the clearing as forcefully as he could. *Eko, eko, azarak. Eko, eko, zomelak….*

By the time he passed over the abandoned farm, his alternate landing zone, his quads and abs burned from the effort of keeping his knees elevated. He couldn't be at more than a couple thousand feet, which at his rate of descent meant about a minute and a half until he touched the ground, and of course even less until he touched the treetops.

This was the deciding moment. Either spin down to the farm's open plot and land safely, giving up on the pilgrimage for today, or spin the wheel of fortune and try to make it. A lake of trees lay between him and the clearing, which looked like a tiny, lonely island. It reminded him of what his father, a naval aviator, once told him landing a plane on an aircraft carrier at sea was like: *trying to touch down on a postage stamp in the middle of a parking lot.*

His better sense told him to touch down in the farm. He wasn't nearly high enough to make it to the forest, and he couldn't keep his legs elevated for another minute and a half. His will to endure the pain had nothing to do with it; his legs already trembled from fatigue, and before long they'd drop and hang. That would slow his forward movement and make his drop into the trees all but certain.

There was no reason to lay it all on the line, here and now, he told himself. He could land here, make a phone call, and someone from Wild Blue would come out to get him. He could go home, order a pizza, and sleep in a warm bed that night. He could always attempt the jump again in a day or two, hopefully without another terrifying canopy malfunction.

But the wind urged him on, strong at his back, and the clearing waited less than a mile away. Roan would never claim to be psychic—not all witches were—but in the course of his tutelage he'd learned to trust his intuition, and right then his intuition whispered to him that he wouldn't get another opportunity as favorable as this one anytime soon. *This* was his moment. He could seize it and accept the risk, or not.

He cried out in pain after he crossed the treeline below. His abs screamed for him to let his legs drop, but he found that he could alleviate the fatigue by letting go of a toggle and using his free arm to help hold one leg in place, then switching to the other arm and leg, and alternating like this every few seconds.

The treetops rustled and swayed in the wind, reminding him of how trees appeared to move when you were peaking on an acid trip. They also reminded him a little of the churning surface of piranha-infested waters during a feeding frenzy…or the horror B-movie version, at any rate.

"Come on!" he screamed, "*Come on come on come on come on come ooooon!*"

As the treetops rushed to meet him, he knew he wasn't going to make it. To prolong his time aloft by a couple seconds, he flared the canopy by pulling halfway on his toggles, causing his flight to steady out and skirt just above the tallest trees.

"Wind! Wind! Wind!" he roared in rage and panic, the sound boiling up from somewhere deep inside him, primal and animalistic. Then, right at that moment, a sudden gust came from nowhere and propelled him forward. His boot tips brushed the treetops, and he prepared to shield his vitals and genitals from the inevitable onslaught of impaling wooden spears when he fell through the trees. However, then the brimming treetops fell away behind him, and his boots brushed nothing but air.

The clearing! Thanks to that weird gust of wind, he'd made it!

His canopy collapsed partially and caused him to lose control of his descent, the price of holding a flare for too long. In an effort to regain control, he let up on the toggles, then eased them down halfway, but he had to make a sharp, hundred-eighty degree turn to avoid flying into the tree trunks at the clearing's far end. As he struck the ground—all dirt, stones, and tall grass—he performed a near perfect five-point roll, ending up on his knees.

Despite the waves of pain that wracked his body from his toes to his eyes, he laughed and stumbled to his feet on spent and unsteady legs. He whooped in joy for all the gods to hear, arms raised to the sky. A trio of crows perched on a nearby elm eyed him curiously.

His reserve canopy lay collapsed in a bundle. He gathered it up before it could catch the wind and take him for a ride across the ground. He'd already acquired more than enough cuts and bruises for one pilgrimage.

He sloughed off the waves of pain, and drew in a deep, satisfying breath. Elated, he took a minute to absorb his good fortune, and to absorb the forest's feral, untamed beauty sprawling all around him. Against all odds, here he stood in the middle of the forbidden forest, his oath to Epona intact and his body battered, but unbroken.

There was no part of him that was not of the gods! The pilgrimage was on!

Roan set up his camp, such that it was, upon an acceptably level spot within a copse of maples. It consisted of a hastily constructed lean-to fashioned from fallen branches, leaves and dark mud, a bed of grass and moss spread upon cleared ground, and a firepit which he dug with a sharp stone.

He hadn't been able to pack much in the way of camping gear, but he'd managed to stuff a decent inventory of items into his rig's Velcro pocket and the various zippered pockets on his pants and fleece jacket—a headlamp, a palm LED light, his phone, a charger cord and charged battery pack, a bag of trail mix (extra chocolate thrown in), various other sundries connected to his pilgrimage's purpose, and a can of bear spray, just in case.

Once settled in, he began his communion with the land by sitting with his back straight against the trunk of the nearest tree. He closed his eyes and began to breathe slowly and rhythmically. Allowing his mind to grow still, he grounded himself in the sensation of the firm earth beneath him, the sturdy, rough tree bark at his back. He reached out with his awareness to touch the land and its secrets.

I call to the spirit of this forest. Hail to you, and blessed be.

I, Roan, son of the moon, humbly come to commune with you, bringing offerings to nourish and heal this land.

I would redress whatever harm humanity has done to this place, and to the creatures that dwell within, as far as I am able. I ask that you accept my presence in this place for the next day. If I am not welcome, only make it known to me, and by my word, I will leave in peace, forever.

He waited for a while. He wasn't sure how long, exactly; it didn't really matter. All that mattered was just being with the surroundings. Just being within the moment. Just being.

He felt no sense of malevolence from the forest, observed no physical sign that suggested it would prefer him to take his offerings and get the bloody hell out. He felt nothing in this place other than what he felt in other wild places—tranquility, balance, beauty, the natural cycle of life and death.

So far, so good.

The first step in working any sort of witchcraft was to put oneself in the proper headspace and charge up on the Earth's vital energy. So he slowed his breathing further, and allowed his mind to sink into trance. He visualized his backbone fusing with the maple's tall trunk, his legs and feet morphing into its roots and twisting down through rich, nourishing earth. He visualized his arms becoming one with the tree's multitude of branches and leaves, reaching toward the sun and basking in all its life-giving splendor.

His imagined branches stretched up, up toward the brilliant ball of fire in the sky, into the stratosphere and even into the bright cold of space. His roots sucked upon the soil's nutrients, the milk of the Mother, and they probed downward, down deeper into the earth, past the river's surrounding water table and below.

At once, a vivid, wet vision possessed him and all his senses. *A car plunged into the river on a stormy night. Roan now sat inside it on that night, felt its weight submerging as the interior filled with dark water. Four panicked teenagers screamed and sobbed and splashed and scrambled over each other, grasping in the darkness for the latches to locked doors, gagging, choking on the muddy water, praying, convulsing, drowning, the young life running out of them and into the river, into the soil, into Roan's roots, delicious, narcotic and sweet, milk of the Mother, the natural cycle of life and death....*

"Jesus H. Christ!"

Roan burst from the vision, gasping for air as though he'd just escaped from that same car.

He remembered the names of those four kids—Andrea

Cornish, Michael Kumar, Laura Tisch, and Bret Hammond—as he remembered the names of everyone who'd died in auto accidents within the forest's borders. That only made the vision more disturbing. He'd researched all of their deaths, all of their stories for weeks before, not out of ghoulish fascination, but rather out of a desire to honor the dead with his remembrance. That was part of his purpose here in the forest.

Then it occurred to him: of course. His pilgrimage should really begin there, at the roadside shrine that had been erected in memory of the twelve people who'd lost their lives to the forest along Brock Bridge Road. To ignore them was to ignore the forest's history, and to ignore the very reason the forest had earned its reputation as the most haunted wood in the state.

That road, which followed the Patuxent River, lay maybe half a mile to the north. It would be easy enough to get there using his phone's GPS. Not that he needed it. Roan prided himself on his ability to read and remember natural landscapes as easily as some Christians seemed able to read and remember passages from their Bible's vaunted, often contradictory pages.

He set out for the memorial, the sun already banking toward the horizon through the trees. He followed a meandering route through where the underbrush grew thinnest, the path of least obstruction through the wood. He almost walked into a few spiderwebs along the way—huge, intricate tapestries the size of doors, with rainbow-colored spiders nearly as large as his hand reposed at their center. No species he'd ever heard of. He'd be sure to look it up after his pilgrimage was over, but for now he felt content simply to bear witness to the forest's strange wonders.

The ground sloped ever so slightly downward, a telltale sign he was approaching water, since water always flowed to and through the lowest parts of the landscape. He didn't see Brock Bridge Road until he practically stepped onto it, so well did the scrub hide the paved asphalt. But there it passed through, a bona fide double-yellow, two-lane state route, replete with the obligatory sprinkling of roadside litter—mostly wrappers, cigarette butts, and plastic bottles. A sign stood about two stone throws to his left, a yellow diamond presenting a curved arrow and the number "15". It sported a scattered trio of bullet holes. As the only artifact of human civilization there in the forest, the road felt almost comically out of place.

Roan's GPS app put the roadside memorial about three miles to the west. Zero sweat. Just a walk in the haunted park.

A pickup slowed along the road, and its burly, bearded driver motioned towards the truck's bed. Roan held up his hand to signal thanks, but no thanks. The driver shrugged and gunned off. Not that Roan had a problem with the burly and bearded, but he was upon sacred business. That usually meant refraining from doing things the easy way.

Be careful on this road, brother. Goddess speed, he silently bid the driver.

The shadows had passed from long to gone when the memorial came into his view just around the bend. Past a one-lane bridge, a group of homemade wooden crosses stood in a rough circle, at varying heights. Some draped garlands, others Mardi Gras beads, others wore colorful mylar balloons, and a bed of dogwoods, roses, and lilies lay at their center. A couple stuffed animals of unknown species, matted and ravaged by the elements, sat up against the tallest of the crosses. Pinwheels, hearts, butterflies, doves, and solar-powered string lights completed the ensemble, with a dark wooden slat staked off to the side and listing those who'd lost their lives in the forest along Brock Bridge Road, twelve names hand-painted in white. Whomever had painted those names apparently had the good sense to leave room for several more below.

Roan approached and touched the name plank with his fingers. After he spoke each name aloud, he assured the dead with a soft murmur that he would always remember their names, their faces, and their stories. To the shrine's motley assortment of items, he added a small, tied off mesh bag of ground yarrow root, a charm which he'd fashioned himself. Yarrow was an excellent herb for dispelling sorrow, persistent melancholy, and negative energy. Also good for protection, especially against faeries, if you believed in such things.

Roan entered the forest on the north side of the road, just a few paces past the so-called "Crash Test Oak." Over the past decade, four vehicles had collided head-on into the tree's massive trunk as they slid off the road, coming around the bend. Five of the twelve names painted on the plank.

Roan felt nothing sinister from that proud old oak, but a sickly bare spot in its bark marked the common point of impact. A vertical streak of fluorescent orange paint marked the county's intention to cut the tree down. Who would erect a memorial for the oak when *it* was killed?

Before long, he came to a glade within earshot of the river. Fireflies danced fluidly through the air here to a gentle chorus of crickets, flashing their beautifully eerie yellow-green light. He felt a shiver cascade down his back. The invisible fabric between the mundane world and the spirit world, what witches called the "Veil," thinned considerably in this tiny clearing, zero doubt. This would be the place for his blood ritual.

He ventured down to the river's bank, a section where the water flowed strong and deep, roaring over and around tumbles of huge rocks. He bent down to scoop up a helping of water with his Sierra cup, thanked the river for its bounty, and returned to the glade.

Dusk had come, staining the world in shadow and shades of mushroom blue. Sitting with his back against the base of a hawthorn tree, he repeated his grounding meditation, this time without visions of drowning teenagers or anything else so grisly. Once done, he arose, centered and aware, his mind completely focused on the present. In the center of the glade, he stripped nude ("skyclad" in witchspeak) and neatly arranged his folded clothes and the ritual's several implements.

First, to prepare his ritual space, he mixed a pinch of salt into the water in his Sierra cup, and walked clockwise in a large circle as he sprinkled the water, chanting:

Salt and water, where thou art cast
Let no adverse spell nor purpose last
Hear my will addressed to thee
And as my word, so mote it be.

He lit an incense stick with his lighter and repeated the circuit.

Creature of fire, this charge I lay
No phantom in thy presence stay
Hear my word addressed to thee
And as I will, so mote it be.

He chose a fallen stick at the glade's edge to serve as his wand, paused a moment to mentally infuse it with his intent, and took a breath. He followed his circular path slowly, deliberately, pointing the wand and envisioning a stream of blue flame springing from its tip and licking the ground. The rest of the world fell away, as he enunciated his words and plotted his steps:

At this time, and in this place, I define a circle:
A sacred space that lies neither here nor there, but somewhere between the worlds
Of the possible and the impossible, of the visible and the occult,
Of the mortal and the immortal, of humanity and the gods.

The wand's flame was imaginary, of course. It didn't set the ground ablaze or leave a charred line in its wake. But within Roan's circle, the air smelled electric, as though a thunderstorm were about to barrel through. A host of fireflies, wholly unimaginary, gathered within the circle's borders, flying in a clockwise spiral.

Beginning in the east, he invited the elemental sovereign of Air, to bear witness to the rite and to bring Air's clarity. In the south, Fire and its passion, in the west, Water and its compassion, and in the north, Earth and its steadfastness.

Finally, from the circle's center, he called to his favorite aspect of the Goddess, Hecate, queen of magic and the night, and his favorite aspect of the God, Dionysus, lord of fertility, frenzy, and the world's wild places. He announced his ritual's purpose—to nourish and heal the spirit of the forest—an end which Dionysus especially would appreciate, and he invited them to join him.

Roan had to say he appreciated the witches' relationship with their gods. As a kid, Sunday church service had always scared him—how a congregation of adults could transform so quickly into a crowd of whiny, spineless children.

Witches didn't *worship* their gods. Not really. Working witchcraft, addressing the gods went a little more like this:

Hey big sister. Hey big brother. What's shakin'? As you can see, we're crafting a spell to achieve this thing we want. Thought you might get a kick out of it. It may get a little wild—these things often do—but it would be great if you wanted to hang out and take part. Or just pull up a comfy chair and watch.

If Hecate and Dionysus had decided to sit this one out, someone or something else had certainly decided to come watch the show. Roan felt otherworldly eyes upon his bare skin, tall shadows looming always just outside his peripheral vision.

A screech owl watched from its perch to the circle's north, trilling hypnotically as he took a seat cross-legged in the circle's center. The orbiting fireflies made way for him.

He picked up a handful of black, silken satchels, and held them up in his palm. "To nourish the forest, I offer these eight charms, crafted by my own hands beneath the new moon. Mandrake and mistletoe, feather and bone. Hyssop and horehound, saffron and stone. Spit and sperm, coin and claw. Fertilizer and cannabis, spider silk and barley straw."

Continuing the chant, he rose and buried the satchels at each of the circle's quarters, two per, starting in the east and working his way clockwise.

He returned to the center and sat. He picked up his wooden flute in both palms, facing up. "To heal the forest, I offer the gift of music, made now with my own breath, and my own lips."

He played the melody of "Lovely Joan," an old English folk song, throwing in a bridge he'd composed himself since the original song didn't include one.

Once done, he placed the flute down and paused. Now came the tricky part.

He opened his knife, and felt the sharp Damascus steel edge against his fingertips, against the skin of his left palm. The movies always made this look easy, cutting one's hand open to obtain blood for some ritual purpose—blood bonds, blood oaths, or just some good old-fashioned Hollywood Satan summoning. Slice, squeeze, drip drip drip, done.

In reality, it took some practice to get it just right. Knives varied in sharpness, and skin varied in toughness. Most of the time, one's instinctive aversion to sharps caused one to cut as lightly as one thought one could and still draw blood. That usually resulted in nothing more than a scratch dotted with beads of blood, or a red line of unbroken skin.

Or, especially if others were watching, one might err on the side of pressing too hard, so as to ensure a satisfactory cut on the first try. Roan had seen the result of that in ritual, once or twice. Wounds that sprayed blood all over the place, or sometimes kept on bleeding long after the required volume had been drawn and applied as needed. Then trips to urgent care, stitches, and later painful infections.

"As humanity had bled the Earth," he proclaimed, "I offer the spirit of this forest my own blood. Life, and symbol of life."

He closed his eyes. He pressed the blade to the meaty flesh below his thumb, just until it felt like the pressure itself might break the skin, then he eased up a little and drew the blade across with a flick of his wrist trying not to anticipate the pain.

The bleeding came in distinct drops, a good sign that he'd cut just right. He rose and circled the perimeter, starting in the east, squeezing his fist in front of him, allowing each drop to fall upon the dirt and rock. The ground quivered beneath Roan's bare feet. The wind picked up, cool on his skin, permeating a chill throughout his body. By the time he came three-sixty, the blood had started to clot and ceased to drip from his fist, now sticking to his skin and trickling down his wrist and forearm.

Done and well done. Perfect, even. Roan smiled, already basking in the magick's afterglow, savoring the cool wind as it brushed across his skyclad body and slid through his hair.

I call to Earth to bind the spell.
Air, speed its travel well.
Fire, give it spirit from above.
Water, quench this spell with love.

He bid hail and farewell to Hecate and Dionysus, to the elemental sovereigns, and brought the circle down with a final incantation.

I race the circle round,
And let it fade beneath the ground,
And all things are as they have been since the beginning of time.

Dusk faded into night, and it grew difficult to see. He brushed himself off, bandaged his hand with some antibiotic ointment, and got dressed. Minus the buried charms, he gathered up everything he'd brought into the glade with him and stuffed it into his pockets. Best to get back to his camp on the other side of the road and get a fire going, he thought. If the breeze didn't die down at some point, it promised to be a chilly night.

He stuffed his mouth with a handful of trail mix as he started south toward the road. Witchcraft had a way of stoking your appetite. He heard a dog bark in the distance behind him and, looking over his shoulder, spied flames through the trees headed toward the river. Sparks flew upward from the impact of someone piling more logs on the fire. There was no way he would have missed firelight while he was working the spell in the glade, so they must have just started that fire while his back was turned.

Who else was nutty enough to camp here, in the most haunted wood in Maryland? Plenty of people, he reflected after giving the matter just a little more thought. Especially high school kids with cheap beer and little sense of fire safety. It would suck donkey dick if he'd boldly fallen from the sky and successfully dispelled whatever negative energy tainted these woods, only to wake up later in the middle of a raging forest fire.

And it would suck an even larger and nastier dick to *die* in said raging forest fire. Since open fires were illegal here anyway, maybe it wouldn't hurt to swing by, say hello to these mystery campers, and take a discreet looksee.

Just off the river's bank, the fire burned inside an ornate, mobile firepit, producing little smoke. A pair of director's chairs sat a couple feet from the pit, and a dark-colored dome tent stood with its front access zippered open. As Roan crunched forward, trying to spot humans by the flickering light, a large dog charged him from the woods to the right, barking savagely.

The dog! In his curiosity, he'd forgotten all about the dog whose bark had drawn his attention in the first place. He fumbled at the zipper of his jacket pocket. Once inside, he fished for the can of bear spray, buried deep behind his trail mix.

The stocky beast was almost upon him when a young woman's voice called out, "Bear, hold!"

The dog immediately slowed and sat not an arm's length from Roan, panting. It sported a striking, almost absurd collar about its muscular neck, a thick, pink, sparkly affair with white tassels.

"Sorry," its apparent owner offered with a tentative smile, a fit young woman about Roan's age, with stylishly unkempt dark hair, wearing a green wrap sweatshirt. "He wouldn't eat you. Not unless I told him to."

Roan couldn't quite tell Bear's breed. He almost did look part bear. Whatever he was, he wasn't about to take his eyes off Roan.

For his part, Roan found it difficult to take his eyes off Bear's owner. He didn't mean to be rude, but besides making one hungry, working witchcraft tended to make one rather horny, after being bathed in all that primal, creative energy. Especially in a setting like this forest, surrounded by so much beauty and life.

"I didn't mean to startle you," he said, holding his hands up and laughing in relief. "I was heading back to my camp and noticed your campfire. I Just wanted to say hello and warn you that fires aren't exactly legal in this forest."

"Neither is public nudity," she quipped as she took a seat by the fire. "But hello. Welcome to my camp."

Roan tried not to blush. "Oh. *Oh*. Um. So you saw. I'm sorry, I didn't hear your dog, so I didn't think anyone else was around. I hope you didn't—"

She dismissed his apology with a wave and a smile. "It's all good. They're both kind of stupid laws, in my opinion. I didn't catch an eyeful, if that's what you mean, but I did hear the lovely song you were playing on the flute. What was that?"

"An old English folk song," he said. "Also a synth tune from around the Eighties, I think. Take your pick."

"Bear, go play," she commanded the dog, who rose and lumbered off into the woods. "Please, sit if you'd like," she told him, gesturing to the other chair. "I was just heating up some coffee, since the wind's been picking up."

"Who else are you camping with?" he asked as he sat, holding his hands out to the campfire to warm them up.

"Oh, no one. It's just me, and my baby hunting mice out there."

Weird, then, that she'd bothered to bring two chairs with her into the woods. Weirder still that she'd set both of them out by the fire, unless she'd been expecting company.

"I'm Roan," he said. "Nice to meet you."

"I'm Brin. Nice to meet you as well." She glanced at his bandaged hand. "I would ask you to play that song again, but it looks like you hurt your hand. Would you sing it for me, instead?"

Roan was no stranger to come-hither looks, but oh, man. Those alluring eyes across the fire…he felt as though he could dive into them.

"Careful what you wish for," he laughed. "I could sing it, but it might make your dog howl in pain before long."

"Please. The folk song. I'd love to hear the words, if there are any."

"Oookay," he said. "Don't say I didn't warn you. This is called 'Lovely Joan.'" He sat up in the chair and cleared his throat and sang from his diaphragm in smooth tenor.

> *A fine young man it was indeed,*
> *All mounted upon his milk white steed,*
> *He rode and he rode, he rode all alone,*
> *Until he met sweet lovely Joan….*

When he finished singing, Brin clapped softly, tittering in delight. "I love it! That was great!"

He nodded with a smile, brushing windblown bangs out of his eyes. "What's not to love? Rich jerk meets pretty peasant girl. Rich jerk offers girl money for sex. Rich jerk gets played. It's a feelgood for the ages."

Brin stretched, arching her back. "Mm. Maybe he should have offered to sing for her, instead."

Her come-hither eyes had graduated to come-hither talk. Roan groaned to himself. *No, witch. No, no, no. You're on a pilgrimage. That's not what you came here for.*

"Right? That, or just suggested that they get coffee together sometime, at least," he said.

"Speaking of which," she returned without breaking stride, "I think the coffee's ready. Would you like to come inside the tent and have a cup? It's getting cool out here."

Deflection failed.

"Thanks, but that's okay, really. I don't mind the elements."

She said nothing as she poured herself a cup from the kettle on the grill. She held the kettle up to him in offering, which he politely refused by holding his hand up.

"Well, that trail right behind you leads to a waterfall that looks absolutely stunning in the moonlight. I was going to walk down there in a few minutes. Would you care to join me?"

He sighed. "I'd so love to join you, Brin, but I really can't. See, I'm sort of on a personal retreat here. Connecting with nature, no comforts, that kind of thing. To be honest, the only reason I came by your camp was to make sure it wasn't a bunch of drunk kids about to burn the forest down."

The barely hidden scowl on her face told Roan that she wasn't accustomed to having her invitations declined. He could sympathize. So rare were the times women declined his advances that it sometimes left him mystified and stung when they did.

"But when I'm done, I'd really like to see you again. Are you on Instagram? Messenger?"

She smiled slightly as she sipped her coffee and considered his rain check, as it were.

"Swing by in the morning, if you like. If I'm still here, I'll tell you then. And If I'm not, oh well. But you can always follow the trail and check out the waterfall by yourself. It'll take your breath away. I promise."

Bear appeared out of nowhere, panting and drooling. He plopped down at Brin's side and cast a sideways glance at Roan. Roan couldn't get past his over-the-top collar, pink and sparkly and full of chichi tassels. If Brin was going for irony, mission accomplished.

Sensing his bemusement, Bear growled, which Roan took as his cue to go.

He stood and nodded. "Sounds amazing. Good night, Brin."

"Thank you, Roan. It's been a long time since anyone made music to me. For me, I mean. See you later, maybe."

She spoke so soft and succulent that his will liquefied, and he almost changed his mind. No one told him he had to abstain from sex during his pilgrimage, after all. But this pilgrimage was for communion and healing, reflection and solitude, an opportunity to withdraw from everyday life and all its distractions.

This was his pilgrimage. If he really needed someone else to tell him what was needed in order to get the most out of it, then maybe the Craft wasn't for him.

The trek back to his camp promised to be an interesting challenge in the dark, especially with those massive spiderwebs and their rainbow-colored residents. Along the road, the full moon provided enough light that he could turn his headlamp off, but the wind blew stronger than inside the trees. His entire body throbbed in pain, dull and relentless as a bad toothache, not from the canopy malfunction and his rough landing earlier in the day, but rather from the cold that seeped into his fleece jacket, as well as from the arousal he'd so cruelly denied. Walking a brisk pace kept the shivers at bay, at least, but did little to alleviate his fuckstration.

At the roadside memorial, solar-charged LED lights illuminated the ensemble in red, purple, yellow, and pink, creating a more festive atmosphere than during the day. Distracting for nighttime drivers, no doubt…the dead beckoning the living to come join the party.

Since he'd stored the GPS coordinates of his camp, he didn't really have to retrace his steps. However, he'd hiked a winding route through the trees from the south, following where the vegetation grew thinnest and most passable. Going back, it wasn't going to be so easy to see, even with his headlamp at full brightness.

He decided he'd walk the road until dead north of his campsite, then turn south into the forest and find his way through the undergrowth there. Not a perfect plan, but the one with the least amount of forest ground to cover between the road and his camp. Hopefully the route from there would be more or less direct.

He spent maybe five minutes on Brock Bridge Road, though, before an impalpable urge struck him to go back and get Brin's contact info. An invisible fairy godmother whispering in his psychic ear to leave no chance for Brin to vanish from his life, never to be seen again, even if a more intimate connection between them wasn't in the cards for this particular night. She wouldn't expect him to return so soon, but Brin struck him as an unconventional woman, and in his experience, unconventional women (*most* women) tended to enjoy the unexpected, especially if it came along with a splash of charm. So, he about-faced on the asphalt, and started back toward her camp.

Once again, he turned into the woods from the Crash Test Oak, and when he came to the grove where he'd performed the blood ritual, he witnessed a most extraordinary sight. Fireflies still inhabited that enchanted clearing, but they no longer pulsed their familiar yellow-green bioluminescence. They'd all changed to a deep purple, the color of those black light tubes you saw sometimes in dance clubs. Passing through a particularly dense swarm, Roan could make out glowing white bits of lint on his jacket. As far as he knew, no firefly species in the world glowed purple. In the virtual world of a couple console games maybe, but in the real world? No.

He couldn't see Brin's campfire from the small glade, as he had before. He strained to spot sparks, glowing coals, anything, but he could only make out the light of the full moon through the forest, a circle of silvery fire through the foliage. He switched his headlamp from red to white, and stepped towards the babble of the river's current.

Roan remembered the exact spot where her tent had been, the exact spot where he'd sat at her fire and sang "Lovely Joan". Yet, to his surprise and disappointment, not a trace of the camp remained. No ashes or blackened bits of wood. No flattened grass or ferns, no imprint of the tent, firepit, or chairs in the dirt. No footprints or pawprints. In the span of maybe ten or fifteen minutes, she'd apparently doused her fire, dumped its remains into the river or somewhere else, cooled the firepit's metal to the point it could be carried, broken camp, humped out all her gear, and erased any sign that anyone had ever been there. Marines in the field would have been hard-pressed to vanish a woodland camp so quickly and completely.

Well, fuck. If she'd wanted to get away that badly, he wasn't about to get his stalk on and try to find her. There'd be other women. Maybe none quite so intriguing, not for a while, but he'd never lack for companionship. This much he knew.

As he turned back, he noticed a trail running parallel to the river, faint, but clearly trodden more than once in a blue moon. Was this the trail Brin had mentioned, that led to the waterfall? It had to be. She'd told him it lay right behind him when he'd been sitting, and it was the only real trail in this forest that he'd seen so far.

Should he follow the trail? Why not? His pilgrimage called for connecting with this land, honoring this land, and what better way to honor it than to immerse himself in its power and beauty? After tonight, he wouldn't get another chance to see this reputedly stunning, moonlit waterfall for years, if ever. If it turned out to be as breathtaking as she'd claimed, it might prove a perfect spot to meditate, and reflect. Odds were, he wasn't going to get a whole lot of sleep this night, anyway. So he switched his headlamp back to red to restore his night vision, and followed the path upriver.

The river meandered to his right, twisting away then turning back, undulating like a belly dancer. When at last the foliage cleared and the waterfall came into sight, he halted with his boots fused to the ground, and felt his jaw go slack. He blinked, cleared the debris from his lashes with both index fingers, and looked again. *"Maiden, Mother, and Crone,"* he whispered.

The view before him framed like something out of a forgotten dream. The moonlight revealed level banks carpeted in flowers and grass. The boulders strewn about, composed mostly of quartz or soapstone and adorned with glowing, phosphorescent moss, seemed as though they'd been deliberately positioned by a landscape artist. The waterfall itself fell from an escarpment two stories high, baby pines growing out and up from the crags here and there, the contours of the cascading water captured almost perfectly by the reflection of the full moon.

Good thing he'd come alone. If he'd taken Brin's invitation and come here with her, lain eyes upon it for the first time in her company, he would have forgotten all about his pilgrimage, literally torn the clothes from her body, and spent the night discovering all the things that made her whimper and moan. Preferably in a warm sleeping bag.

The place felt as enchanted as places came. A natural temple, not just for meditation, but for visions and visitations, a place to be touched by the divine. Yes, he would connect with the goddess and god here, but first, he had to get pictures on his phone to bring back to Epona and the rest of the coven. Not that a jpeg could possibly capture the aura of this place, but if he could capture a decent enough image, he just might convince them to come see it for themselves and add it to the coven's list of ritual locations.

Still a hundred or so yards away, he continued forward along the path looking through the phone's display, trying to frame as crisp and clear a picture as he could. He glanced downward to make sure no roots or rocks lay in his way for him to trip over, only to discover that, a single step ahead of him, the path kept going right over the edge of a steep rock face.

"*Fuck!*" he screamed as he dropped his phone and tried in vain to throw his body backward. His momentum carried him straight over the edge and into black, empty space.

Having jumped out of airplanes with a parachute strapped to his back a total of fifty-two times, Roan's body reflexively tried to assume a skydiver's arch as he fell. That reflex, unfortunately, only took a dire situation and made it worse, by exposing his vital organs to the rocks below and focusing tension in his lower back. His ribcage impacted the first ledge he passed on the way down, instantly fracturing three ribs. The shock of the injury made him curl into the fetal position as he tumbled along the rock face. Something hard sliced his back open, from waist to center, up and across. His head grazed the face, halfway from his left ear to his crown, then he landed, hard, on his ankle, which broke with a meaty, muffled crack, and he passed out.

When he came to, he looked upon two full moons, and two identical clouds glowing gray in the inky sky. The world spun fiercely, as though he were trapped in the centrifugal force of some psychotic amusement park ride, and his head threatened to explode with each heartbeat.

He rocked onto his side, each movement setting his back and his ribs on fire and forcing a painful grunt from the deep of his throat. Beneath his fleece jacket, his long john top, and his t-shirt, a layer of cold, wet, sticky blood blanketed his back.

"Help!" he cried out. The hurt that simple word put upon his torso made him double over. Amidst his limbic mind's inner screams, his rational mind scrabbled for purchase.

"Anyone…please…help me," he strained between breaths. The crickets and frogs alone replied in their eternal chant, followed by a lone whippoorwill.

"My name is Roan," he whispered to himself, trying unsuccessfully to stave off delirium. "Son of the moon."

A foot-long, bright pink dildo, garbed in a priest's frock, stood before him just a foot or two away.

"How long since your last confession, my son?" It asked him.

Not your son, Father Peter, Roan tried to answer.

The dildo twirled the noose it wore as its fascia. "I meant: *confess,* witch. How often do you suck Satan's cock?"

"*Fuck you. Your faith…not mine,*" he whispered back.

"You really need a bath," the dildo said. "You're filthy."

It pointed to the waterfall's pool, where a pair of monks stood on the bank, torturing a sobbing young woman lashed to a dunking chair. Down into the water…and up. Down into the water…and up.

Roan knew he was hallucinating. The moonlight was hardly bright enough to distinguish colors in the dark, let alone the detailed shapes and outlines of the monks and their victim on the pool bank.

He'd lost both his phone and headlamp in the fall, but he kept an LED palm light in his inside coat pocket, as a tertiary backup. Slowly, he dug it out and shined it on the pink dildo. In the light, it revealed itself to be just a phallic rock formation, jutting from the ground in front of him.

I don't have to talk to you, he thought. *You're just a rock.*

He gingerly pulled himself upright, and slowly his vision righted itself. The two moons that hung above the waterfall drew close, and at last merged into one. The excruciating pulse in his temples made him want to puke, but taking a look at his immediate surroundings helped to orient himself and dispelled most of his brain fog.

He began to take stock of his wounds, starting with the wet, plum-sized lump on his scalp. All of the hair on the left side of his head matted with half-solid, congealing blood. He wretched in dry heaves, and his rib cage felt like kitchen knives scraping his insides, front and back. As soon as the spasms passed, he found that keeping his breaths shallow and rhythmic kept the pain down to a dull roar.

So much blood, already cold and pasty, soaked into his hair and his clothes, spackling his skin. Judging from his dizziness and the sharp pain in his abs, he sported a bad concussion, maybe even a skull fracture, and he was likely bleeding internally. He had to find a way back to the road and get help somehow.

He shined his palm light up the rock face behind him, trying to judge just how far he'd fallen, but it wasn't bright enough. He chalked the height up to *higher than I wanted it to be, but not nearly as high as it could have been.*

Using the dildo rock for support, he tried to stand. A bolt

of agony shot from his ankle all the way up to his neck, and he collapsed with a scream. The grapefruit swell in his boot and his foot's odd angle told him his ankle was broken. Only then did he begin to grasp what might happen to him if he couldn't find help.

Some cloud cover had rolled in while he lay passed out. He was already shivering in the night air. A good rain would surely chill him to the bone. He dragged himself through the rubble to a spot under a low overhang in the rock face, gritting his teeth with every inch.

Roan had sprained that same ankle once during a skydive. Using a daily routine of healing magick, he'd managed to repair the injury in just a couple of weeks, when his doctor had told him it would take at least a couple *months*. He certainly didn't expect to mend the break now with a snap of his fingers, but maybe magick could help. He definitely had nothing to gain by not trying.

He lay his left hand upon the rock, his right hand upon his ankle, and quieted his mind of fear and anguish as best he could. "Bone, like rock. Strong and whole like rock. Bone, like rock. Strong and whole like rock."

He closed his eyes and whispered the incantation over and over, paying attention to the stone's feel and its sturdy structure, eventually trancing out to the syllables' rhythm as to a drumbeat, allowing it to take on a life of its own.

After an unknown time, the syllables lost their momentum. He opened his eyes and felt the circumference of the grapefruit swell in his boot. Maybe the swelling had shrunk, maybe it hadn't; he couldn't tell, but it no longer felt so tender to the touch. Taking a knee, he set his good foot flat on the ground and stood, cautiously transferring weight to the other. It took a couple attempts, and he had to crank the suck-it-up factor to eleven, but at last he managed a couple of limp, upright steps.

Modern medicine would have told him that his impromptu spell amounted to a placebo, not magick, but he didn't really give a rat's ass. He could walk. However that worked, he'd take it.

A dog barked from somewhere inside the tree line by the waterfall, sweet as a ballad to his ears. His heart did a Snoopy dance, and his gut fluttered with hope. He dug into his pant pocket and pulled out a metal whistle, and blew three shrill, short blasts, the universal distress signal. The dog barked three times in seeming response, and Roan laughed in relief. He let loose another three blasts, and again the dog responded, this time a little closer.

Then Roan's intuition took him by the throat, and a sense of dread dried his mouth like a breath of hot, acrid smoke.

You fucking idiot. Shut! Up!

He recognized that deep, curious bark. It belonged to Brin's dog, Bear. He remembered now that the trail he'd followed went right over that escarpment, with no danger sign posted, or any warning whatsoever to hikers. The same trail Brin had so casually encouraged him to follow. She'd been there before, so she must have known about it; how could she not? So why hadn't she warned him? And why on Earth would her dog be here *now*, if she'd already broken camp and left?

All of these rational questions muted against his primal instincts, which urged him to dig a hole deep, deep into Mother Earth and bury himself there. Which howled of epic danger, m*ortal* danger…and maybe even worse.

The creature that emerged from the tree line was like nothing Roan had ever seen in waking life. At least as large as a bull elephant, it downed a set of trees on its way out, sniffing at the air in mammoth huffs. Lumbering and massive, it traced the outline of a prehistoric bear. As it padded towards the rock crop where Roan stood, he felt the thuds of its enormous paws in the ground below him, and watched bats take flight above the trees. The wind carried its sour, musky scent.

This was no hallucination.

If the creature relied on smell, finding him was going to be no problem, from all the blood smeared on and around him.

He overcame his natural urge to freeze in place and looked wildly about for a grotto or a cranny to squeeze into, something to hide behind.

Nothing. He stood with his back literally to the wall. Nowhere to go but left and into the forest, blind, and given the speed with which the giant creature approached, he'd never make it there in time.

On impulse, he produced the can of bear spray from his coat and flicked off the safety cap. Which felt almost as ridiculous to him as going for his four-inch knife, but as though he'd stepped outside of his body, he observed himself infusing the can with his magickal will, declaring the metallic cylinder a weapon, an extension of him.

In his other hand, he directed the palm light at the beast as it charged. With a head as large as a compact car, its jaws stretched wide enough to snap the Crash Test Oak itself in half. Around its impossibly thick neck it wore a collar—a pink, sparkly collar, with huge white tassels hanging like church-bells.

Bear. This thing was Brin's pet, he somehow knew. And maybe some part of him had known all along that her pet wasn't a dog, even if it hadn't quite jibed with what he'd *wanted* to see at the time, which was a gorgeous, available, nature-loving female, just camping and enjoying a night in the great outdoors with her pet dog.

Back in his body, he desperately tried to imagine what he was supposed to do with the bear spray, which was bound only to piss the creature off. Only when it came in range, maybe thirty yards, did Roan remember the commands that Brin had used on it.

He leveled the can and fired a steady burst at the creature's yawning maw.

"*Bear! Hold!*" he bellowed, ignoring the stabbing pain it caused in his ribs.

Bear slid and came to a stop, just a couple arms' lengths away from where Roan stood and tried to maintain his balance.

The thing looked down at him and smiled, actually *smiled*, baring rows of pointed, lime-white teeth the length of his forearm.

"Bear! Go play!" He bellowed again, firing another volley straight into its eyes and muzzle. It might have winced; he couldn't be sure, but at his command it spun and trotted away with a dissatisfied huff, then turned and galloped off into the trees with a loud crash.

Roan dropped his arms and fell back against the rock face. He swallowed, and tried to slow his machine-gun heartbeat.

"Now, why did you have to go and do that?" a soft, feminine voice sighed from above and behind him. "Bear makes a ginormous mess playing in the forest when he's that big."

Brin sat upon a middling ledge of the rock face, the same one he'd scraped his head against on the way down, completely nude except for a bone necklace. She slid off the edge and drifted down to him, her deep brown hair trailing upright as though she were sinking through water.

"I'm so sorry, Roan. I never wanted you to suffer. But you made it here, that's the important thing, and it took your breath away, like I promised it would. No?" She spread her arms and smiled, fake-shy.

Even now, Roan couldn't help but take in her curvy, alluring form. She made a twirling gesture, and suddenly the air filled with fireflies of red, yellow, purple, and pink. She nodded toward his palm light, which he trained on her. "Please turn that ugly thing off. We don't need it now."

"Brin," he began, at a loss for words. She waited politely for him to find them. "Why do you want to hurt me?" he finally asked.

Tears flowed from her large, ice-blue eyes, and she put her fingers to her throat. "Hurt you? I want to *kill* you," she corrected him. "How can you even ask that? I don't want to *hurt* you! For thousands of moons, no one's made me cry me like you did, Roan. You came to me from the sky, to love me, to nourish me, and you didn't let anything stop you. You sang for me. You bled for me."

"No, I didn't. I came here on a pilgrimage, to connect to and heal this forest."

She regarded his wounds and his precarious stance with genuine compassion. "Don't you understand, Roan, son of the moon? I'm the river. I'm the land. I *am* this forest. And I *hate* seeing you hurt. It didn't have to be this way. If only you'd come into my tent when I invited you."

Roan laughed bitterly. "Right. So you could kill me."

She rolled her eyes. "Yes, but why do you have it say it like that? It's only so that we can have *all* of each other. I love you, Roan, and you love me, too. I can feel it!"

He realized that she was right. He *did* love her, or at least, he wanted to. Even over his broken body's anguish, even over the flood of crazy spilling out of her mouth. The longer he took in her nude, nubile physique, the more open and connected he felt to her. It hurt to be so far away from her. He longed to take her into his arms, inhale the scent of her hair and skin, breathe in her love and drown in it. Gods, it felt as though he'd been dosed with an extra potent batch of molly, his brain swimming in a well of oxytocin.

Only then did he understand.

"Mother goddess," He gasped. "You're an ondine!"

"I don't know what that means," she shrugged with a frown. "I'm the river. I'm the land. This is my forest."

Until then, Roan hadn't believed that ondines—water elementals—actually existed. When Epona taught about the elemental spirits of air, fire, water, and earth, Roan had written it off as bullshit. Magick was real enough, sure, but that hardly meant that unicorns, faeries, or elementals must also be real. In the course of one's studies, the smart witch made an effort to distinguish the literal from the symbolic, especially in the twenty-first century.

And yet there he stood, seriously entertaining thoughts of dying for this (lovely, heart-rending) creature he barely knew.

Water was the element of love and the emotions, and in folk tales around the world, water spirits were famous for falling in love with humans, as well as the power to make humans fall in love with *them*.

He took a breath and centered himself, then stood back and assumed a protective magickal stance, arms crossed mummy-style.

"I can't die for you," he proclaimed as firmly as he could. "I don't want to die. I have a life to live."

"You think I would just devour you? Like the car people?" She exclaimed in wounded disbelief. "I want you for my lover, not for nourishment! I need to feel you inside me. Die for me already, and I'll show you love like you never thought possible. On my name, Brin-teh-owah-meme-gwesi, I swear you'll wonder why you even hesitated!"

Roan felt himself sinking further under her spell. His will was eroding, along with his physical strength, little by little, as he coughed up blood. Soon he would become too weak to stand. It would feel so right to embrace her, to love her, to relinquish the remaining life in him that was gradually draining anyway.

However, her heartfelt and persuasive pitch failed to address a couple elephants in the room. "You tried to kill me, Brin, *three times*. You failed. Only now does my free will matter to you? And even if we became lovers, that list of names at the memorial would just keep growing, wouldn't it? I could never be with you, knowing that."

Brin gritted her teeth and clenched her fists, and her eyes filled with the fearsome rage of a flash flood. A deep peel of thunder rolled lazily across the sky.

"'As far as I am able,'" she hissed. "That's what you said when you first spoke to me. Remember? *I would redress whatever harm humanity has done to this place, and to the creatures that dwell within, as far as I am able.* And you're able to give me your life."

Roan swallowed.

"You won't deny me, my love. I'll have you, one way or another. A witch's word is a witch's *bond*. That much I know."

"That was never his intent behind those words, to die for you," an assured voice stated, as a familiar figure strode out of the darkness behind Brin with a flashlight in hand. "But that's what you do, Brin-teh-owah-meme-gwesi, Hungry River Water Woman, isn't it? You take. You drown. You consume. That's what you've always done, as the people who lived in this forest long ago understood."

"Epona!" Roan lit up at the sight of his high priestess, dignified and poised even in a bulky coat and worn denim jeans.

Brin narrowed her eyes at him jealously, before she turned to face her enemy, square.

She smirked with raised eyebrows. "Well, well, well. If it isn't the skanky trailer trash witch queen herself, sneaking around my forest like a rat. You're breaking our truce by being here, you know. So now I'm going to kill as many travelers as I want, starting with you. I wonder how much your children will hate you for abandoning them, after your wet, stinking corpse is finally found hanging from one of these trees with a suicide note."

Epona sighed. "Making a truce with you was a mistake. I realize that now. My coven wanted to leave you in peace, as a goddess of the people who once lived in these woods, but your hunger for life is only going to keep growing. Innocent people are going to keep dying. We should have burned this forest down long ago."

Brin laughed contemptuously. "Pony-bitch, please. As if you had the mojo."

Epona held her ground. "Give me my witch back, and maybe we won't need to find out just yet."

"Oh, Pony. I'm so going to love watching the life run out you. But all that aside—excuse me, *your* witch? He fed me his magick. He fed me his cum. He fed me his blood. He's *mine*."

Epona whirled to Roan. "You fed her your *blood*?"

"In ritual, to heal the land, yes," he replied weakly. "Blood's the essence of life. It felt like the right thing to do."

She glared at him, curling her knuckles on her hips. "Anything else you've tried to heal out here by offering your blood, hon? A poor swarm of horseflies? A starving bear, maybe?"

As Roan drew breath to reply, Brin washed up to within inches of him, and tracing satin fingers across his trembling lips, stole his breath away. As Epona moved to come between them, Brin shoved her away with her other hand, arcing the priestess airborne like a rag doll toward the tall grass.

"Tell you what, love," she whispered to Roan, nearly brushing her lips against his. "Stop fighting. Give yourself to me, and maybe I'll let her walk away."

And that really was the right thing to do, wasn't it? Epona shouldn't have had to come to save him. Above all else, the witch's path centered around taking responsibility for one's own fate. How one's life unfolded sat not in the hands of some god or goddess with a master plan, but rather in one's own hands, alone. That was the price of becoming a witch, and of receiving access to the invisible—to lose the right to claim helplessness, forever. To accept that there were no victims, only volunteers.

"I can't let you risk yourself for me," he struggled to tell Epona. "You warned me, and I chose to come anyway. Let me own this. Let me accept the consequences and die honorably, as I should."

"Hon," Epona growled as she got back to her feet, brushing off the dirt and grass, "Snap out of whatever ridiculous *Game of Thrones* trip you're on, and stand with me now...or *neither* of us will ever leave this forest."

"Why are you doing this? I'm not your responsibility. I'm just—"

"You're not *just* anything, Roan!" she fired back. "You *are* a son of the moon! You *are* my brother! The Craft isn't some elite club you get voted into, I thought you understood that by now. You either are a witch, or you aren't, and like it or not, you *are*—even if sometimes you have the common sense of a brain-dead jackass!"

Brin gestured to the sky with a flick of her wrist. A low rumble echoed across the clouds, and slivers of hail began bouncing off the rocks around them in quickening staccato. Within seconds, the wind went wild, and the ice bits grew to the size of marbles, then golf balls, and all around their impact upon the rocks reported like enthusiastic applause. By the time the hail grew to the size of apples, the applause waned as the bulk of the hail concentrated upon Epona's body and began to pummel her with meaty thuds.

"Pelting you to death now," Brin announced casually, without bothering to look away from Roan. With the sweetest smile, she pressed her mouth to his, her tongue probing softly behind his teeth.

He bowed his head and squeezed his eyes shut. He pointed to Epona with his index finger and sent her all of the magickal energy he could using the first image that came to mind, as ludicrous as it was. He envisioned texting her a string of emojis: a heart; an eye shedding a tear; a huffing bull poised to charge; the waxing, full, and waning moons; a lightning bolt; a blue flame; a fist; a dragon breathing fire; and finally, a gift-wrapped box. In his mind, he hit "send". Then Epona gasped and fell to her knees.

Brin interpreted her gasp, wrongly, as pain. She blew a kiss to her and giggled. "Daughter of the moon, we bid you *hail*, and farewell."

Then Epona leapt to her feet, and reaching with both arms toward the clouds, she issued a throaty shriek from the realm of nightmares. Flashes of lightning strobed through Roan's clamped eyelids, as though an army of paparazzi giants were snapping off photos of Epona as she held the pose. The world exploded in a cacophony of deafening thunderclaps that echoed her shriek, the concussions rippling through air, ground, and flesh.

Roan opened his eyes and watched as Epona repeated that terrifying shriek, her nails raking towards the sky. Again the world strobed as brilliant white threads of lightning arced from above and struck throughout the forest. The closest lightning bolt left vines of orange flame along the trunks of three nearby trees. With the storm's winds to fan them, the flames quickly crawled across the underbrush, and blossomed in the trees' dense foliage.

Roan had never witnessed such a terrible display of magick as the lightning storm Epona unleashed by redirecting the power of Brin's hailstorm. A day prior, he wouldn't have imagined such magick was even possible. Hollywood on a blockbuster budget would have been hard-pressed to match such a spectacular and destructive scene.

For as far as Roan could see, patches of wildfire began to sprout throughout the forest. The ondine screamed in rage and anguish, twisting in circles as she tore out fistfuls of her own hair.

Epona sucked in breath to call the volley of lightning a third time, and Roan felt his hair stand on end, smelled the bitter tang of ozone on the wind, telltale signs that lightning was about to strike nearby, and he hit the ground. Again, a dozen brilliant forks of light stabbed down from the clouds throughout the forest, instantly accompanied by sustained, ear-shattering explosions.

Already the eye-stinging miasma of wood smoke, strangely homey in smell, set both Roan and Epona coughing. Firelight began to illuminate the waterfall pool and the surrounding woodland, and Brin evaporated, leaving Roan with a final, pleading look of confusion and betrayal.

"Come on!" Epona yelled, blood trailing from her nose and mouth, bruises pocking her hands as she extended them both to help Roan stand. "My car's not far from here, there's a path!"

Hacking violently, she draped his arm behind her neck and wrapped hers around his waist. She used her free hand to cover her mouth and nose with a soaked piece of flannel torn from her shirt. Roan followed suit by slipping his arm out of his fleece jacket and biting on the empty sleeve, breathing through his mouth. Together they did a three-legged race up a winding, narrow path through the trees, as the heat from the nascent forest fire caused their hair and clothes to steam.

Epona's aging green Prius waited along a service vehicle trail with hazards blinking. She opened the passenger door and gently helped Roan collapse into the seat. Spitting gravel and scraping the undercarriage, she reversed up the service trail until the rear tires bounced up onto the asphalt of Brock Bridge Road. She threw on the high beams and the wipers, thrust the car in drive, and fish-tailed heading east. Fallen branches and downed trees littered the road as Patuxent River Forest burned around them, a midnight drive through an idyllic, wooded hellscape.

"Stay with me, hon," she urged Roan, gently squeezing his arm. "The hospital's not far."

"How…h-how did you know where—" he began.

"We share our phone locations on the 'Find My' app, remember? I checked to see where you were at sunset. No surprise, I'm sorry to say, you were in the one place I told you not to go."

Stupid hurts. The popular skydiving maxim wasn't just for skydiving anymore. He gazed silently out the window at the spreading flames, and tried not to think of Brin. He sent out the last fumes of his magickal strength to the night, to help anyone else who might be caught in the blaze to escape.

"By the way. I hope it goes without saying that you'll be re-doing your pilgrimage," she said.

Roan said nothing, and only squeezed her hand. Keeping her eyes fast to the road, Epona squeezed back.

WIDDERSHINS

Hollie Snider

Humidity rose from the ground in opaque rainbow wisps. Gentle rain ticked against verdant leaves and cascaded along smooth tree trunks. The surrounding jungle smelled of green, growing things in rich earth with an underlying tang of decay.

The scent reminded Dara Kincaide of greenhouses, hot garbage, death…and life. Unseen flowers bloomed within the Peruvian cloud forest, sporadically filling the air with phantom sweetness. Its effect was akin to catching an occasional breath of fresh air while standing waist deep in a rotting refuse pile.

"Our first day," Dara said. She smiled at the student expedition group. Susan, Edgar, Jimmy and Francine grinned back at her, excitement shining in their eyes.

Kevin, Dara's husband, checked the packs on the four guanacos one last time. "Let's get going. Those ruins aren't going to inspect themselves." He snugged his rafting hat on and picked up the lead rope belonging to the nearest guanaco. Kevin led a train of three llama-like animals down the well-used path.

Dara picked up the fourth animal's lead, then swatted at the back of her head, shooing the guanaco away from her hair. The curious beast stepped faster, moving to walk beside her, sniffing. She looked into its large, brown eyes, noting the extraordinary length of its lashes and feeling a little jealous. *Why is it animals and boys always get the longest eyelashes?*

Scents of hot, wet hay and damp fur tickled Dara's nose as the guanaco nibbled her shoulder. She shrugged the lips away. "Just don't spit on me." Long lashes closed in a slow blink, then the animal's ears pricked. Dara listened too, wondering what the animal heard.

Droning sounds of insects thrummed in the air. Then something else, something…slithering crossed her path. The noise came from deep in the soil. Dara stared at the dark earth, trying to see into its depths. Nothing met her intense gaze. Wary, she stepped wide and continued, throwing a nervous glance over her shoulder. The guanaco hopped across the implied snake trail, refusing to set foot on it.

Rain stopped and itchy moisture settled on Dara's skin. She felt like ants crawled along her spine, and wove through her scalp. Knowing scratching would only add to the discomfort, Dara sought to ignore the sensation. The prickling strengthened, and she still tried not to scratch, instead rubbing calloused palms along both arms. Even the smallest abrasion could open her skin to infections in the jungle.

Why did I plan an expedition into a South American cloud forest in December? Sooner or later, I'll remember seasons are reversed down here.

Their expedition moved along the snake- and spider-infested trail, winding ever-deeper into the hellish environment. Kevin led the way, hacking at the overgrowth in places. After two hours of walking, he called back, "Do we need to stop and rest? You all looked a little winded."

Dara glared at him as he stood, auburn hair plastered to his head. Sweat ran along the sides of his face and dripped from his rounded chin.

"Yes," called Susan, one of the students. She dropped her

backpack with a heavy thump. "Please."

"All right. But just a quick break," said Kevin. He flashed a boyish grin. "I want to see these ruins before the world ends in three days."

Susan and Francine swayed on their feet. Edgar sipped from his canteen, looking for all the world like he wanted to gulp the entire contents.

Dara took a drink from her own and almost choked. Water, ice cold this morning, now tasted metallic and stale. The tepid fluid did little to quench her thirst.

Their last student, Jimmy, stood next to Kevin, showing no apparent signs of suffering. Sweat stains spotted his shirt, but he breathed easy and didn't touch his canteen.

Jimmy's from the Louisiana bayous, Dara reminded herself. *This is probably like home to him.*

"Okay, let's move on," said Dara.

Designated P42CF, the newly discovered ruins appeared to show traits not belonging to South America, according to the preliminary reports. Claims of unusual findings, such as Egyptian styled hieroglyphics and Sumerian cuneiform writing made up the majority of the missives filtering back to the USA. Those determinations brought Dara and Kevin, along with his top four archeology students, to the Andes—the most beautiful hell Dara had ever seen.

With a collective groan from three of the students, the group moved on, heat and humidity combining to keep a ponderous pace.

Some distance ahead, Dara heard running water. The sound reminded her of wind through aspen leaves. A longing surfaced for the cool, dry air of the Wyoming Rockies. Imagining snow, she put one foot in front of the other, occasionally pushing the nosy guanaco away from her hair.

Broad-leafed trees towered above, stretching to the heavens and blocking most of the sunlight. Dara looked up, knowing the sun was there in that azure sky, yet not having visible proof other than a muted greenish light. The cloud forest felt darker, more menacing than it had previously. A quetzal called, its sudden voice startling Dara. She looked around, desperate to acknowledge the bird's existence. She needed to know her little group wasn't the only living thing, outside of snakes and spiders, in this jungle of giants. The bird eluded her, well-hidden in the dense, intertwined treetops like some colorful haunt.

Dara stepped off the trail, hoping to sight its bronze, green and red plumage from a different angle. The guanaco balked at first, then followed with hesitant steps.

Thick undergrowth closed around her. Faint voices spoke, words unintelligible, hideously luring, reminding her of the infernal susurrus of orchid bees and other winged insects. Leaves rustled, the innocent sound somehow ominous now. Heavy panting and coughs came from behind Dara, and she turned to find the guanaco, sides heaving and eyes rolling in fear. She struggled to calm the beast even as her own panic rose. The animal screamed, a high, bleating call. Maguey rope scraped skin and burned palms as the guanaco pulled free and bolted.

The deep, slithering sound returned. Dry skin against dry earth. Noise sizzled in Dara's ears. Blood pounded through her veins as if searching for escape. Pressure rose and throbbed in her skull. Neck muscles tightened and shoulders hunched. Dara's body drew in upon itself, curling toward defense.

Sibilant voices grew louder, chanting monotones. Dara strained to listen, to understand the almost recognizable words. Her brain screamed to get out, get away from the menacing chorus. Dara couldn't move, as rooted to the soil as the trees caging her.

Vines shifted and fell, coiling at her feet like fat green serpents. Loops of the ropy tendrils dropped all around, entangling her in their serpentine grasp. Leaves quivered in anticipation. Tree branches bowed and bent, groaning as if under a tremendous weight. Psithurisms rose from faint, buzzing murmurs to incomprehensible gibberish. No human mouth could ever form such words.

Dara raised her hands to cover her ears. Sounds felt like they reverberated deep in her bones. The ominous droning thrummed beneath skin and sinew, threatening to shatter joints. Then a new demand broke through, banishing the chanting to the background.

Kevin! Calling my name!

He sounded muffled, faraway somehow.

Why does he sound so distant?

"Kevin?" called Dara, voice weak with fear. She turned and saw Kevin stalking toward her, leading the escaped guanaco.

"Dara, you've got to keep up," he said. "If you fall behind and get lost, we'll never find you." Kevin thrust the animal's lead at her. "If Peggy here hadn't tried to bolt past me, we'd never even know you were gone until we made camp."

She hugged him, wrapping her arms around his strong torso.

"Hey, what's wrong?" Kevin stroked her hair.

"Nothing," she said. Dara looked over her shoulder, expecting to see something creep from the undergrowth. Only the trail and dripping leaves met her fearful gaze. "Let's keep going. And who's Peggy?"

Kevin pointed at the guanaco. "Don't you remember her name?"

"Oh, right. Yeah." Dara studied the path behind. Nothing. "Peggy. Sure, I remember."

"You sure you're all right?"

Dara winced as Kevin squeezed one hand. He looked at her palm. Angry rope burns met his gaze. "Why didn't you just drop the rope?"

She snatched her hand away. "There wasn't time. Peggy was fine one minute, then freaking out the next."

"Why aren't you wearing your gloves?"

Dara pushed past him. "Gloves? In the cloud forest? As if it isn't hot enough." She turned and walked backwards a few steps, still moving away from him. "And I thought you were in a hurry to get there. Doctor Halsey and the other teams are supposed to meet us there the day after tomorrow so we can officially start this dig."

Kevin followed, shaking his head.

Finally, after almost a day's travel, the group reached the perimeter of the dig site. Fire, in the form of sunset, raged across the small, treeless depression in the mountains, glistening off clouds blanketing the opposite forest, and licking around the plateaus. Just beyond the forest's edge stood the discovery of the century.

Dara gazed at the sight before her. *They look like some Andean Brigadoon. I wonder if the ruins will vanish in the morning.*

Ruins glowed orange and shadowy, ominous and forbidding. They shimmered in the oppressive humidity, a spot of surrealism in a valley of green and bronze and copper reality.

Unlike other Peruvian ruins, these were not separated into an agricultural sector and a citadel. Buildings of various sizes dotted the area. Houses and stables intermingled with temples and storehouses. A small amphitheater squatted central to the surrounding buildings. Curved stone benches wrapped around a raised dais looking to be about twelve feet in diameter.

Terraces traced horizontal lines across the cliffs, stepping down to a river gurgling below. Verdant grasses grew in the *andinas*, overtaking what had once been farmland for sweet potatoes, onions and maize, along with other crops. Below, nearer the river, only circular depressions resembling meteor craters remained of ancient farming experiments for crops with different water and temperature requirements. Aqueducts, carved through whole rock in some places, hugged the sides of the fields, still carrying thin trickles water from mountain streams to irrigate the fields.

Ground fog curled about the buildings and crept over terraces, caressing stone with cold fingers.

"How are the aqueducts not clogged with plants with no one to clean them out?" Susan asked softly.

The expedition of six crept forward, light and shadow playing tricks with vision. Shapes shifted and roiling gloom appeared to reach for the group as they passed.

"There are ghosts here," Dara murmured. "P-forty-two-C-F belongs to the dead."

"And the dead keep it," said Jimmy. The group snicked at the *Lord of the Rings* reference, breaking the supernatural spell.

Since no explorations could begin until sunrise, Kevin, Jimmy, and Edgar set up camp with a mixture of eagerness and disappointment while Dara, Susan, and Francine collected firewood and prepared the evening meal.

"So, what do you think this place is?" asked Susan.

"Given the andinas and aqueducts, this place had to have been a farming community along the lines of Machu Picchu," said Jimmy. "Only I think this place may be older."

"What makes you say that?" asked Kevin. "We haven't seen much yet."

Jimmy shrugged. He stirred the dried beef stew for a moment. "I don't know, really. Just a feeling." He raised one hand. "And before you say anything, no, I don't know any more about the feeling, no, I don't know where it's coming from, and yes, I will pay attention to it as we're digging."

Kevin smiled and shook his head.

Quiet solitude reigned over the evening. Somehow, after Jimmy's statement, conversation seemed blasphemous in the midst of ancient relics from a bygone civilization.

Kevin banked the fire and everyone retired to tents for the night.

Morning came sooner than expected, sun rising red and raw over the site.

Surveying the area, Dara wondered just who had sent the findings back to the university. The dig site was still pristine, and the ruins appeared to be untouched. Mosses and lichens covered the stones and spread over the nearby land, surrounding the structures in a living moat of green. No sign of human activity—much less active digs in the area—existed and yet the reports came.

Directly addressed to me, not Kevin. Strange since he has the doctorate and I'm not even a full professor yet.

She pulled out the crumpled letter and re-read it. The brief missive contained the standard greeting, a line of information about the site and GPS coordinates. Only an illegible signature scrawled across the bottom.

The return address had no sender's name—only Bradford College in Haverhill, Massachusetts. The school's seal made up most of the letterhead.

Dara stuffed the letter back in her pack with the report folder, renewing her mental note to figure out why the accounting had been sent to her, and why it had come as a letter instead of the more typical email.

Kevin had done some research after she'd shown him the letter. The coordinates were valid, and he'd found references to others planning an expedition to the same area, including a group led by his mentor, Doctor Halsey. Dara had doubts when they started, but now, being here, seeing the ruins, those feelings fled. She looked around the site.

A swath of about two meters separated the forest from the ruins on three sides. On the fourth—to the west—rose steep, rocky cliffs, jagged and towering; angles so severe in places, they gave the impression of being paused mid-topple. Native grasses and scrubby bushes stuck out from gray crags, both holding the rock together and tearing it apart. Below, the moraine stretched across the valley, full of glacial till. Dara suspected she would find stone from the till had been used as building materials.

Treeless valleys in the middle of the cloud forest were not a common site. Someone had to have spent much time continually pushing back the growth, and yet there was no remaining evidence.

No tree stumps, no tire tracks, not even a little-used road anywhere, thought Dara. *Just a trail we followed that's more a glorified cow path.*

Dara ignored her husband and the students plotting excavation grids. She walked through the remains, noting what she thought was a temple with four outer buildings. The layout would form a rough cross if drawn on paper, she noted. And they seemed to date from different time periods in the Inca civilizations, with the sacred building being far older than the others.

As she explored further, Dara concluded the ruins did not belong to the Inca.

"Did you find something, Professor Kincaide?"

Dara started at the voice and turned. She hadn't heard Susan's approach. "Just call me Dara. I've told you this, Susan." She smiled at the younger woman. "I'm not a professor yet."

"No, but you will be. Anyway, did you find something?" Susan studied the wall behind Dara. "I noticed you weren't laying out grids, so I thought you might have found something and might need my help."

"Maybe." Dara turned back. "Let me show you and you tell me what you think." She held out a page with quick sketches covering it. "First, if you mark each building on paper, they form a cross shape, like a Tau."

"It looks like a T, not a cross."

"This would be a Greek cross, not the Latin one you're more familiar with."

"Ah. But why would these buildings be laid out in a cross

of any shape?"

Dara smiled. "That's the first question I have. Look at this architecture too."

Some of the designs matched Inca style, such as the elongated trapezoidal windows and doorways, but the large frescoes were reminiscent of those found at Jericho.

"Why would the Inca paint their walls like this?"

"A better question is, why are the colors still so bright?" asked Dara. "We shouldn't be still able to see these colors with the naked eye."

Before she could continue, flapping came from overhead, and both women looked for the source. A red kite hovered in the currents, the attached camera snapping photos for the aerial documentation of the site.

Dara studied the movements of the kite, then waved when the lens turned toward her.

"And my second question is," said Dara, attention returning to Susan, "we know the Inca painted murals, but why would *these* be so similar to the ones at Jericho when none of the others at different sites are?" She took Susan by the arm, leading her through a low doorway. "Come with me."

They walked through three more rooms before exiting and heading to a wooden structure. Sunlight streamed in, unhindered by the thatched roof, painting bright swipes on the dirt floor. A long trough lined one wall, and pegs stuck out at regular intervals from the walls.

"This is a stable," said Susan.

"And look over there." Dara pointed to the far corner, beneath one end of the trough.

Still buried up to the nose, a human skull stared back at the two women. Clay covered the bone that could be seen, and the eye sockets had been inlaid with small clam shells. Again, reminiscent of those found at Jericho and not native to this side of the world.

Could there have been other civilizations here? Could the Sumerians or the Babylonians have reached South America?

Susan bent to study the skull, reaching out, then stopping herself before making contact. "The skull seems to have Caucasian markers, not the Mongoloid associated with these people."

"Remember though," Dara said, "that mummies with Caucasoid features were found in the Paracas burial caverns in the nineteen-twenties. And those skulls showed evidence of trepanning too." Her words felt at odds with her thoughts, and she wanted to share the latter with Susan, but couldn't. Dara had to remain the teacher and not fall victim to excited speculation.

Susan looked up at Dara. "So, you're saying these oddities can be explained through diffusion theory?"

"No. I'm pointing out that a few inconsistencies have been found at other sites, but none seem to have the number found here."

"You haven't shown me much that couldn't be explained by either diffusion, or previous, unreported discovery or even a hoax," said Susan. She studied the skull further. "You just said other Caucasian mummies were found in Peru, and these shells are bean clams, common on sandy beaches all over the world."

Dara smiled. "The central building here seems to be a temple. Let me show you something else."

The women walked to the temple and entered.

"We know the Inca had no written language," Dara said.

"Right," replied Susan. "They relied on quipus to keep track of time and events. We'll probably find several once the grids are laid and digging starts."

"If the Inca had no written language, who did that?" Dara pointed to a wall in front of them.

The symbols bore a resemblance to Egyptian hieroglyphics, yet the characters were alien. Men with tentacles for arms or legs, animals the likes of which were never born on this Earth. Serpentine horse-like beasts, arachnids with long, jointed legs, a worm, barely recognizable as such behind the gaping maw.

"What the hell are these?" Susan asked. "Is this some kind

of joke?" She studied the carvings. Then her manner changed. Susan's face slackened and she stared at the wall. She reached to touch the images and a soft snap sounded. She pulled her hand back, shaking it like she'd been shocked. "It's like I want to remember these. I feel like I should, but there's a blank spot where the knowledge would be." Words came out soft and hypnotic, barely above a whisper.

Dara traced them with reverent fingertips, knowing she violated preservation rules yet not able to stop herself. *Could these be gods lost to the ravages of time? Maybe from a sub-race of Inca? One that* did *have a written language?*

"I know."

Susan stepped back a few paces. "I don't want to be in here anymore." She rubbed her arms and looked around. "Come on." Susan grabbed Dara's hand and led her to the surrounding buildings.

These didn't share the same careful construction. Blocks didn't fit together as well, doorways and windows were more irregularly shaped. Everywhere, on the inside and outside of these four buildings, faces leered with mocking grins. Some of the visages were human, some might have been. All were only simple stone carving chiseled into the walls, yet ominous and knowing. Chills raced along Dara's spine as she studied them, glad for Susan's presence.

"We need to excavate this," said Susan. "Make sure this isn't a hoax."

Under about two feet of soil, at each of the four temple corners, they found bowls. The clay vessels had been buried upside down. Carefully, Dara removed one then another, until all four bowls rested in front of the two women.

Each vessel had words inscribed inside, beginning at the rim and spiraling down to the center of the bowl.

"What are they?" asked Susan.

"I have no idea." Dara picked up one and stood. "I'll be right back. See what else you can find." She carried one of the bowls to Edgar, their language expert.

He studied the bowl, then looked at Dara. "Is this for real?"

"Susan and I found it, and three more like it, buried at each corner. Why?"

"The language is Akkadian. It hasn't been used since about the Eighth century, when Aramaic became the primary language of Mesopotamia. And judging by the words, this is a Devils Trap from Babylonia." He pointed to the words. "See how the words run widdershins into the bottom?"

Dara nodded.

"This is a spell, essentially a contract to divorce a spirit. If the words ran clockwise, it would be a spell to connect a spirit. Was it right side up or upside down when you found it?"

"Upside down. Why?"

"Burying a Devil's Trap right side up divorces a spirit from the ground. Burying it upside down divorces the spirit from the air or the surface."

Nothing is quite right about this site, Dara thought. "How did it end up here?"

Edgar shrugged and handed the bowl back to her. "You're the expert on ancient cultures. You tell me."

Dara turned the bowl over a few times, considering, only to realize she had no immediate answers.

Phantoms plagued Dara's dreams that night. Creatures not known to this world filled her subconscious. They spoke to her, the language familiar. She knew she'd heard it before, but couldn't remember.

She woke with panic twisting her stomach. Dara tried to remember the dreams, the words spoken, but vivid images faded too fast. A scream ripped the night, followed by another. They didn't sound human. Dara considered waking Kevin to investigate, but unease stilled her hand.

Instead, she zipped the tent open, wincing at the harsh noise, hoping it didn't attract whatever lurked in the dark.

Dara pulled the .357 revolver from its holster, pointing the muzzle toward the ground. The weight of the Ruger reassured her, and Dara peeked through the flap.

Nothing waited to pounce, nothing lay in wait. The guanacos hadn't raised an alarm. If some predator prowled in the night, the pack animals wouldn't remain quiet.

Dara eased onto her sleeping bag, lying on top of the slick nylon. Beside her, Kevin snored softly. She poked him in the ribs, and he turned over then settled in to sleep once more. Dara blinked in the night air, every slight noise sending her pulse racing. Sleep eluded her. Picking up the gun again, she made her way to the banked fire, intending to get an early start on the day.

Then, the entire world dissolved in sound.

Voices, hundreds of them, came from the forest. Low and guttural and ugly.

Recognizable as human, each word spoken clearly but with no intonation. Heavy black clouds rolled in, blocking out the stars and moon. The chanting grew louder, and the wind picked up, threatening to tear the meager tent shelters away.

Kevin and the others stumbled into the night, awakened by the shrieking wind.

Words came faster, growing higher in pitch, seeming to be meaningless phrases of power so ancient they were almost unpronounceable. Speech increased in volume and velocity until Dara was sure the sounds couldn't emanate from a human tongue. Words became little more than a raucous cawing, melding to a single, grating note.

Tree branches smacked and clacked together, sounding like wooden chimes. Roots ripped free of the thin topsoil, flailing and smacking, reaching for the group. The forest advanced on the tiny camp in leaps and bounds.

One heavy limb crashed against a neighboring tree and broke, its splintered end sprayed red. The smeared traces of gore running down the smooth trunk resembled macabre trails left by bloodied snails.

The banked campfire flared and soil erupted in a flaming fountain, allowing everything to be seen in gruesome bas-relief. Earth shifted, spitting out grisly remains of previous sacrificial victims, somehow not fully decomposed even after the passage of centuries. Smells of death and decay found Dara's nostrils. She vomited. Air around the site thickened to a gelatinous feel, active with unseen creatures walking, crawling, slithering through.

A root grabbed Kevin by his ankle and wrenched him off his feet, dragging him away. Dara grabbed for his outstretched hand and missed. Branches of a cannonball tree grasped his arms and legs, hoisting him upside down against the balled trunk in a grim rendition of a living crucifix. Vines snaked down from the treetops and wound around his head, pulling Kevin tighter against the tree, halting futile struggles. He screamed then, horrible keening sounds. His chest heaved with the effort just to breathe.

Dara tried to crawl to her husband. Skeletal hands held fast, tying her to the soil. They pulled on her legs, bony fingers digging into flesh. Blood ran red and warm down her calves, and it energized the decayed digits. They gripped harder, dragging her to her knees. She reached toward Kevin, trying to stretch herself, to pull free despite the burning sensation overtaking her lower body.

More hands grabbed at her clothing, twisting the fabric into tattered shreds. They snatched her hair, pulling strands out by the roots. One gripped her throat, jerking her face to the earth.

Dara raised the gun. Shaking hands aimed the muzzle at Kevin, and squeezed the trigger.

The Ruger roared once, twice, before ancient teeth bit down on Dara's wrist. She dropped the weapon. Bullets ricocheted, deflected by wood and stone.

Blood sprayed as a rusted knife ripped through Kevin's thigh, then a second through the right side of his chest and still he screamed. Terrible, tortured sounds.

Two pre-Columbian warriors stepped from behind the tree and retrieved their weapons as Dara stared. Flesh hung in tattered rags, fluttering around their limbs. Mouths still full of stained teeth opened in rictus laughter. Bone rasped against bone with each stuttering step. Sleeveless tunics, more hole than fabric, stuck to ribs in large, wet spots while cloaks, tied at the neck, drifted lifeless behind. Moldy leather boots thumped against the earth, sounding a cannibalistic cadence.

They strode toward Susan, blades raised. The girl had nowhere to run.

Helpless tears, hot and salty, poured down Dara's cheeks. They washed away dirt and grime, love and life and happiness. Her chest ached with guilt. Anger and sorrow as tore sobs free. She gulped great breaths of air.

Kevin's eyes bulged then popped free. Nerves dangled them against his cheeks. Fleshy worms with grapnels lining their underbellies burst from the sockets, waving fat, white bodies in newfound freedom for a moment. Their tiny hooks tore at Kevin's eyelids as the worms pulled free, crawling toward his chest. Blood flowed.

Still, he screamed.

Dara tried to cover her ears, but she could not raise her hands. The very voice that had saved her sanity just two days ago now drove her crazy.

Kevin's screams stopped and he hung limp, head lolling. All tortured cries ended. Silence reigned for precious seconds.

Then the ground split in a raw, ugly wound in front of Dara. Leathery tentacles slid out, searching, flailing, grabbing whatever came within reach. A thick, sandpapery scraping grew louder. Names filled Dara's head, buzzing with intensity. Odd names, ones with too many consonants and not enough vowels to be human. Names like *Ghisguth, Naggoob, Snireth-ko and Yhoundeh.* There were more—hundreds, perhaps thousands—all speaking and screaming at once, desperate to be heard, needing to be recognized, wanting to be welcomed, to be embraced as they had before.

Dara fought against the skeletal hands holding her. Bone snapped and cracked. Shards flew, imbedding themselves in earth and wood. She strained against the hold, ignoring tearing skin. With an agonized scream, Dara broke the last hold.

She ran before even trying to stand, an awkward skittering, pushing, pulling movement that carried her toward Kevin.

The jungle shifted again—changing, growing, moving. Moaning came from within the trees themselves. An overhead branch broke as it slammed into another, spraying Dara with more blood. The tree bellowed as the campfire flared again, this time igniting some of the tumbling, squirming vines. Smoke rose dense and acrid, filling the air as green plants smoldered and writhed.

Another figure appeared and blocked her path.

Dara skidded to a halt, legs splayed for balance. The mummified apparition shambled toward her.

Clay crumbled and fell from the skull. Firelight glittered off bean clam shells covering eye sockets. Blood and fur clung to its mouth and chest. It dragged a mutilated, panting guanaco.

Dara's heart wrenched at the sight, and she cried out. Gulping sobs tore through the air and dizziness tilted the world. She fell, landing hard on one hip and wrist. Pain lanced through her arm.

More unidentifiable creatures emerged from the open gash in the Earth, pulling themselves up with whatever appendages they had; some with huge claws, others with too many arms and hands, all moving within the smoke and fog like wraiths. A single bulging eye glared at Dara before fading. She heard chittering behind her, and jointed legs covered with coarse hair caressed her slick skin, then pulled back.

Vaporous air swirled and churned in new patterns. A sinewy purple-red arm, veins standing up like cords, stretched out, fingerless tip testing the air. Thin tentacles unwound, adding to the thing's length, and small suction cups shuddered, straining to move further. The tentacle pulsed and swelled as the suckers widened, searching for prey. Suction cups gripped and released, gripped and released, sliding forward.

Pop.

Pop.

Pop.

Dara watched, unable to turn her gaze, unable to move. Horrors surrounded her, then Hell itself stroked her body.

ABOUT THE CONTRIBUTORS

Robert Lewis is a Colorado-based author, editor, publisher, magician, scholar, podcaster, YouTuber, entrepreneur, and more. He holds degrees with Latin honors in Biology, English, Mathematics, and Psychology from the University of Colorado Denver (where he also took an Astrophysics minor) as well as a Master of Education in Science and the Public from the University at Buffalo. A dedicated polymath, he likes to tell people that his hobby is to collect new hobbies. Among his current favorite pastimes are chess, cooking, woodworking, tinkering in his workshop, collecting bizarre artifacts and curiosities, and (re) learning his musical instruments. By the time you read this, he'll assuredly have added some more to the list.

Professionally speaking, he is the founder, owner, and executive editor of Polymath Press, host of the YouTube channel *Phobophile*, co-host of the *Do You Like Scary Movies* horror podcast, member of the Rocky Mountain Paranormal Research Society, co-author of the *Case Files of the Rocky Mountain Paranormal Research Society* series, and he performs as a magician at Bob Lewis Magic. By the time you read this, there's a good chance he'll be in the process of adding something to this list as well. Learn more about his work at robertlewisauthor.com.

John H. Howard lives in Dayton, Ohio with his wife Melanie and four cats and has two wonderful daughters, Kaitlyn and Sarah. He grew up on fantasy fiction and it's still his go-to genre when he needs to unwind. John primarily writes fantasy and horror, but has recently been experimenting with magical realism, which he has discovered he enjoys a great deal. His short stories have been featured in *The Ladies and Gentlemen of Fantasy* anthology series, *The Ladies and Gentlemen of Horror* anthology series, the *Fiction Foundry: One* anthology, and *The Horror Society Presents: Forgotten Places* anthology. He is also the author of the novella *Ordinary Heroes,* and most recently, his short story "Midnight Train From Tokyo" appeared in the anthology *A Walk in a City of Shadows: Tales of Urban Legendry*. Find out more about John and his work at johnhhowardbooks.com.

Wordsmith **Dr. Sangita Kalarickal** has been published in several e-magazines and anthologies worldwide. Her most recent publication is a poetry chapbook, *Mamina,* published by Adisakrit Publishing in Chennai, India. She lives in Minnesota, USA, with her husband, kid, and the several fantasy characters she writes about. She can be contacted on Facebook and Instagram via the username skalarickal.

Josh Snider is a multi-genre author from a family of writers and editors. He has participated in professional writers'

groups for his entire life, being the youngest member of his first group, the award-winning Colorado Springs Fiction Writers Group, and a founding member and former president of Fiction Foundry. He has a background in poetry and has since moved into prose.

From an early age, **Carolyn Kay** has been steeped in the worlds of fantasy and science fiction. Legos and *Star Wars* figures were her favorite toys, and Madeleine L'Engle and Tolkien graced her bookshelves. So it's no surprise that she writes stories in a variety of genres, or that her first novel was an *Avengers-Star Wars* crossover fanfic. Carolyn melded two of her favorite genres—steampunk and fantasy—into a trilogy titled *Galessel's Tale*, set in the world of Ashelon, co-created with her husband and award-winning illustrator, Chaz Kemp. Her foray into military sci-fi, *Gunpowder Geishas*, was released in 2023. She's also authored multiple short stories and a sci-fi novelette.

A government drone, she carves out time to write between the day job, belly dancing, gardening, photography, and herding two independent felines. You can find her at carolynkayauthor. com and on most social media platforms under the username Bewitchinghips.

Charli Cowan considers herself a lifelong bookworm and artist. Some of her earliest memories consist of setting up a desk in her grandmother's bedroom, where she would write and illustrate stories. Her favorite themes include romance, history, adventure, and anything paranormal, but she'll explore anything that seems intriguing. When she isn't writing, you can find Charli wandering new places, gardening with peculiar vegetables, ghost-hunting with her team, or spending time with her plethora of pets. She has been published twice in the UCCS literary journal, *riverrun*, as well as in an anthology entitled *Colorado's Best Emerging Poets*, both for her poetry. This is her first time publishing fiction.

For over 25 years, **Henry Snider** has dedicated his time to helping others tighten their writing through critique groups, classes, lectures, prison prose programs, and high school fiction contests. He co-founded Fiction Foundry (est. 2012) and the award-winning Colorado Springs Fiction Writers' Group (1996-2013). Thirteen years to the month from founding the CSFWG, he retired from the presidency. After a much-needed vacation, he returned to the literary world. While still reserving enough time to pursue his own fiction aspirations, he continues to be active in the writing community through classes, editing services, and advice. Henry lives in Colorado with his wife, fellow author and editor Hollie Snider, son, poet Josh Snider, and numerous neurotic animals, including, of course, Fizzgig, the token black cat.

Shiloh Silveira is a Canadian born, Oregon raised writer. Her biggest passion is writing non-fiction focused on mental health and self-improvement, though she sometimes dabbles in romance, fantasy, and children's stories. Shiloh put together the graphic novel script adaptation for author Bryan Davis's book, *Raising Dragons*. She has two certificates from The Children's Institute of Literature and is nearing completion of her Associate's degree in Psychology.

Her free time is primarily spent re-reading the *Harry Potter* series with her children. When not reading or writing, she can be found running around the streets of Grants Pass, Oregon and getting shin splints for the umpteenth time.

Kari J. Wolfe writes horror and weird fiction from her home in the foothills of the Rocky Mountains with her husband, daughter, and cat if she is not out on the eastern plains of Colorado with a herd of Skipper W quarter horses. Growing up, she read everything *Nancy Drew* and all the Newberry Medal Award winners she was given. *Pet Sematary* was the book that cemented her love of horror.

Her interests range from most things horror and weird fiction-related to Western horsemanship. She also plays video games such as the *Resident Evil* series and *Final Fantasy XIV* where she plays a Level 90 Dancer named Kips Sanguine on Odin, a European server. In one of her past lives, she received a degree in mathematics and physics from Marshall University in Huntington, WV. She can be found online on Facebook (facebook.com/kari.wolfe), Bluesky (@kariwolfe.bsky.social), or on her blog/newsletter (kariwolfe.com).

Christophe Maso is a conduit of dark visions and a teller of dark fantastic, paranormal, gothic, and sci-fi tales. He's the former fiction editor of *The City Morgue Magazine*, and a member of the Horror Writers Association, Horror Authors Guild, Brooklyn Speculative Fiction Writers, the Denver Horror Collective, and Fiction Foundry. His short story "Feast of the Senses" can be found in the horror anthology *Consumed: Tales Inspired by the Wendigo*. His first published novella, *Scream of the Butterfly*, was released in 2022 by D&T Publishing.

He lives with his wife Katherine Navarrete in Silver City, New Mexico. When not writing, he enjoys jumping out of perfectly good airplanes, acting, riding horses, volunteering, playing guitar and hammered dulcimer, ranging into New Mexican backcountry, hosting barbecues, and walking betwixt the worlds. See his author page at christophemasoauthor.com.

Hollie Snider writes horror, dark fantasy, and high fantasy. In 2012, she co-founded Fiction Foundry, a critique group dedicated to helping authors improve their writing in anticipation of publication. When not working on her own writing, Hollie leads creative writing workshops and participates in lectures and panels. She is currently at work on several novels and short stories. Hollie lives near Colorado Springs with her family and neurotic pets. Learn more about her work at holliesnider.com.

Leighton Buxman is a Colorado-based artist who creates illustrations for books, comics, and concept art for games. Ever since they got their first drawing tablet at 13, they have been enamored with digital painting and visual storytelling. Their work often features elements of Dark Fantasy or Horror and is stylistically known for its ethereal brush work and distinctive use of contrast and shadows. Leighton has worked with various clients such as Source Point Press, Polyverse Publications, and many others. Learn more at leightonbuxman.com.